HAPPENSTANCE

HAPPENSTANCE

MELVILLE JONES

Matador
Unit E2 Airfield Business Park
Harrison Road,
Market Harborough. LE16 7UL
Tel: 0116 279 2299
Email: books@troubador.co.uk
Web: www.troubador.co.uk/matador
Twitter: @matadorbooks

ISBN 978 1800465 398

British Library Cataloguing in Publication Data.
A catalogue record for this book is available from the British Library.

Printed and bound in the UK by TJ Books LTD, Padstow, Cornwall
Typeset in 10pt Petersburg by Troubador Publishing Ltd, Leicester, UK

Matador is an imprint of Troubador Publishing Ltd

To Sylvia

ONE

It was not much of a day. The jolly weatherman on Radio Kernow had spoken of sunny intervals and a chance of an isolated shower. Showed what he knew. Perhaps, Steve thought sourly, if he spent less time indulging in leaden banter and more time studying his charts, or whatever they looked at these days, he might have a firmer grip on meteorology. Not, Steve had to admit, that predicting the weather in Cornwall was easy, especially down at the far end. They had all told him that when he moved down. "If you don't like the weather, hang around; it will change in half an hour." Another favourite he had heard too often was "If you can see St Michael's Mount it's going to rain, and if you can't see it then it's raining already." As if on cue, he glimpsed the Mount now as the A30 swung around the last bend before the bay. It rose mistily out of a sullen, monochrome sea, and across the bay, through the murk, the distant rooftops of Penzance were slate bleak.Not a view to put in the brochures to entice the tourists; not that you could expect many of them in late January. Steve recalled a useless item of trivia that stuck in his memory: a claim that the 16th January was peak suicide day. Some sad loser must have worked that out, but it made a sort of sense. The excitement of Christmas and the New Year

1

over – for those who got a buzz out of such events – and only foul weather and accumulated bills to look forward to.

As his car joined the queue awaiting a chance to edge into the roundabout and onto the bypass, Steve reflected on when he had last enjoyed Christmas and the New Year. As a kid, Christmas had been bearable, he supposed; the presents a fair trade-off for domestic incarceration and family tensions. In his student days the New Year had had its moments; getting pissed and, he now shamefully remembered, presenting opportunities to snog some equally ratted girl whom you would never see again. Seemed a whole lifetime away now.

The impatient blast of a car horn interrupted his musings. Raising an apologetic hand, he took his chance on the roundabout. They'd warned him that in the summer it could take an hour to negotiate this last mile into Penzance. It was the Poldark factor, they said. Cornwall had always sunk under the weight of its summer visitors, but of late the popularity of the TV series with its presentation of a remote and romantic never-never land, as Steve categorised it, had doubled their numbers as the credulous jammed the country lanes in the search for the particular cove where Ross had tumbled Demelza.

Linda had loved Poldark. Steve had needed to be careful not to be too snooty about it as it would have given them something else to argue about. Not passionate vase-throwing fights, but simmering resentments and muttered asides. He knew that she was disappointed in him. His lack of enthusiasm and sense of adventure were high on her list of disappointments. "We never do anything," was a familiar lament. It was true, of course. But what were they supposed to do? He was too wearied after a day with his hopeless students, and strap-hanging home on the Tube, to face much beyond a glass or two and then a doze in front of the box after

2

he had groaned his way through the sheaves of paperwork required to keep Ofsted at bay. 'Outstanding' was the verdict the fawning headmaster had been hoping for after the last inspection. Instead they had just avoided being put in special measures. The head had made it clear that he felt let down by a colleague. When he said as much at an emergency staff meeting, Steve had been sure that he was the one getting the eye contact. So with all that going on, it was hard to whip up much enthusiasm for going out. Anyway, he reckoned that Linda didn't really need him to take her out. She had plenty of girlfriends from the leisure centre and the tennis club. They were always socialising. Not quite the Tupperware parties his mother had patronised, but some other excuse for a glass of wine and a gossip. Linda was certainly a liberated woman in his view. She did what she liked; had her own car, her own bank account. And why not? She earned more than he did, although he was never quite sure how much more, or exactly what she did. Human resources was not his area of expertise, and when he had feigned interest she had squashed his insincerity with her bored response.

Steve turned off the bypass when it abandoned Penzance and headed west as the drizzle turned into more serious rain. The windscreen wipers thumped a rhythmic soundtrack to his thoughts. He suddenly wondered what Linda would be doing now. Friday night. She would be going out somewhere, for sure. He tried not to think of her too often. Everyone had told him he must move on, but now he pictured her clearly in his mind. Still strikingly attractive; all that time at the gym. Bubbly is what people called her; blonde and bubbly. It was hard to imagine what she had seen in him. He allowed himself to believe that perhaps in his twenties he had not been bad-looking. He even had the photographs to prove it; of him in his rugby kit. That was how they'd met: at a rugby club disco. She had been the sister of the team's hooker, which was the source of many ribald comments. She was still at university then – or uni, as they call it these days. They seemed a good match, people said. They were both sporty and uncomplicated. Friends told them their characters were in sync. She was lively and spontaneous whereas he was more grounded and sensible. Perhaps they'd believed those judgements too readily and sailed into marriage on a sea of optimism. To begin with it had been fine; better than fine: passionate and carefree. Linda had found a good job in what Steve understood to be personnel management and he had taken the first step on the rickety ladder of his teaching career. What could possibly go wrong?

It was a question he had pondered many times but now it froze in his mind. A car had pulled out of a side lane regardless of his approach. Instinctively he flattened the brake pedal and palmed the horn button, but the wet road offered no instant traction and the skid made steering useless. The car slowed, but not quickly enough to avoid the other vehicle, which was now stationary across the road as if petrified. Weirdly, in the instant before the collision, Steve pictured the rabbit in front of the stoat. Then his car scraped sides with the other before jolting to a halt. Now there was silence apart from the still-insistent whump of the wiper blades. Steve was shaking; he could feel his heart pounding. There was no sign of movement in the car he had slammed into. He tried to slow his breathing to regain some control over his disordered senses. He turned off the wipers, and that mundane action seemed to put him back in at least partial charge. He was able to think rationally now. He was aware of other cars stopping; people getting out and coming to the crash scene. He tried to open his door, and it responded. He stepped out shakily onto the wet tarmac, indifferent to the rain.

"You all right, mate?" This from a man in painter's white overalls.

Steve noticed the van parked alongside: 'Pasco Home Decorating', and underneath that the promise 'No job too small.' He tried a smile. "Thanks. I seem to be OK."

He was aware now of people getting out of their cars. An elderly couple were peering through the windows of the other vehicle. Bizarrely, they had a small dog on a lead with them: too precious, Steve supposed, to be left in a car. As its owners struggled to open an unresponsive door, the dog lifted its leg against the front tyre.

"I can't open the door. It must be jammed." The old chap wrestled with an unmoving handle.

"Are you hurt?" His wife, or so Steve presumed, shouted her inquiry with lips almost pressed against the window glass, but there was no movement or response, although it was now just possible to make out two people inside. They were sitting upright but motionless. The elderly couple looked at others for guidance.

Pasco the painter was the first to react. "I'll get my toolkit. We'll have to smash the window." He sprinted back to his van and quickly returned with a bulging canvas bag. He rummaged in it and produced a lump hammer. The small crowd that had now gathered stood back as he approached the car with the hammer raised. He paused to consider his options.

Steve ventured a suggestion. "The rear window, I think. In case..."

Pasco nodded his agreement and moved to face a window. He raised the hammer, but before he could swing it the driver's window slid down. Pasco froze, hammer still raised in a pose reminiscent of statues of noble labourers in Stalin's Russia.

"We are not hurt. We are OK." The voice was accented but not heavily. The speaker was a woman, her features hidden by a muddy balaclava pulled down just above her eyebrows.

There was an almost palpable sense of anticlimax amongst the gathering. No drama, no first aid, no mangled bodies. The elderly couple were the first to leave, after their dog had a final pee against a tyre. The rest drifted back to their cars and engines started up.

Pasco looked embarrassed as he returned his lump hammer to the canvas bag. "Over to you, mate." He nodded cheerily at Steve. "You'll have to call the police; get the road cleared."

Steve fumbled in his damp jacket pocket for his phone and joined Pasco by his van as he repacked the canvas bag.

Pasco watched him for a few seconds. "No signal, mate?"

"No." Steve felt less and less in control of the situation.

"Well, there won't be. Not down here. I'll call them up when I get to the top."

"Thanks. I suppose—"

"Get her to move the car." Pasco nodded towards the vehicle straddling the road. "We can push it if it won't start."

Steve felt increasingly indebted to Pasco. He was clearly a man of action; someone who took control of situations. Someone Linda would admire, was the fleeting irrelevance which slid unbidden into Steve's subconscious.

"And take some pictures. You can still do that on the phone."

Steve tried to pull himself together. "Yes, of course." He prodded vaguely at his phone.

Pasco shook his head. "I tell you what, mate: shall I do that for you? I reckon you're still a bit shaken up."

Meekly, Steve handed his phone over.

Pasco slammed his van door shut. "Right. Let's see if we can get these cars shifted."

They turned to cross back to where the two cars obstructed the road, but they had to pause to allow a slow-moving farm tractor carefully to navigate its passage. The cloth-capped driver obviously knew Pasco, who shouted up to him a few words of explanation which Steve lost in the roar of diesel. As the tractor trundled off with its yellow hazard lights flashing in the deepening gloom, the two men crossed back to the cars. Steve noticed that the window of the other car was now closed. As they approached there was the sudden blast of an engine firing up unevenly but powerfully.

"Good," Pasco shouted above the noise. "They've got her started. Perhaps we can get her onto the verge."

It seemed that might also be the intention of the balaclava lady at the wheel, as her car scraped clear of its embrace with Steve's.

"I'll tell her to pull over to the side." Pasco walked towards the revving vehicle, but before he could approach, the car, with tyres squealing and exhaust backfiring, raced away and was soon over the hill and out of sight. Pasco was momentarily speechless. "Bugger me," he muttered after a pause. Then, gathering himself, he turned back to Steve. "Bugger me," he said again.

Steve seemed incapable of thought. "What now?"

Pasco was quickly back in master-of-the-situation mode. "You wait here and I'll call the police. She can't get away with that."

"But she just has," Steve offered bleakly.

"Not quite." Pasco held out Steve's phone and smiled widely. "I snapped her number plate."

TWO

The radio alarm should not have been set. It was the weekend, for God's sake. But in his shattered state last night, Steve had forgotten to switch it off. So now, as he tried to force his eyes to focus, he had to endure the inane burblings of Mandy Trewellard listing the attractions on offer in West Cornwall over the weekend. Steve lay supine, not yet ready to attempt movement, as she gushed over the prospective delights of a male voice choir singalong in Camborne, a bring-and-buy sale in Newlyn, and a talk on Celtic crosses in the community hall at Connor Downs. All events dangled the promise of a pasty. Steve wondered if any event in Cornwall could proceed without a pasty. Perhaps they handed them out with the service sheets at the crematorium.

"Not a good day for the garden, so maybe a chance to tackle that bit of DIY you've been putting off for—"

The voice of the bloody weatherman was enough to galvanise Steve into switching off the radio. He sank back onto his pillow. He didn't have a garden and the sound of the rain on the bedroom window was all he needed to know about the weather. As for DIY, he wouldn't be doing any of that in the scabby cottage he was renting for an outrageous sum. 'Holiday lets' was the excuse the shark at the estate agents had offered. They pushed up the rental market prices. He'd implied that Steve was lucky to find anything, and Steve had accepted that he probably was. He had left London at short notice and taken a step down the career ladder and several steps down the pay scale to take a job on a twelve-month-only contract to cover maternity leave in a failing – if not already failed – comprehensive in a depressed and depressing post-industrial town which would never feature in any Cornish Tourist Board brochure. The odd thing was, when they'd interviewed him no one had been surprised by his kamikaze career move. His rehearsed explanation of wanting a change in lifestyle had raised no eyebrows. That was what people did, it appeared. Cornwall seduced those looking to escape urban stress, pollution, capitalist materialism. The irony was that those who came to find a Zen life of inner truth in Cornwall needed at least half a million of accumulated capitalist wealth to buy a house there. Once they had made it there were plenty offering help along the Path of Alternative Enlightenment – at a price. Steve was familiar with Pilates and yoga, of course; Linda had been a dutiful follower of both. Not, in her case, because she was seeking spiritual regeneration, but because she still wanted to fit into her Size 32 jeans. At least Steve could get his head around that, but in the few weeks he had been in Cornwall he had become aware of a whole new world of alternative therapies. At the newsagent where he bought his Sunday paper the window was covered in notices advertising specialist routes to wellness and mindfulness. He could almost construct an alphabet of therapies: you start with acupuncture or aromatherapy and work your way to Zen via homeopathy, reflexology, reiki and so on. He could not always comprehend what was on offer in some of the more arcane adverts. What, in God's name, went on at a transgender workshop? It was not really something you could ask without seeming prurient.

The chime of the doorbell shocked Steve into movement. Who the hell was calling at this time of the morning? Blearily checking the fly of his pyjamas, he stumbled down the narrow, creaking stairs and eased the front door open enough to show his face.

"Need a signature." The postman thrust a large brown envelope forward.

Steve signed for it and watched the postman stride off bare-legged through the rain. That was another mystery of contemporary life for Steve. He was only forty-three but sometimes felt as if he was a Victorian. Why did all postmen and postwomen, he wondered (or should that be postpersons, or even mail delivery officers?) wear shorts? Did it make dogs less likely to bite their ankles? Or was it some macho statement: I may look like just a postman but don't mess with me!?

Sometimes, Steve had to accept, life was just questions. No answers. He looked at the envelope he had been handed. He vaguely recalled some lines of poetry about being unable to hear the postman knocking without a quickening of the heart. He looked more closely at the envelope but felt no quickening of his heart; instead he suspected a rising of his blood pressure. Smithers & Nash. He knew the imprint. He childishly dubbed them 'Sausage & Mash'. He had a drawerful of communication from them. They were acting for Linda over the divorce settlement – or, to put it more accurately, they were crucifying him financially. Neutral observers would describe the divorce as amicable; a term clearly coined by someone who had never experienced one. Amicably, Steve had had to agree to continue to pay the mortgage on the family home until their seventeen-year-old daughter finished her education, and to contribute to her maintenance. He was OK with that last bit. Hannah was the joy of his life; perhaps the only joy in his life. Leaving her had been gut-wrenching; far worse, even, than leaving Linda. He was allowed access but his decision to get as far away as possible from the scene of his misery made that impracticable. He had managed to see Hannah for a few days over Christmas but living out of a hotel room had made their meetings awkward and stilted, and Hannah had been clearly upset to see him but not be a part of his life any more. He had come back to Cornwall early for her sake and now they communicated by letter. Steve could not bring himself to express his feelings in the sleazy world of social media. He was familiar enough with the technology – he had done dozens of PowerPoint presentations and the like in the classroom – but the online world was steeped in criminality and depravity by his reckoning: scamming, grooming, trolling and so on. Not to be touched with a barge pole. Nor did they speak on the phone; that would have been too painful: to bring her close yet still inaccessible. Hannah seemed to accept his Luddite sentiments and her letters were both a pleasure and a pain to him.

Steve wondered constantly if Hannah suspected the truth behind the divorce. Linda had decided that they should maintain the official line: that they had simply grown apart to irretrievable breakdown; gone their separate ways and become different people. But Steve had not gone anywhere, whereas for over two years Linda had gone at least twice a week to the fetid bedsit of her young tennis coach, Jason. Steve had met him unsuspectingly at several social events at the club. He came across as a muscle-bound dimwit but Linda had obviously seen a different side to him, and Steve didn't want to dwell on which side in particular. It seemed that all their friends knew, but not Steve and possibly not Hannah. Eventually Linda broke the news to him, in case, he suspected, someone let the cat out of the bag. His reaction was one of bewilderment rather than rage, but then Linda tried to explain. She was over forty and afraid of their future together. What had they to look forward to? That was not a question Steve had ever addressed. He had just assumed that they would bumble along as always. More fool him. He could acknowledge now that he should have been more sensitive to Linda's needs; made more of an effort to be the partner she deserved. He could only excuse himself by accepting that life had ground him down and routine had dulled his feelings.

Linda seemed to bear him no particular resentment. It was what it was. Their parting was as flat and unemotional as their last years together. She laid down the ground rules. They would cohabit until Steve decided his next move, which she expected him to organise within weeks rather than months. She would stay in the house with Hannah, whose A Level preparations must not be disrupted. Steve would need to move into the spare bedroom; not that there had been much activity in the nuptial bower of late, he tacitly conceded. The financial arrangements would be sorted out by Sausage & Mash. With no trace of a blush, Linda assured him that after he had moved out she would not bring Jason into the house. She spoke as if he was an incontinent puppy, but claimed it might be distressing for Hannah. At the time Steve had been grateful for her sensitivity, but now, with cynical reflection, he could see that if Jason moved in it could affect the maintenance payments she could claim.

Events had moved at the pace Linda determined. Steve had handed in his notice, which the weasel headmaster snatched from his hand with unconcealed pleasure. Then it was a question of scouring the Times Educational Supplement to find a job – any job. The only requirement was that it should be as far away from Linda, and therefore London, as possible. A vacancy in Carlisle looked promising but a requirement to participate in girls' pastoral care implied that a woman applicant might be at an advantage – although, of course, no advertisement was allowed to be gender specific. Putting that one aside, there was, at first glance, a possibility at a comprehensive in Aberystwyth but on reading the small print it transpired that the medium of instruction was Welsh. Another one crossed off the list, which left only maternity cover at Trengrouse Academy. Checking online, Steve discovered that the academy status had been awarded for sports provision, which in his experience was usually a sign of failure in every other provision. However, he had got the job. When he'd told his colleagues in London about his move, they, knowing nothing of his changed domestic circumstances, had assumed that he must be having some sort of midlife crisis. "Cornwall?!" one had said. "The graveyard of ambition?"

Before his interview Steve had only been to Cornwall once before. That was on a college rugby tour, so any recollections were fogged in alcohol fumes. Apart from that, insofar as he'd had any view of the Duchy, it had been through the distorting fantasy lens of the likes of Poldark and Doc Martin and other such mush. Now he could see the reality, and it was not so pretty.

As he fumbled to stuff a slice of stale bread into the toaster, Steve looked again at the damp envelope in his hands. He decided he didn't have the strength to open it before a cup of tea. Waiting for the water to boil, he tried not to register his surroundings too closely. The Formica-topped table with a wonky leg, melamine cupboards holding just a few tins, and a noisy fridge holding even less; only a carton of milk on the turn, a rasher or two of bacon hardening in their plastic wrapping, and some indeterminate fragments of greenery in the salad drawer. Steve was embarrassed to confront his pathetic housekeeping. He must try to pull himself together. The trouble was that he ate lunch in the school canteen, where the food was surprisingly good. After that he had little appetite to cook for himself in the evenings. He had got used to grabbing just a slice of toast for breakfast before the drive to work. He sometimes read with incredulity the breakfast habits of the famous, or infamous, who happily splashed details of their personal lives across the pages of the Sunday supplements. He often failed to identify some of the ingredients they claimed to be consuming. Granola and quinoa he knew about; Linda had dabbled with those. But chia? What was that? And would an almond milk antioxidant blueberry smoothie really be as satisfying as a cup of PG Tips? Would the local Co-op stock the ingredients for him to start his day with figs on toast with goat's yogurt labneh? He didn't care for the sound of labneh, whatever it was; particularly associated with goats. Another irritant for Steve was that these people didn't just have a cup of coffee for breakfast; it had to be freshly ground, thrice-roasted, fair trade organic beans from Machu Picchu or wherever. Should he ever be asked for his daily routine – nought out of ten on the scale of probability – he would have to admit to a slice of three-day-old rubbish bread, some ersatz butter substitute, and supermarket own brand marmalade, all washed down with two strong cups of builder's tea with a dash of full-cream cow's milk. "Nothing like it, Gwyneth Paltrow. You should try it." With this small act of defiance Steve sat down with his tea and, with the marmalade-smeared knife, opened the brown envelope.

It was not good news. Sausage & Mash's designated specialist in family, domestic and marital law had taken several pages of closely typed legalese basically to inform Steve that he was skewered. There was no escaping the fact that he must fulfil his statutory duties under the Matrimonial

Causes Act of 1973 in order for a court to issue a Consent Settlement. Relevant passages of Section 25 of the said Act were highlighted for his attention. There was an emphasis on 'Financial needs, obligations and responsibilities'. In detail, the solicitor enumerated Linda's needs and Steve's obligations and responsibilities to pay for them. There was a reluctant acknowledgement that when Hannah completed her education it might be possible to consider an equitable division of property assets, but until then it was pay up and pay now. There were forms for him to sign and, in an act of magnanimity, a stamped and addressed envelope for their return. He was already paying the mortgage but now there were other bills to which he must contribute, all of which must come out of his reduced salary, in which rent for this hovel was already making a considerable dent. He scribbled a few calculations on the back of the brown envelope. If he reduced his present spartan lifestyle to hermitic levels he could just about keep afloat. The prospect was not an enticing one but what choice did he have? If he attempted to contest the figures it would involve solicitors, and they were the most fearsome of participants in the money-sucking stakes. He would, anyway, be hampered by having no real idea of Linda's earning capacity. It had never been a topic of detailed conversation. His was a generation which still saw the husband as the provider; not quite a hunter-gatherer, but the payer of bills. There was another problem with fighting the demands: Hannah. The last thing Steve wanted was for her to be caught up in squabbles about money. That would be too demeaning. With a deep sigh of resignation, he signed on several dotted lines and sealed the return envelope. Now he was really up the creek without a paddle.

Sometimes, Steve had to accept, when you think things can't get worse, they get even worse. After he had found the energy to dress and shave, he was bracing himself to face the driving rain to take the envelope to the postbox when his mobile jauntily let rip with the first bars of 'I Do Like to Be Beside the Seaside', which Steve had selected in an ironic moment as his ringtone. It was the mechanic from the local garage where the car had been towed late last night. It had failed to start after the collision, making only a metallic groaning when Steve had tried the ignition. He was an innocent in any matters relating to the internal combustion engine. He had once been told by a grease monkey that he had a serious case of 'tappet slap', which for a chilling moment had sounded like a terminal illness. This time, he was told, the problem involved the cylinder block, which Steve was familiar with as a concept if unclear as to its precise function. "Cost an arm and a leg. Not worth it. Not with your motor." The tone was dismissive rather than supportive. "Leave it with us and get the insurers to check it out. They'll write it off, with any luck."

Steve failed to grasp how he would be lucky to be deprived of his car, but reminded himself that he must contact the insurance company. That was what the policeman had told him last night and given him a reference number to quote. That was about all he had done. Pasco the painter had warned him that it would be a long wait for the law to arrive. He claimed there were only about three policemen in West Cornwall and they were usually drinking tea behind the locked doors of redundant police stations. Certainly there was no sense of urgency in the manner in which PC Basset had handled the situation. After slowly taking down details of Steve's date of birth, ethnicity, occupation, place of residence, and email address, he next required him to puff into a breathalyser, and seemed disappointed to find that it indicated no presence of alcohol. Only then did he allow Steve to give an account of the accident and his brief contact with the other driver. Steve expected an outraged reaction from this enforcer of the law when he told him the other car had driven off, but PC Basset simply noted the fact laboriously in his notebook.

"No one was injured, sir. Is that correct?"

"Yes. Fortunately. But that—"

PC Basset interrupted him. "Technically they should have waited, but you know how it is." He shrugged and made to close his notebook. "Not really a matter for us. We haven't got the manpower to chase all these road traffic violations." And then, as an afterthought, "Sir."

Steve made an effort not to shout. "But I have their registration number. Surely you'll follow it up?"

With exaggerated weariness, the constable reopened his notebook and made a note of the number Steve gave him. "It'll be up to my sergeant to decide what action is appropriate, sir." He closed his notebook and turned to his car with its slowly revolving blue light. He got back in and wound down his window for a final word of advice for Steve. "I should get on to Roadside Recovery if I were you, sir." He started his engine and, as he wound up his window, offered a parting shot. "Because technically you're causing an obstruction."

Steve felt his luck might be changing when he contacted the insurance company. There was actually a real person answering the phone, rather than a disembodied voice telling him how important his call was, but not answering it. He explained why he was telephoning. There was a muttered "Oh dear" when he came to the bit about the other car absconding. That would complicate things.

Steve passed on the police reference number and asked what happened next. It seemed that, under the terms of his policy, which Steve was ashamed to admit to himself he had barely studied, he was entitled to the use of a replacementcar until the loss adjuster could examine the damage to his vehicle. That might take a few days. Then the decision could be to repair or to write off. It would be to Steve's advantage to attempt to contact the driver of the other vehicle so that a knock-for-knock agreement could be reached with her insurance company. Steve explained that that was highly unlikely to happen, and that, at a guess, he doubted the other vehicle was insured. That possibility was accepted at the other end of the phone, but with a sober warning that in cases like this there were implications for a client's no-claims bonus and premiums. Steve put the phone down feeling like his luck had not changed; the gloom had just deepened.

THREE

The pretend weather forecaster on Radio Kernow had offered the hope that early persistent rain would give way to frequent heavy showers. It might be hard to detect the difference but at the moment a feeble sun had emerged, with its rays just able to penetrate the grime on the kitchen window sufficiently to pick out the dust on the cabinet tops and the unwashed dishes by the sink. Steve reproved himself. He really must make an effort to spruce the place up. Linda would be appalled at the squalor of his surroundings and no doubt attribute it to his besetting inertia. She had always been an energetic 'homemaker', as she liked to put it, and their house was always immaculate. Steve had been paranoid about incurring her wrath by spilling coffee, or not putting on slippers before treading the Axminster in the lounge. It was hard to credit that only a few weeks ago his surroundings had been so pristine, and now he had sunk to the sort of grubbiness he would have found hard to tolerate even in his student bedsit days. It would not do. Finding space on the already annotated brown envelope, Steve jotted down a list of basic cleaning items. He might as well spend a wet weekend on housework. He had no car to go anywhere. Indeed, he reminded himself, he had no car to get to school on Monday. Something else he would need to sort out.

The frequent showers had merged into a longer period of rain by the time Steve had finished his shopping. Clutching several plastic bags full of abrasive detergents and aerosol cans for furniture and windows, he had taken shelter in a shop doorway, waiting for the cloudburst to ease to a downpour. He stepped to one side as the shop door opened behind him.

"Bugger me. Some rain, boy."

Steve turned with a start of recognition. "Hello. Mr Pasco, isn't it?"

Pasco paused for a moment and then remembered. "It's you. The bloke in the car. You got home all right, then?"

"Yes. Eventually. You were right about the police."

"Waste of space, they are. Useless. You got problems round here, you got to sort them out for yourself. Know what I mean?"

Steve was not sure if he did know but put speculation from his mind. "I never got a chance to thank you for your help. I'm most grateful."

"No problem." Pasco peered out at the rain, which still thrashed down.

"Perhaps I can buy you a drink sometime?" Steve was not sure where that idea had come from but it was the sort of thing people said, never expecting to be taken up on the offer.

"I won't say no to that. The Miners keeps a nice pint." Pasco pointed across the road to a pub.

Steve was momentarily taken aback. "Fine. What's a good time for you?"

Pasco grinned at him. "Now, if you're free."

Steve collected his thoughts. He was certainly free. Free not to start scrubbing floors and polishing furniture. He had not been to a pub since coming to Cornwall and lapsing into monastic purity. He felt a pulse of pleasurable anticipation. "Why not? I'm not doing anything that can't wait."

The pub was welcoming. It even had a real log fire; not one you switched on. The few men who leaned against the bar were clearly on familiar territory. They bantered with each other and the amiable landlord, who looked as if he was his own best customer. They laughed noisily and frequently at some sally or other which Steve could not quite catch at the table where he and Pasco sat with their pints, drying out by the fire. Steve had been nervous about entering the pub as a stranger, but with Pasco at his side there were nods and smiles from the other drinkers. Pasco clearly knew them all and had a teasing word with most. He looked completely at ease, and Steve felt a stir of envy for a man who seemed so comfortable in his own skin.

"Cheers!" Pasco raised his glass to Steve and sipped his beer appreciatively. "Not a bad pint, this. You a real ale man?"

Steve tasted his pint. "In theory, but, well, I haven't been much of a pub man lately." He looked around at the low beams and polished mining paraphernalia mounted on the walls alongside framed sepia photographs of stern-faced Victorian tin miners gathered at tall-chimneyed engine houses. "We didn't have pubs like this in London."

"That where you're from, is it?"

"Yes. I'm sorry, I should introduce myself. It's Steve. Steve Milton." Awkwardly, he stretched out his hand across the table, aware of how absurdly formal that seemed.

"They all call me Pasco. I have got another name: Peter. But no one uses it. Even the wife calls me Pasco." He laughed and shook Steve's hand.

Steve felt he should offer more. "I moved down a couple of months ago. I'm a teacher."

Pasco nodded as if not surprised. "Where you teaching?"

"Trengrouse Academy. You know it?"

"They got a good rugby team. Some of their lads play with Selwyn."

"Selwyn?"

"My boy. He plays county under-eighteens."

Steve nodded approvingly. "He must be good."

Pasco allowed himself a smile. "Not bad, though I say it myself." He drank some more of his beer. "You a rugby man?"

"Used to be. Long time ago. Still follow it on the box." Steve felt as if the beer was loosening his tongue. "Never lose a game when I'm a spectator; a real armchair critic."

Pasco nodded in agreement. "Me too. And I still get wound up if the Pirates are losing; shout the odds. Tamsin tells me I should grow up."

"Your wife?"

"Of twenty years." Pasco smiled as if at some private joke. "She's in education too."

"Really? Where does she teach?"

Pasco laughed at the notion. "She cooks. School dinners at St Mary's. Little kids."

"Oh." Steve smiled. "Probably more useful than what I do."

"She doesn't need to do it, it's not about the money, but she says she'd go round the twist if she stayed in the house all day. I'm out working; Selwyn's at sixth form. She's not one to sit around."

Steve felt confident enough to offer a character assessment. "I don't imagine there's much sitting around in your family?"

"No chance. Work is what I know. I'm not one for sitting on my arse. Don't watch telly much; don't read books." He offered Steve an apologetic smile. "Shouldn't be telling a teacher that, should I?"

Steve raised a hand in airy dismissal. "Feel free."

Pasco leaned forward. "What's odd is Selwyn. I don't know where he gets it from but he's always reading, studying.

He's got his rugby, of course, but the rest of the time he's up in his room with his books. A Level stuff, not that I understand a word of it. He'll be off to college soon enough, I suppose. Then get himself a proper job."

"You must be pleased."

"I know I should be. He won't have to earn a living stuck halfway up a ladder in the freezing rain, but..." Pasco broke off in reflection, frowning.

"But?" Steve prompted.

Pasco leaned forward, and when he spoke it was softly; confidentially. "I know how hard it is to make your way in the world."

"Not easy."

Pasco paused as if debating whether he should say more. When he spoke again it was almost tentatively. "Look, Steve, I'm a one-man band. I've worked bloody hard to build up my business. I was out of school at sixteen; never did any good there. But I was strong and liked being outside, so my dad fixed me up with work as a general labourer with a builder mate of his. I settled into it and they showed me how to paint and plaster. I did all right, but then there was a bit of a problem." He paused and looked at Steve, perhaps gauging whether he had already said too much.

Steve smiled encouragingly. "What was the problem?"

Pasco decided he could press on. "I worked out the foreman was on the fiddle. Nothing big, but knocking stuff off, making out dodgy receipts for the petty cash – that sort of thing. I reckon the other blokes knew but didn't care." He stopped and sighed wearily.

"But you cared? Is that it?" Steve guessed.

"The boss was a mate of my dad's. He'd taken a chance on me. I owed him. I was only a kid, really." Pasco seemed to be asking for Steve's understanding. "I know now I should have handled it better."

"How did you handle it?"

Pasco's demeanour suddenly changed from apologetic to cheerful. "I decked him!"

Steve tried not to express his alarm. "Oh, I see."

"I didn't plan it. I told him I knew what he was up to and that he had to stop."

Steve smiled. "That was brave of you."

Pasco laughed. "Bloody stupid, more like. He was a big bloke. Nasty piece of work. He came at me, so I took a swing at him and got lucky. He went down. Down and out. All hell broke loose then. The boss told me I was lucky he wasn't calling the police."

"But surely once you explained—" Steve protested.

"I never told him."

"What?" Steve was astonished. "Why on earth not?"

Pasco shrugged. "I didn't like the foreman but his family were all right; his boy had been at school with me. They'd be the ones to lose out if he was in the shit. And I was pretty sure the fiddling would stop."

Steve looked at Pasco in amazement. "So you said nothing."

"It wasn't that big a deal. I got sacked, of course, but I'd learned enough by then to start up on my own, in a small way." He laughed. "In fact, you could say it was the making of me. Funny how things turn out."

"Happenstance," Steve mused.

Pasco raised an eyebrow. "What?"

Steve explained. "Happenstance – when a chance event leads to a good result. Sorry, I sound like a teacher."

"Well, you are a teacher. Happenstance. Good word. I'll remember it." Pasco looked down at his wristwatch. "Blimey, is that the time? Tamsin will kill me." He got to his feet and, for the second time since they had met, offered his hand for Steve to shake. "It was good to meet you. I hope I didn't talk too much."

Steve stood up and shook hands. "Not at all. I enjoyed it. Made a change."

Pasco pulled on his donkey jacket; still wet from the rain. He waved a farewell to the drinkers at the bar and moved towards the door, but then paused and turned back to where Steve was struggling to sort out his soggy plastic bags. He came back to the table, and Steve stopped his repacking.

"You said you was a rugby man, didn't you?" Pasco reminded Steve.

Steve was surprised by the question, and considered the suggestion. "Well, yes, I suppose I am."

"I got a couple of season tickets for the Pirates. Selwyn usually comes with me but he's got a county match next Saturday. Shame to waste the ticket. You fancy it?"

Steve felt an emotion akin to pleasure; an alien experience of late. "Thank you. That would be great."

Pasco smiled. "Good. I'll pick you up here, then. Twelve o'clock."

FOUR

Steve had had no idea housework could be so exhausting. Two hours of it had just about done for him, but he had to admit the results were impressive. He had started upstairs, scrubbing the rust marks from the bath and eradicating dubious stains from the porcelain of the lavatory bowl. Then he had lugged the ancient Hoover from the kitchen cupboard up to his bedroom and unleashed it on the sticky carpet. He surprised himself with his technical expertise in twice emptying the dust bag into the outside bin. The spare bedroom, which barely had room for him and the vacuum cleaner, was less of a challenge, as the only covering on the bare floorboards was a bedside rug which looked as if it had died there. Steve was not overly concerned about that as he was not anticipating any guests. The sitting room (or perhaps it was a lounge; he had never been sure of the difference) now looked, if not exactly inviting, at least not repellent. The windows shone; the once-upon-a-time Ikea coffee table had not only been polished but supported a vase of flowers upon which Steve had impulsively splashed out after leaving the pub. The sagging sofa was no longer lopsided, thanks to a conveniently sized textbook courtesy of Trengrouse Academy subbing for a missing castor; the clunky television set, which looked as if it had been a John Logie Baird prototype, at least had a gleaming screen; and in a moment of triumph Steve had found a light bulb in a kitchen drawer to bring a spindly standing lamp back into working life. The kitchen – or 'kitchen-diner', as it had been ludicrously described in the property details – was, Steve reckoned, his greatest achievement. The dirty crockery had been stashed away in cupboards relined after vigorous scouring with ozone-damaging substances. The draining board and sink had responded well to the stainless-steel cleaner and almost sparkled in the late winter sun now flooding in through windows free of accumulated grime. The tiled floor had yielded most of its ingrained gunk to Steve's determined mopping, and the kitchen table, although still wonky, was at least sanitised and fragrant after being sprayed with harmful chemicals. Steve even believed that the wonkiness might be passed off as artisanal, in a poor light. "Not bad," he said to himself. "Not bad at all." His mood had lightened in step with the vanishing dirt.

He had spent a productive afternoon not only with his cleaning blitz, but in sorting out a replacement car. A hire company in Penzance would drop it off in the morning. It seemed that Steve's insurance cover was generous enough to secure home delivery on a Sunday morning, although not enough, he was advised, to qualify for a top-of-the-range model, for which he was truly grateful. He could not envisage rolling up to Trengrouse Academy in a brand-new BMW.

He convinced himself that his hard work deserved a reward. He had a bottle of single malt stashed away. He'd bought it months ago on special offer in Sainsbury's, intending it for Christmas celebrations at home, but of course they'd never happened. At Christmas he had been in London to see Hannah, staying at a Travelodge next to an industrial estate. Not a place to celebrate anything.

Steve had lived long enough to know that pleasure was never unalloyed; it came at a price. As he savoured his whisky, the price of this indulgence was the means to pay for it. There was a bundle of essays to mark stuffed in his briefcase. With admirable self-discipline he pushed the whisky bottle to one side and spread out the scripts in front of him. 'In Pride and Prejudice, how far does Elizabeth Bennet defy social conventions?' Really! It was absurd to expect his rough-hewn Cornish kids to engage with the mannered niceties of Miss Austen's prissy world. As he ploughed his way through the barely legible responses, placing the odd tick or encouraging comment in the margins, he was increasingly aware, as the stack of paper gradually diminished, that he was reading the same essay repeatedly. He was not surprised. In his schooldays it would have been called cheating and punished, but in these more enlightened times it was called 'online research'. With no attempt at concealment, his class had obviously found the relevant model answer and reproduced it. Some of the more conscientious, or devious, had bothered to shuffle some of the paragraphs about and add the odd original connecting sentence, and on those grounds he awarded them a higher grade than the straightforward plagiarists. He found it difficult to be too censorious. In their own ways, he and his students were all playing a game, and the important rule was not to ask the point of it. Therein lay madness.

With the last essay marked and bundled with the rest for returning on Monday, he felt justified in topping up his glass. He would need to get some supper together. He had grabbed a packet of sausages along with the cleaning fluids, and even an adventurous choice of a sweetheart cabbage to meet at least one of the requisite five a day urged on him by the government, or possibly the National Greengrocers' Association. After supper he might fall asleep, after his unaccustomed domestic exertions, in front of Casualty or Match of the Day. He was surprised that the prospect did not depress him unduly. Perhaps for the first time since he had come to Cornwall, there was a tiny flame of contentment flickering in his psyche. Apart from the therapeutic effects of spring-cleaning he could only attribute the lightening of his mood to his lunchtime drink with Pasco.

His introspective musing was brought to a stridently unphilosophical end by a tinny burst of 'I Do Like to Be Beside the Seaside'. He checked the number of the incoming call; not one he recognised.

"Hello?" Steve offered.

"PC Basset, sir." The tone was familiarly weary.

Steve waited for more but nothing came. This was clearly going to be a slow business. "Have there been any developments?" He hoped this might set the ball slowly rolling.

"In a way."

Steve allowed a further few moments of silence and then tried again. "Have you managed to trace the car?"

Basset was now positively upbeat. "We have, sir. It was in the system."

Steve felt praise was due. "Good. Well done. I can tell my insurance company and they—"

Basset seemed to be clearing his throat. "Not as simple as that, sir," he interrupted. "The vehicle was registered to a lady in Truro." He paused, and Steve thought he could hear the rustling of paper: the notebook, no doubt.

"A lady in Truro, you say?" Steve prompted. "It was a lady driving – well, I say, 'lady'..." He broke off before saying something Basset would deem inappropriate and ending up in front of a tribunal.

Basset now seemed to have found the right page in his notebook. "I can't divulge the name, of course, sir."

"No, of course not," Steve agreed meekly.

"But I very much doubt she was the lady you described."

"Oh." Steve felt guilty for even assuming she might be.

"What I can tell you is that the registered owner is aged eighty-two and a retired social worker," Basset proffered.

"Well, I didn't get a clear look but I think we can assume that the woman driving was not eighty-two and probably not a social worker." Carelessly, Steve blundered further into dangerous territory. "Although you can never be sure these days."

Basset, after a pause, seemed to overlook the frivolity on this occasion. "We know it was not the registered owner driving, sir."

Again Steve had to draw blood from the stone. "How is that?"

Basset played his ace. "The vehicle was reported stolen two days ago."

Steve let that sink in. "I see. Not good news. That makes things a bit more complicated."

Basset now trumped his ace. "We have recovered the vehicle, sir."

Steve was stunned. "That was quick. Most impressive. Have you made an arrest?"

Basset reverted to weary mode. "Inquiries are ongoing."

"But if you have recovered the vehicle you should be able to..." Steve broke off for fear that Basset might take umbrage at being chivvied by a civilian.

"When I say we have recovered, sir, I mean we know where it is."

Steve was not sure of the distinction but decided it would be unwise to ask for clarification. He waited patiently.

"Two walkers rang it in early this morning. Up at Ding Dong."

Steve wondered if Basset, in a moment of aberration, was now speaking in code. "Ding Dong?" he ventured.

Basset spoke slowly, as if addressing a small child. "Ding Dong Mine, sir. Old workings up on the moors. It was up there, burnt out. Torched."

"So what happens now?"

"Not a lot we can do, sir. I expect they'll have legged it back to Poland or Romania or one of those sorts of places. EU passports; they can come and go as they please." Basset's tone made it clear which way he had voted in the Brexit referendum.

Steve felt his liberal hackles rise but managed to disguise his disapproval. "How can you be sure?"

"You said she spoke in a foreign accent and was wearing a balaclava?" Paper rustled.

"Yes," Steve admitted, "but—"

"And they were coming out of a farm lane. You said that too, didn't you?" Basset's tone was almost accusatory now. "I may not be in the CID, but put all that together and what have you got?"

Steve kept quiet but readily caught Basset's drift.

"Migrant workers, sir; makes it tricky. We try to keep out of it unless things get too heavy."

"So nothing can be done? Is that it?" Steve tried not to sound critical.

Basset adopted a more conversational tone. "We'll keep it on file, of course, sir, but between you and me, no one's going to lose any sleep over it. No one was injured; you and the old lady get replacement cars from your insurers."

Steve could not help himself. "So we're all winners? Is that it, Constable?"

He could almost feel Basset snapping his notebook shut. The tone now was distinctly formal. "Just one more thing, sir. Be sure to notify the DVLA of your change of vehicle when you get one." With that, he hung up.

FIVE

For once the weatherman had good news and, in between his leaden jests with Mandy Trewellard, was able to confirm that a ridge of high pressure was building over the south-west. "A good day to be out and about," he suggested. Steve had to agree he might be right. If there had been a fine Sunday since he'd arrived in Cornwall he could not remember it, but now the sun shone through his newly cleaned kitchen window and the sky was an unbroken blue. He knew that somewhere he had stowed away his old walking boots.

In the brief years before Hannah had arrived he and Linda had taken to Sunday walks. Nothing too strenuous in the well-manicured parklands of London's Green Belt, but vigorous enough to justify a leisurely late Sunday lunch in a faux-rustic inn. Happy days. He remembered them now as if watching a film of someone else's life. When Hannah arrived there were no more country hikes. Carrying her, kangaroo-like, in a baby pouch around Clapham Common and, as she grew older, supervising her on the swings and slides of the play area became the new Sunday routine. They had tried to take her on the odd long walk and she'd struggled gamely to keep up, but it was a bit of a chore for everyone. In a careless moment Steve had suggested that they might make more active use of the holidays and they had attempted one disastrous camping week (it was supposed to be a fortnight) in Wales. Hannah had remained bravely cheerful as the rain fell unceasingly, but Linda's confinement to wet canvas had been traumatic. "The worst week of my life," was her verdict. So they had bailed out early and found a late online deal to Tenerife, where the sunshine was unbroken. Steve had to admit its warmth overcame his reservations about mass tourism. He could hardly complain about the English abroad if he was one of them, and if the Germans really did bag the sunloungers by the pool it was their reward for getting up early. In subsequent years Linda had researched more upmarket, and hence more expensive, destinations. They had graduated from Turkey and Cyprus to Florida, where Steve had to admit he enjoyed the rides in Disney World with a childlike delight far in excess of Hannah's, who said that reading about Snow White was better than seeing her.

Their last family holiday had been to the Maldives, at outrageous expense in Steve's view but Linda had insisted. They had booked into a chalet hotel on an atoll which Steve nervously imagined would be submerged at the next high tide. It was certainly a setting most would describe as romantic, but its magic did not rekindle any passion in their marriage. Then, he had blamed the sunburn and mosquito bites; now he knew it was Jason. Linda, he had noticed, seemed more distant than usual; not unfriendly but a bit wistful, as if something was not quite right. At the time he had put it down to the fact that on an excursion in a glass-bottomed boat around the lagoon they had found themselves sitting next to their London window cleaner. In the mutual shock of recognition Steve was able to murmur some platitude about it being a small world, whilst Linda seemed transfixed by a purple jellyfish bumping against the bottom of the boat.

Steve wondered if Hannah had noticed any changes in his relationship with her mother. She had always been a quiet child; never any trouble, not even in the pubescent turmoil of her early teens. She had friends, of course, but not really close ones. She seemed quite content with her own company and worked without complaint at her schoolwork. Her reports were always excellent. Their friends told them how lucky they were to have such a child, and regaled them with horror stories about their own delinquent offspring. In recent years the familiar litany of complaints about untidiness, ingratitude, laziness and so forth had given way to darker concerns around drugs and underage sex. Hannah was seventeen now. Steve tried to reassure himself that she had travelled through the badlands of adolescence unscathed, but how well did he really know her? If he was guilty of taking Linda for granted, had that also been true for Hannah? Perhaps it was only with distance – albeit enforced – that you gained perspective. However, he must not try to delve too deeply now. That would be like picking up the proverbial flat stone to reveal those sinister wriggling creatures underneath.

Sunday was the day he wrote to Hannah. Chewing on his biro, he wondered if he had anything to say that could conceivably be of interest to her. He always confined himself to dull factual accounts of his week because at least that precluded any real expression of the frustrations of his banishment. He didn't want her to feel sorry for him; to burden her with his depression. So he wrote about the ordinary; the mundane. The weather was a safe and constant topic for correspondence, as was how he was getting on in his new job. He asked her how she was coping with her A Levels and if there was anything he could help her with. At the end he told her he loved her, which was achingly true, and that he hoped her mother was well, which was also true but more of a formality. Today he could write in an altered mood. He told her how cheerful it was to see the sun shining, and how it would have amused her to see him cleaning and polishing the house. He had brought only one framed photograph with him from London. It was of Hannah; taken with a slew of holiday 'snaps' (as he still called them) on the ill-fated Maldives holiday. She was sitting on the white coral sands under a sunshade and had a book open on her lap. She had paused her reading to smile dutifully at the camera. The smile was more quizzical than expansive; hard to read the emotions behind it. Steve wondered again if his daughter had, unbeknown to them both, been for some time a silent observer of the gradual erosion of her parents' marriage. He looked now at the photograph he had hung from a convenient nail on the kitchen wall. "Hannah, I hardly knew you." He spoke out loud. He half remembered the words as some corruption of a popular song he had once hummed along to. On reflection it had been Jonny and not Hannah in the song but it seemed apt all the same, and he recalled something Noel Coward had said about the potency of cheap music.

Putting these distractions to one side, Steve resumed writing. For once he did not have to strain for material to pad out his narrative. He told Hannah about the car crash and assured her that no one had been hurt, and tried to amuse her with an account of his dealings with PC Basset. He explained his debt to Pasco and attempted to capture the character of the man, which was not easy, but although he had barely spent an hour in Pasco's company he had come across as someone without guile, without social inhibitions. Steve was not used to people like that, he reminded his daughter. They could be disconcerting as well as refreshing. Did she understand? Finally he told her that Pasco was taking him to a rugby match next weekend, and that he was looking forward to it. He didn't elaborate to Hannah that for the first time in months he had something to look forward to. That would seem pathetic.

With the letter ready for posting and the sun still shining, Steve hunted down his old walking boots. The leather looked a bit worn but he tried them on and they seemed comfortable enough when he took a few practice steps around the kitchen. The car hire company had been true to their word and a modest family saloon was now parked outside. He would take it for a drive to get the hang of it. He had found a dog-eared Ordnance Survey map of the local area in one of the cupboards; left behind, no doubt, by the summer holiday letting brigade. He had been intrigued by Basset's mention of Ding Dong Mine, which he had found marked on the map. It was only a few miles away, high up on the moors. The views up there should be good, and a bracing walk was something his parents had always recommended when he had slumped, festering, in his bedroom in an adolescent stupor.

The views were good; Steve could not deny it. The sharp light, honed by a keen northerly breeze, picked out St Michael's Mount in stark relief on its rocky outcrop in the crystalline blue sea. 'Blue', Steve accepted, was a totally inadequate word to do justice to the colour of that sea. Fortunately he did not have to describe it, just marvel at it, and if he turned his back on Mount's Bay and the Mount he was rewarded with a view across the moors to the distant glint of the Atlantic. Only a mile or two separated the English Channel and the Atlantic here. Steve knew that, of course, but the visual evidence of it was more impressive than the textbook fact. He was standing next to the towering old engine house chimney; unused for over a century but still defying the gales which blasted over these moors. Fenced-off and capped shafts were the reminders that once men had trudged up here from the villages in the valley, guided by the ding-dong of a bell in misty weather, to descend into the darkness and crawl along narrow passages to hack at the lodes of tin. What a bloody life. Steve contrasted his own meek existence with those poor wretches to whom, he had read, Methodism denied even the comfort of alcohol. That was probably too cynical. The promise of paradise in an afterlife was, he accepted, better compensation than a pint of watery beer for life like pig in this one.

Taking in the wild, treeless grandeur of the moors, Steve found it hard to remember that this timeless landscape was PC Basset's crime scene. The burnt-out car had obviously been towed away. There were heavy tyre marks in the mud which had probably been left by the recovery vehicle. He tried to imagine the scene barely more than twenty-four hours ago when the car would have been driven up here over the stony, potholed track which connected the mine to the tarmac lane where he had parked the courtesy car. It would have been dark, wet and misty. No one would have seen the blaze of the abandoned car up here in those conditions. How had they got away, the lady in the balaclava and her passenger? Did they have accomplices? Or did they walk? If Basset was correct and they were farmworkers, perhaps they knew their way on the many paths which criss-crossed the moors. It was all a mystery, and PC Basset had more or less admitted that it would remain so. Yet Steve felt somehow that that could not be right. People were always being told they needed 'closure' before they could 'move on'. They were usually talking about bereavement; sometimes violent and sudden death rather than the loss of a car, but he could still feel dissatisfied that there were unanswered questions nagging at him. Who were the people in the car? Had they left the country by now as Basset had implied? What were they doing driving a stolen vehicle? He would never know, of course, so he told himself he might as well stop fretting, but that was easier said than done.

The light was fading now and the air cooling. Steve started back to the car. He paused at the end of the rough track and looked back at the sentinel chimney stack silhouetted by the fast-setting winter sun. Perhaps he was being fanciful, but now its brooding presence seemed slightly menacing. He hurried to the car and was happy to switch on the engine and the heater.

SIX

And shall Trelawny live?
Or shall Trelawny die?
Here's twenty thousand Cornish men
Will know the reason why!

It was the fourth time the massed and swaying ranks of drinkers had burst into the chorus of what Pasco had told Steve was the unofficial Cornish anthem. In the noise and confusion Steve had found it hard to follow the explanation of who Bishop Trelawny had been and why twenty thousand Cornish men had cared about his fate, but after two pints of Doom Bar he had joined in the chorus with gusto. The beer tent was in full celebratory mode after the Pirates had triumphed, particularly as the victory had been over a London side. "Posh public-school boys," he had been told, but in truth most of the opposition seemed to be Fijian or Australian, though Steve had not been foolish enough to point that out to Pasco and his many celebrating friends.

Pasco had warned Steve on the drive to the ground that he might get carried away and to shut him up if he was making a fool of himself. Shutting Pasco up would have been a Canute-like task. His exhortations to the home side and denigrations, albeit good-humoured, of their opponents were leavened with loud sallies about the referee's eyesight and partiality. Initially Steve had felt embarrassed by Pasco's pungent running commentary, but it was soon clear that this was no more than the home fans expected. He was their cheerleader, and they laughed and applauded as he offered passionate instructions to his team and lived every moment of the contest. At half-time he instantly reverted to calm normality, as if he had been unplugged from the National Grid. He offered Steve a swig from his hip flask and hoped he was enjoying the game, which he certainly was; not just the match but the whole uninhibited atmosphere. It was, he had to admit, good fun. Fun. Not a phenomenon he'd been familiar with in recent years. Nobody here knew who he was or what was going on in his life. He didn't have to conform to any norm. It offered at least a temporary liberation, and when the match resumed he surprised himself by venturing an occasional involuntary cheer, and when in the last minute the Pirates ran in the winning try, he found himself on his feet celebrating with the rest of the crowd and returning Pasco's jubilant high five.

Eventually the throng in the beer tent began to thin out. With much backslapping and laughter, the hoarse and well-lubricated choristers drifted out into the cold and dark night. Pasco made his round of noisy farewells and indicated to Steve that it was time to go. Once they had left the town, the lights on Pasco's van picked out the twisting road back home. Before they got there, they passed the scene of the crash. Steve found it hard to believe it was barely a week ago. He told Pasco about his call from Basset, and about the burnt-out stolen car and how no further action could be expected. Concentrating on his driving, Pasco did no more than nod in confirmation of his estimation of police capabilities. "Useless buggers," was his muttered verdict.

Pasco insisted on driving Steve home, and followed his directions to the mean street and even meaner hovel. He parked outside and switched off the engine. "Thanks for your company, Steve. Hope you enjoyed it."

"Very much. A real treat." Steve made to open the van door, but paused. "I've got a half-decent bottle of whisky inside. Can I offer you a nightcap?" Then he remembered. "But of course you're driving; probably not a good idea."

Pasco had opened his door almost before Steve had finished speaking. "One won't hurt and, as I told you, you're more likely to see a camel crossing the road up here than a policeman."

As Steve fumbled with his front-door key, Pasco looked up and down the street. "Didn't know you lived here. Quiet, isn't it?"

Steve stopped with the key in the lock. It was not something he had considered; he had been barely aware of his surroundings when he shut the door behind him after the daily slog at Trengrouse. "Yes, now you mention it, I suppose it is." He looked down the street. "Not many lights on."

Pasco laughed. "Not in January!"

Steve poured Pasco a generous measure of the malt and listened to his explanation of the unlighted houses. It was obvious, of course, but it had somehow not impinged on his preoccupied mind.

"You'll have plenty of company in the summer. Kids everywhere; no parking. Nightmare."

"But they bring the money, don't they?" Steve felt as if he was apologising for his fellow invaders.

Pasco shrugged. "Can't do with them; can't do without them. When they're shouting the odds in the pub in August I say to them, 'You can moan as much as you like but you'd moan a bloody sight more if they stayed away.'"

Steve raised his glass in mock salutation; the alcohol was making him almost playful. "Well done. You are the voice of reason, sir."

Pasco laughed. "Never been called that before." Then he leaned forward, his elbows on the table. "Look, Steve, I'm Cornish. I was born here and so was my dad, so I suppose I qualify, but his dad came down here from Birmingham to work in the mine. Half of the lot that go on about being 'proper Cornish', if you go back a generation or two you'll find they've had family come from all over the place." He was in full spate now. "And what about the Cornish who buggered off to Australia and South Africa and all over when the mines closed? Can't blame them: they had to go where the money was. They didn't say, 'Oh, I'm sorry – I'm Cornish and I can't leave Cornwall, so I'll stay here and starve'!" He sat back and drained his glass. "Sorry, Steve, got a bit carried away."

Steve smiled. "I guess you won't be voting Mebyon Kernow, then?"

Pasco laughed at the idea. "I tell you something, Steve: I've never voted for anyone. Ever." He sighed. "I suppose I should be ashamed of myself."

Steve reassured him. "Well, I have voted for three different political parties in my time and they have all been a bitter disappointment. So perhaps, like you, I shouldn't have bothered."

Pasco shook his head. "No. It wasn't that I couldn't be bothered, but they all make these stupid promises which you know they can never keep; it's like writing to Father Christmas. If you want to change things you can't rely on that lot."

"Are there things you want to change?"

"Christ, yes. All round me." Pasco spoke with an unexpected intensity. "In this street, even."

"This street?"

"These empty houses. Miners' cottages, they were. Thirty years ago you could have picked one up for a few thousand. Now? You'd be lucky to get any change from two hundred grand. No young people down here can afford that. Selwyn will have to move away to earn that sort of money if he ever wants to buy a house, and he's one of the bright ones; perhaps he can do that. But the rest? And they can't even rent. Not at these prices."

"Tell me about it," Steve sighed.

Pasco nodded. "And who's making the money? Not just the holiday companies and the estate agents. Think about who sold these houses. Locals. They took the money and ran. It wasn't 'Cornwall for the Cornish' then. 'You want my cottage for a second home? Certainly... and here are my bank details.'" He slumped back in his chair.

Steve looked at him. This was a different Pasco.

Pasco offered Steve an apologetic smile. "Must be your whisky talking."

Steve pushed the bottle across the table. "Have another."

Pasco looked at his watch. "Better not. Tamsin will murder me." Then he took the bottle and poured himself a generous measure. "What the hell. I'll leave the van here and walk home; it's only five minutes. Cheers."

He raised his glass in salutation and Steve did the same. They savoured their drinks and then Pasco put his glass down and folded his arms theatrically across his chest.

"Right, Steve. Your turn."

"My turn?" Steve said nervously.

"I don't know much about you; only that you're a teacher at Trengrouse and a bit of a rugby man, but I'm a nosy bugger and I ask myself, What brings a bloke like you down to the Wild West? And another thing." He pointed. "For the last ten minutes I've been wondering who that lovely girl is."

Steve turned and looked at the picture of Hannah.

He was not sure for how long he spoke, with Pasco a silent listener offering only an occasional nod, frown or smile as a counterpoint to Steve's narrative. It was the first time he had confided in anyone about the events which had brought him to Cornwall. He told Pasco about Linda and Jason and admitted that he had not seen it coming and could not really blame her. He confessed to his own lethargy; his too-early descent into middle-aged tedium. He explained that he was now having to adapt to what genteel people called 'reduced circumstances'. Pasco nodded sympathetically at that, but smiled encouragingly as Steve spoke of Hannah and his love for her in words which he hoped were not mawkish. He had not spoken at such length and in such personal detail to another human being for as long as he could remember; perhaps ever. Maybe it was the whisky talking, or maybe something about Pasco that prompted plain, unvarnished speaking; a built-in bullshit detector.

When at last he sat back, his throat dry from his monologue, Pasco said nothing. Then he stood up and carried his glass across to the sink. As Steve watched, anticipating some comment or reflection, Pasco put on his overcoat and walked to the door, where he stopped and looked back.

"See you Saturday, then; same time." With that, he opened the door and walked out into the silent street.

SEVEN

Steve had to admit the cottage pie was good. He thought perhaps Trengrouse should have applied for academy status on the strength of its school dinners, but maybe that was not a qualifying category. Not only was he enjoying the food, but his lunch break had been enlivened by the company of another member of staff. Usually he found a table where he was not obliged to make more than minimal contact with his colleagues; not because, as far as he knew, there was anything wrong with them, but because he was wary of invasive questions to which, he felt, he would offer only minimal response. Thus, he confined himself to bland pleasantries and, when necessary, conversation on curriculum-related topics. So he was startled when the head of the PE Department, Taff Evans, sat down opposite him and asked him what he had thought of the game on Saturday. He had spotted Steve in the beer tent but had not come over because it was too squashed to move, and anyway, he could see that Steve was in good company with Pasco. Was there anyone in Cornwall who did not know Pasco, Steve wondered? After the initial surprise, the two of them chatted easily enough about the game, and Steve was even asked if he would consider lending a hand with the after-school rugby coaching, and was too taken aback, and possibly too flattered, to rule it out completely, which the PE man seemed to take as a yes.

There was no doubt that Steve's mood had lightened a touch in the past few days. He had to admit that he did not feel the same dread hand of gloom constantly squeezing any enjoyment of life out of him. He was not at a stage where he leapt cheerfully out of bed in the morning to welcome the jocund day but at least he did get out of bed without wishing he could lie there forever, which was how he had felt in his first weeks in Cornwall. Maybe the improving weather helped. The anticyclone was proving stubborn and keeping the Atlantic troughs and fronts and depressions at bay. There were definitely signs of spring in the fields as he drove to work. Daffodils were flowering in Wordsworthian loveliness and were being harvested by teams of pickers bent double in their high-visibility yellow. The sight of them brought Steve back to the car crash. Was Basset right? Did someone out there picking daffodils know about the stolen car? He put these thoughts aside as pointless. It was over; finished.

Except, of course, there was the matter of his car. The loss adjuster had visited the garage and confirmed the mechanic's diagnosis that Steve's car was not worth repairing. It was written off and Steve received a cheque for the second-hand valuation, which was less than he might have hoped for but, as the mechanic had so eloquently put it, "better than a poke in the eye with a sharp stick". Now he would have to buy a replacement. He could only keep the courtesy car until the weekend, so he had earmarked Saturday afternoon to go into Penzance to look at second-hand cars; not an expedition he anticipated with any pleasure, as in a recent newspaper survey he had read that second-hand car salesmen had ranked only above estate agents and politicians in the nation's list of least-trusted occupations.

Thinking of Saturday was a reminder that he was meeting Pasco in the pub. There was no home match for the Pirates this week but it would still be good to meet, although Steve was a little nervous at the prospect. He could not quite remember all he had said across the kitchen table but he suspected that it was too much. He barely knew the man and yet he had laid bare his soul, and if that sounded a bit melodramatic, he had certainly discarded his customary reserve and spoken of feelings and emotions he scarcely ever allowed even himself to dwell on. Had Pasco been embarrassed by all that soul-baring? He was a hard man to read. He had shown that there was another side to him, too, behind that apparently chirpy and uncomplicated front. He had spoken with real anger and conviction about what was happening in the town; blighting the future of the next generation, in his view. What should Steve make of that? Perhaps the Romans had got it right: in vino veritas.

The pub regulars were at the bar again. Perhaps they had been there since last Saturday. Steve had arrived before Pasco but the landlord, who introduced himself as Sam, was friendly enough, and some of the others nodded in recognition as Steve carried his pint across to a vacant table and unfolded his copy of the local newspaper. The Penwith Packet would not have been his usual choice of reading matter, but with barely a glance at the front page he turned to the classified ads and stared in some confusion at the listings of used cars. Reading the descriptions, he wondered why anyone would ever consider selling such exemplary vehicles. Many were alleged to be in immaculate condition and some were given additional acclaim by belonging to a 'local owner'. From his experience of Cornish driving habits, that seemed more of a disqualification than a recommendation. Further bafflement was provided when the permitted word counts were insufficient and a car's attractions were spelled out in acronyms: 'FSH' and 'CL' piled on top of 'RVW' and 'HDS' and so on. Steve wondered if Bletchley Park would have cracked it. He accepted that he was about as far from being a petrolhead as it was possible to be. Linda had the use of a company car and his car (now waiting to be crunched in the scrapyard, no doubt) had spent most of its life parked on the concrete of what had once been their front garden. Linda had acquired it with the help of her mixed doubles tennis partner, who knew more than you could ever possibly want to hear about the internal combustion engine. Steve had to admit that it had been a good buy. In the five years before he collided with the old lady from Truro's stalled automobile there had never been a problem with it, largely because he rarely drove it. He had seen similar cars advertised as being ideal for 'running about town'. Whoever wrote that was living in Fairyland rather than London, where you could not 'run' anywhere in a car and the best pace you could hope for was a shuffling stumble. Rather than face daily road rage, Steve had braved the subterranean horrors of the Northern Line, which was good for his carbon footprint but bad for familiarity with what lay under the bonnet of a motor car. Indeed, on the very rare occasions when Steve had needed to open the bonnet – to attempt something as intricate as replenishing the screenwash – he'd needed to consult the handbook to find out how to do it.

"What you got there, boy?" Pasco said as he sat and raised his glass in greeting.

"Cars. Used ones." Steve pushed the newspaper towards Pasco, who picked it up and studied it for a few moments before handing it back.

"What you looking for?" Pasco asked.

"Wish I knew. Something to get me to work and back as cheaply and reliably as possible."

"How much you got to spend?"

Steve was not surprised that Pasco, in his forthright manner, had come straight to the point, and he told him how much the insurers had paid out. Pasco agreed it was not much but said it ought to be enough to pick up something a year or two away from the knacker's yard.

"But what? It's all a mystery to me." Steve gestured helplessly at the car ads.

Pasco gave the matter thought for a moment or two. "When you going to do this?"

"I'll have to sort something out this afternoon, after I've dropped off the car." Steve sighed at the prospect.

"I'll come with you." This was not a suggestion but a statement. "Don't reckon cars are your thing."

Steve felt inadequate in the face of this blunt if accurate assessment. "You must be wondering what is my thing. Me too."

Pasco smiled. "You're a good teacher. That's worth a lot."

"That's kind of you to say so but—"

"It's not what I say. Selwyn told me."

Steve was puzzled. "But I don't teach Selwyn."

"No, but I told him I'd met you and he mentioned it to some of the Trengrouse lads at county training. They reckon you."

Steve was unexpectedly heartened by this news. He even sensed a blush.

Pasco continued. "That lady teacher who got herself up the duff?"

"My predecessor, you mean?" Steve offered by way of clarification.

"They said she was useless. Spent most of the time crying."

Steve nobly stepped in to defend a colleague he had never met. "Pregnancy can be challenging, of course, and I believe there were... well... unfortunate issues."

Pasco was prepared to make some allowance. "I dare say. Anyway, she's gone and no one thinks she'll come back." He smiled at Steve. "That would suit, wouldn't it?"

Steve half sensed where this might be going. "I don't know—"

"You're doing a good job. You could carry on."

"It doesn't work quite like that. There are procedures, protocols and so on."

"Bugger that." Pasco was clearly not a man for protocols. "But it's possible, isn't it, that they might ask you to stay?"

"I hadn't really thought. It's been one day at a time for me."

Pasco was not to be deflected. "But it is possible?"

"I suppose it might be," Steve conceded.

"And would you? Stay?"

Steve did not feel he could offer the certainty of a firm response. "I really don't know. I think I've been on autopilot for too long."

Pasco seemed to settle for that as an interim position. He looked down at the car listings again and studied them for a moment. "Load of old bangers, most of them," was his verdict. "I got a better idea. Desi Hosken."

Steve felt more explanation would be helpful, but Pasco merely drained his pint and, with a contented burp, put down his glass. Steve was quickly on his feet. "Let me get you another."

Pasco hesitated. "Better make it a half. Got to be thinking straight for Desi."

Steve made for the bar, where Sam was arranging pasties in the warming cabinet. Whilst he waited for the drinks he caught Pasco's eye and performed an elaborate mime involving pointing at the pasties, putting an imaginary one in his mouth and raising his eyebrows quizzically. The message got through and Pasco raised a thumb in approval. By the time Steve carried the drinks and the pasties back to the table, Pasco was engrossed in the Packet, frowning and muttering as he studied the front page. Steve could make out the banner headline: 'Trevalwith plans turned down'. It meant nothing to him, but clearly a great deal to Pasco. He began to eat his pasty in silence.

With a shake of the head and some indistinct oath, Pasco slammed down the paper. He grabbed his pasty and chewed an aggressive mouthful, and the effort involved seemed to dissipate his indignation. "Thanks, mate," he said, his manner now calmer. "Sam does a nice pasty," he pointed with his half-eaten one at the newspaper, "but that's enough to give you indigestion."

Steve picked up the newspaper and scanned the offending item. To him it seemed remarkably unsensational; basically a bland summary of the council's rejection of a planning application by property developers wanting to build holiday cottages. He looked for clarification to Pasco.

"Do you know Trevalwith?" Pasco asked, and then answered his own question. "No, why would you? About ten scruffy acres on the St Ives road. Never been any good for anything. Not enough grass for cows and too many rocks for sheep. Couldn't do anything with it, but that suited old John Penhaul." He laughed.

"John Penhaul?" Steve queried.

"Part of his farm. The useless part. But the beauty of it was, he got paid for doing nothing with it even though he couldn't do nothing with it anyway. Bloody barmy."

"How was that?"

"Set aside. Money from Brussels. This is what they call an Environmentally Sensitive Area. Hard to believe sometimes

51

but they chuck all this EU cash at farmers to preserve it as it is." He shook his head in disbelief. "They'll miss all that."

Steve looked again at the newspaper. "Someone wanted to build holiday homes there. A dozen of them. Is that right?"

Pasco nodded. "Penpol Investments Limited." He spoke the words slowly and with clear distaste.

"I gather you don't approve?"

Pasco gave a scornful laugh. "You can say that again! Bunch of crooks."

"Well, you should be pleased they can't get planning permission, then."

"That's not how it works down here, Steve." Pasco pointed to the front page of the newspaper. "See what it says there?" He jabbed his finger at the concluding paragraph.

Steve studied the text and read it aloud.

'A council spokesman stated that the application was not acceptable in its current form. For Penpol Investments, chief executive Brian Kingdon said that, whilst he was disappointed in the council's decision, he acknowledged their concerns and his board would look again at the company's plans to see if an accommodation could be reached.'

When he had finished, Steve looked in some confusion at Pasco. "That seems straightforward, or am I missing something? Is there a subtext?"

Pasco frowned. "I don't know what that is, Steve, but what I do know is that it's all bollocks."

Steve waited for elaboration but none came. Pasco made short work of what was left of his pasty and got to his feet.

"We'd better crack on to Penzance if you want to get a car sorted. I'll tell you about bloody Penpol Investments on the way."

EIGHT

Knowing his luck, Steve drove with particular care on the journey to Penzance. He didn't fancy returning the car with a dent in it. The leisurely pace afforded Pasco the time to explain his deep misgivings about Penpol Investments. They were behind a number of developments in the area, most of which he described as "dodgy". They seemed to get away with building on sites where permission had been refused to small local builders. Pasco had done work for some of these firms over the years, and spoke of their dark suspicions regarding Penpol's methods in winning over the council. Nothing could be proved, of course, but he was sure palms had been greased.

Steve was shocked. "Are we talking corruption here?" He risked a quick sideways glance at Pasco before concentrating carefully on the road again.

Pasco shrugged. "Just the Cornish way of doing business, some would say. It's been like this for as long as I can remember. But it was small-scale stuff. If you knew someone who knew someone who might know someone – say, in the Planning Department – then, if you bought them a drink or two they might put in a word to let you, for example, put in a new dormer window or something. Or maybe you had a relative worked in Building Regs who could have a whisper so that you could get away with using one sort of brick rather than another. Nothing major."

"And you? Was that how you worked?"

Pasco smiled. "I probably should have done. Might have made some money. But..."

Steve laughed. "But you decked the foreman!"

"I couldn't do it, Steve." Pasco paused. "I blame my dad."

"Your dad?" Steve queried. "How does he come into it?"

Pasco turned his head and looked absently at the empty fields. When he spoke it was softly; almost apologetically. "He's been dead over ten years now. He and my mum, within a year of each other. But I think of him a lot." He turned towards Steve. "And I talk to him a lot. Daft, I suppose."

"Not at all. Sometimes it's easier to talk to the dead than the living."

Pasco laughed. "At least they can't answer back."

"So what do you talk to your dad about?"

"Everything and nothing, I suppose, but if I'm not sure about the right way to go about things then I'll talk about that." He glanced warily at Steve. "I've never told anyone else this; people would think I was some sort of nutter."

Steve shook his head. "Not at all. My parents are both still alive but I can't talk to them about anything, especially now. I'm sure they feel I've let them down."

"I know I'm only really talking to myself but I still feel my dad's listening; even watching. So I daren't risk it." Pasco smiled to himself.

"Risk what?"

"Letting him down."

Steve was puzzled. "How would you do that?"

Pasco tried to order his thoughts. "You know the Methodists were big down here, years ago? You see these big old chapels all over the place."

Steve nodded. "Yes; most of them shut down."

"Right. Or turned into holiday flats or restaurants or amusement arcades. The ones that are still going get a few pensioners on Sundays if they're lucky." Pasco sighed. "Not that I can say anything. Apart from weddings and funerals I haven't set foot in a chapel since I was twelve."

"And before that?" Steve asked.

"Twice a day every Sunday. Morning service and Sunday school. I hated it; bored stiff."

"So why did you go?"

"My dad was very big in the Chapel. It was his life, really. A lay preacher, I think they call it. So I had no choice: listening to all those sermons; singing all those hymns."

Steve was puzzled. "But when you were twelve?"

"Father realised I was a fish out of water. He knew I'd rather be out with the other kids; on the beach or kicking a ball about. So, one Sunday morning as I was getting my best gear on to go to chapel, he came into my bedroom. I thought I must be in some sort of trouble, but he sat down on the bed and just looked at me for what seemed forever and said, 'You don't want to do this, do you?' I was too surprised to make anything up so I just told him he was right. I was scared he would get mad, but he just said, quite calmly, 'I hope I've shown you the right way. Now you're old enough to find your own way.' Then he went off to chapel with my mum and we never spoke of it again. I can still see them walking out the door and leaving me sitting there in my Sunday best."

"So what did you do?"

"Changed and went off to the beach." Pasco looked abashed at the memory. "But sometimes I think maybe I've left the Chapel but perhaps it never really left me. All right, I know I drink too much, swear too much, lose my temper too quickly, but I hope I can tell what's right and what's wrong."

Steve nodded. "I understand. 'Give me a child until he is seven' and all that. Sounds as if your dad knew when to let you go; trusted you. He was a wise man."

"A good one too. I see that now, of course. More than I did at the time. Perhaps this talking to him is trying to let him know or something. Weird."

"Far from it," Steve reassured him. "He would be pleased. He'd see that you have found your way."

"Thanks, Steve." Pasco paused. "So now you see."

"See what?"

"Why I decked the foreman and why I get so wound up by the likes of Penpol bloody Investments."

"Because it's what your dad would have done?"

"I suppose so." Pasco laughed. "But I doubt he would have decked the foreman."

Steve was relieved to be able to hand back the car unscathed. Once they had done that, Pasco led him on a few minutes' walk to a large car showroom where expensive new vehicles rested, gleaming with polish, behind glass and the forecourt was packed with an array of cars of lesser distinction. Steve stared in dismay at their serried ranks. Pasco looked already to have several possibles in mind and, oblivious to the residual damp, was actually lying on his back under one of the candidates, shaking its exhaust pipe vigorously with both hands. Steve stared at him in disbelief but was distracted by the opening of the showroom door and the approach of a large, besuited figure who bore down on him with outstretched hand.

"Can I be of assistance, sir?" The tone was deferential and the smile well rehearsed but somehow incongruous coming from this giant of a man whose suit, Steve could now see at close proximity, was liberally stained and blotched; the trousers losing the battle to confine an abundant paunch.

"Thank you. We were just—"

Steve got no further. Pasco had scrambled back to his feet and came towards them shouting out a greeting. "Desi, you old bugger! How you doing?"

"Pasco. What you doing here?" Desi clapped Pasco on the back in hearty recognition.

Pasco gestured at Steve. "Come with my friend here; he needs a car."

Desi turned back to Steve with a reassembled professional decorum. "Well, you've come to the right place, sir. May I ask how much you were looking to spend?"

Pasco answered for him. "A lot less than you were looking to charge." He then named a figure a couple of hundred pounds below the amount Steve had received from the insurers.

Desi looked doubtful. "I'm not sure we have anything I could recommend at that price."

Pasco swept such doubts aside and pointed to the car with the exhaust he had assaulted. "That one; the green one. We'll take it round the block – that's if it will start."

Desi tried to look affronted. "All our used cars are thoroughly checked and serviced."

Pasco laughed. "And I'm the Queen of Sheba."

Desi was not ready to give up yet. "Anyway, that particular car is several hundred pounds more than the gentleman's budget." He smiled apologetically at Steve.

"We'll see about that after a test drive. Keys, Desi." Pasco held out a palm.

Desi accepted the inevitable and shambled back to his office for the keys. When he was out of earshot, Steve spoke anxiously to Pasco. "I really haven't got that sort of money. Not the way things are." Before he could elaborate, Pasco hushed him with a silent finger to the lips as Desi plodded back with a bunch of keys.

Steve hoped sincerely that Pasco was right about the dearth of policemen in West Cornwall as he raced the car furiously and noisily along the Promenade, past the startled walkers taking the sea air. Then he revved the engine deafeningly to get them up the steep hills behind the town, before alternately braking and accelerating fiercely along quiet side streets in a manner which rendered Steve quite nauseous and fearful that he would have to part with Sam's recently consumed pasty. As they motored at a more sedate pace back to the forecourt, Pasco advised Steve to let him do the talking. Catching a glimpse of his ashen features in the driving mirror, Steve was happy to agree; he was not sure he was capable of speech.

Desi emerged from his office in his rumpled suit as they got out of the car. Steve, mindful of Pasco's instructions, leaned in what he hoped was a nonchalant manner against the car door, which helped to support his shaking legs.

Pasco sucked in his breath, made a clicking noise with his tongue and shook his head slowly. He looked reproachfully at the car, and then accusingly at Desi. "If I didn't know you better, Desi, I'd say she's been round the clock."

Desi looked outraged, his florid features reddening. "We don't do that. We're not cowboys, Pasco."

Pasco thought about that for a few seconds. "OK. I believe you, Desi, but she's got no poke at all. Rattles like hell; I reckon the exhaust is shot." He looked warningly at Steve, who was now remembering Pasco's earlier foray under the car. "And look at the state of these back tyres." He kicked one of them dismissively.

Desi hurried round and bent his considerable frame to examine the tyres. "They're legal," he protested.

"Just. Steve will be looking to replace them in a week or two. Couple of hundred quid to fork out."

There was a long silence. Desi spoke first. "So you're not interested, then?"

"Not if it was for me. But Steve needs wheels, so if you forget about this silly price you've stuck on her you might get yourself a deal."

Twenty minutes or so later, after thrust and counter-thrust between Desi and Pasco with Steve merely a silent onlooker, a price was agreed which was the exact amount of the insurer's cheque but several hundred pounds less than the amount which had been advertised on the windscreen. Steve followed Desi into his office to complete the paperwork and, happening to glance behind him, caught a glimpse of Pasco wriggling back under the car. To distract Desi he pointed in admiration at one of the elite models in the showroom and gabbled some inane comment about it. Steve handed Desi a cheque and received various documents in return. Perspiring slightly from the effort of his administrative duties, Desi sat back in his commodious executive-style leather chair and gratefully undid the buttons of his constraining jacket and loosened his constricting tie. His salesman facade thus discarded, he smiled cheerfully at Steve.

"How long you known Pasco, then?" he asked.

"Not long at all. A week or two, if that."

"He's something else, isn't he?"

Steve was unsure if this was a criticism or praise, so looked to shift the focus of the conversation. "What about you? Have you known him long?"

Desi laughed. "Twenty-odd years. He used to be my minder."

"Your minder?" Steve was nervous about where this might be going.

"Rugby."

Steve relaxed. "Oh, I see," he said, but he didn't really.

Desi explained. "He's a couple of years older than me. They stuck me in the team straight from school because I was a great big lump, I suppose, but I was well out of my depth. Not streetwise. Some of the older guys we played against used to try to wind me up – a quick punch or a boot when the ref wasn't looking – and I was stupid enough to retaliate, but by then the ref was looking so we got penalties against us and I got sent off once. That's when Pasco stepped in."

This was beginning to make sense now. "And became your minder?" Steve asked.

"Yes. He was a bloody good player; played for Cornwall dozens of times. Would have been a pro these days. He wasn't the biggest but he was hard. Not dirty, but hard as nails." Desi broke off reflectively; in memory, back again in muddy conflict.

Steve broke the reverie. "So how did that work; being your minder?"

Desi blinked as if waking from a dream. "He gave me a real bollocking and told me to get a grip on myself and if there were problems to leave it to him to sort out." He grinned.

"And how did he do that?"

"If someone was winding me up, Pasco would have a quiet word. No shouting or waving his arms about; just a whisper."

Steve was curious. "And that worked?"

"Not always. Some of the hard nuts told him to piss off. Kept on niggling me." Desi smiled broadly. "More fool them."

Steve was engrossed in the drama now. "What happened?"

Desi leaned forward, his arms flat on the desk, his voice low as if wary that someone in authority might overhear. "He'd bide his time, wait for the moment when it was legal, and then hit them with a tackle like you never saw. Like a sodding Exocet. They'd go down in a heap, all the wind knocked out of them; used to have to call on the sponge man often as not. And the thing is, after he'd floored them he'd get up and just give them a little wink. Just to make sure they got the message." He sat back with a warm smile of appreciation.

"Not a man to mess with, it seems," Steve offered.

Desi nodded. "He did that for most of my first season. Word must have got around because they stopped bothering me. And I tell you what, Steve," first names now replacing salesman formality, "and I can remember it like it was yesterday, before the first match of the next season he took me to one side and gave me a really serious talking-to about how I should handle myself. 'Don't let yourself down,' he said. Talking to me like he was my father."

"That didn't bother you?" Steve asked in some surprise.

"No, not coming from Pasco it didn't, and before we went out on the pitch he said one more thing which I haven't forgotten in twenty years."

"What was that?"

"He said, 'Desi, I've shown you the right way; now you must find your own way.'"

Desi got to his feet and Steve stood too. They walked to the office door, and on the forecourt saw Pasco, now standing by the green car.

Desi gestured towards him. "Hard to imagine him saying that, isn't it?"

Steve remembered Pasco talking about his father. "Not really, Desi, not hard at all."

Steve drove slowly on the way back, getting used to the car, which now seemed to be running quite smoothly. He commented on this to Pasco, who merely smiled enigmatically until curiosity got the better of Steve.

"Tell me, Pasco. What were you doing under the car?"

Pasco laughed. "Just checking the exhaust. I think I've fixed it now."

Steve looked at him doubtfully. "If I didn't know you were a good Methodist boy I might think—"

"As if," Pasco protested. "Anyway, everybody got a result, didn't they?"

"How do you work that out?"

Pasco was patient in his explanation. "You get a decent car at a fair price and Desi still makes a tidy profit. He'll have bought it in at half what he was asking for it." He waited for Steve to grasp the argument. "So everyone's happy."

"You've convinced me. I tell you what, Pasco, I wouldn't like to meet you on a mountaintop offering me all the kingdoms of this world."

"Matthew 4, Verse 8. One of Father's favourite sermons."

Steve stared at him in astonishment. "There's more to you than meets the eye, Pasco."

Pasco shrugged. "All those Sundays on hard chapel benches. I suppose it stays with you a bit."

"More than a bit, I think. Perhaps more than you know."

Pasco seemed embarrassed by the turn of the conversation and sought to change it. "You in a hurry to get home, Steve?"

"Why would I be? Only more marking waiting for me."

Pasco pointed ahead at an approaching crossroads. "If you turn right here you can have a look at Trevalwith. It's only about a mile."

Steve had to think for a moment to remember Trevalwith. "The planning thing?"

"Yes. There's a lay-by you can park in. Won't take a minute."

In fact it took considerably more than a minute. Once they had parked, Steve followed Pasco down a rutted, sunken lane which ended at a collapsing double wooden gate which was easily dragged open to allow them access to an area of overgrown gorse and bracken. The land sloped away here to the edge of the cliffs, and beyond them the sun was beginning to douse itself with an orange afterglow in the steely waters of the Atlantic. Only the occasional rumble of a car passing on the road behind them disturbed the cold silence of the late afternoon. The two men stood and gazed.

Steve was the first to break the silence as he stared at the broad horizon. "Hard to imagine a dozen houses here."

Pasco turned to him. "There won't be, Steve."

"That's good. Isn't it?"

Pasco's smile was without humour. "There was never going to be anything like that."

"But I thought that's what it said in the paper – the planning application?"

"All bullshit. That's how Penpol works."

Steve was lost, and for the moment Pasco was not prepared to offer an explanation. Beckoning Steve to follow, he pushed his way through some obstructive bracken and low clumps of heather until they emerged onto a patch of relatively open boulder-strewn grass.

Pasco scanned the field below them until something caught his attention. "There. Can you see them?" He pointed to a distant corner of the field, where the rays of the setting sun glinted on the pristine corrugated roofs of two low buildings. "Clever bugger."

Steve waited for enlightenment but Pasco was absorbed in his own thoughts. Then he turned abruptly and, with Steve trailing behind him, headed back for the car.

Pasco remained silent for the rest of the journey, and only when Steve asked him where he wanted to be dropped off did he speak. "You can let me out at your place, Steve."

"Are you sure I can't drive you home?" Steve offered.

"No, thanks. There's someone I need to talk to first."

Steve wondered who that might be, but reminded himself it was none of his business.

When Steve had parked, Pasco sat for a moment and then turned to him. "This Penpol business. I suppose I've got a bee in my bonnet. I shouldn't be bothering you with it; I know you've got enough on your plate as it is. Sorry to have dragged you out there."

"Don't apologise. What is on my plate, as you put it, is not exactly exciting. You've got me hooked, to be honest with you, Pasco."

"Well, if you mean that I'll fill you in on it all."

"Thank you."

Pasco opened the car door. "Right. I've got a few people to see and questions to ask, but if I get any answers I'll be in touch." He gestured at the hovel. "I know where you live."

NINE

The chips were good, so Steve accepted that the discomfort he experienced in lifting them out of their greasy bag was just about worth it. "Nothing broken," the blonde Australian lady doctor in A&E had said, and merely prescribed paracetamol which Steve had taken with a shot of what was left of his whisky. He had a vague memory that alcohol and painkillers shouldn't mix but he lacked the energy to study the listed prohibitions, caveats, and details of hundreds of possible side effects jammed into the packet of tablets. He was really past caring. He had spent the obligatory two hours in A&E before the Barbie-doll lookalike, who could not have been more than fourteen in his estimation, sent him on his way. He had explained to her how he had damaged his shoulder and her reaction had been one of disbelief and amusement. "At your age?" she had queried.

Steve should have come up with a ready excuse when Taff Evans (Why are all PE teachers Welsh? he had wondered) reminded him of his vague offer to help with the rugby coaching. Taff had even found him a pair of old boots which just about fitted, and Steve dug out a tracksuit he had barely used. It was left over from his brief flirtation with the fitness regime Linda had urged on him a few years ago. She had warned him that he must not let himself go. She was a fitness addict with her wellness classes and tennis, and whilst her stringent calorie-counting ensured Steve did not put on weight, she told him he should do aerobic work for his lung capacity. She put newspaper articles in front of him which carried grim warnings of the multiple disorders awaiting those who did not run upstairs or walk to a further bus stop. So, to keep the peace, Steve forced himself to go for a run when he came home from work. It was the last thing he felt like doing after the purgatory of the Northern Line. He never enjoyed it; never experienced a 'jogger's high'; never felt the euphoria fitness professionals (how could that possibly be a profession?) rhapsodised about in the weekend supplements; never sensed the surge of endorphins which would banish depression. All he had felt was hot, sweaty, out of breath and self-conscious. It had been a struggle to keep at it and he was secretly relieved when Linda stopped pestering him to continue. He had thought then that she had taken pity on him, but now he recognised that her waning interest in him had probably coincided with her increasing interest in Jason.

In his reincarnated tracksuit and pinching boots, Steve had felt a bit like the spectre at the feast when he joined Taff after school on the rugby field, but the boys greeted him cheerfully enough, and with Taff bellowing the orders Steve quickly settled into the training session. He was pleased to discover that he had not lost all of the proficiency which had once made him a useful player. Taff divided the squad into small groups and entrusted Steve to coach handling skills, which he did with increasing confidence.

During a water break, Taff came across to him and muttered, "Not bad, boyo; I can see you've played a bit."

All of which was fine but, as Steve now reflected, increasing confidence goes before a fall. Taff decided to end the session with a short game, and divided the group into two sides, telling Steve to join in if he felt like it. Initially Steve confined himself to the odd pass and a gentle trot after the ball. It took him back to the days when he had played for real, and this reflection jolted him into more wholehearted participation: his trot became a tentative run and he held on to the ball for longer when it came his way. He even managed a sidestep to thwart an opponent, and then put in a pass which enabled the boy who received it to score.

"There you are," Taff shouted. "That's how it should be done."

If only Steve had bowed out there, but adrenaline was overcoming common sense, so when he received a pass not far from the try line he managed to accelerate towards it with glory in his sight. Unfortunately, what was not in his sight was the team captain, a lad of considerable bulk and a surprising turn of speed, who came out of nowhere to clatter him to the ground with a textbook tackle. The boy had the grace to apologise to Steve as he sat propped against the goalpost, struggling to breathe.

"Don't worry, lad, it's all in the game, isn't it, Mr Milton?" Taff said jovially.

Steve nodded weakly. As the boys trooped away, Taff helped him to his feet and, noticing him wincing, prodded experimentally at his shoulder. Steve yelped at the pain.

"Don't think it's dislocated, boyo, but better pop into A&E on your way home – that's if you can still drive?"

Steve had just about managed to drive and, after his experience in the emergency room, decided he would stop for fish and chips on the way home. It would be an extravagance he could ill afford but he justified it as his reward for his suffering, and anyway, he doubted he would be able to lift a frying pan. The chips were getting cold now, congealing in their bag. The battered cod was finished and Steve looked at the detritus on the kitchen table, trying to summon the energy to clear it away. Supporting himself with his good arm, he stood up and began to gather in the litter.

Before he could edge his way towards the pedal bin there was a rap on the door. Steve managed to open it with his one functioning arm to see a pale, even ghostly figure looking at him.

"You got a moment?" Pasco asked. "Just finished work," he pointed at his white overalls, "so I thought I'd catch you, if that's OK."

Steve dragged the door open. "Sure. I've just finished eating."

Pasco looked at the jumble of packaging in Steve's hand and sniffed the air. "Fish and chips, is it?"

"Yes. A rare treat after a hard day." Steve manoeuvred awkwardly around the table to put the litter in the bin.

"What you done to yourself, Steve?"

"You don't want to know; too embarrassing." Steve pointed to the now-cleared table where only the whisky bottle stood. "There's a bit left."

Pasco hesitated. "I shouldn't really; I ought to be getting home." Then he reached for the bottle as Steve produced another glass. "Well, just a nip, then."

They both sat down and Steve one-handedly refreshed his glass. "I've been half expecting you to call."

"I would have come sooner but it's taken a bit of time, what with work and trying to get hold of people. Didn't help old John Penhaul was in Majorca for a week."

Steve remembered the name. "He's the farmer you mentioned."

"Was a farmer," Pasco corrected. "He's been retired these last couple of years. Built himself a nice bungalow in town. I did all the decorating for him."

"You know him, then?"

"From a long time. He's a Chapel man; still goes. He and Father were good friends." Pasco sipped reflectively. "I felt a touch guilty."

"What about?"

"I called on him yesterday; told him a bit of a story, I'm afraid." Pasco looked down at his glass. "Said I was short of work and I'd heard there might be a big building job coming up at Trevalwith, and did he know who the contractors were?"

"But it's been turned down," Steve protested.

"Yes, but I pretended I didn't know that, so it gave me a chance to ask him all about it."

"What did he tell you?"

Pasco shrugged. "Not a lot. He doesn't have anything to do with the farm now. He left it all to Giles."

"Giles?"

"His son." Pasco spoke the words dismissively. "Not like his old dad. Went to private school and then agricultural college but spent most of his time there chasing women and running up debts for John to pay off. After college he buggered off to London and did something in the City; John never really understood what but he used to tell me Giles was doing well; serious money."

"And then his dad handed him the farm?" Steve guessed.

"Couple of years ago. Giles moved down here for a bit and spent a lot doing up the farmhouse; not that he hangs about here more than a few weeks at a time. Still got his place in London."

"He doesn't farm, then?"

Pasco laughed aloud at the idea. "He's not one to shovel shit. He's got a farm manager to run the place, but when he's down here he likes to look the part. Got a Range Rover, the green jacket, and some fancy bird hanging on his arm."

"His wife?"

"No chance. Old Mrs Penhaul is always grumbling that it's time he settled down and raised a family."

Steve picked up the bottle and drained what was left in it between the two glasses. Pasco nodded his thanks. "So Giles must have been involved with Penpol; the planning application."

"Right on. John didn't really approve but nothing he could do about it. He said he was glad it got turned down." Pasco sighed. "I didn't tell him the rest of it; didn't want to upset him."

"The rest?"

Pasco pressed on. "I did ask him about those new sheds; told him another porky. Said I'd seen them from the road."

"What did he say?"

"Surprised as hell. Didn't know nothing about them. Couldn't see why Giles would need new sheds; least of all in that rough old field."

Steve smiled. "But you, Pasco, you know why they're there."

"I think I do," Pasco drained the last of his whisky, "but I need to dig around a bit more; see if I can get hold of Keith."

"You've lost me."

"Keith Rowe. Good bloke; an old mate of mine."

"Let me guess. An old rugby friend?"

"I can see you've got me sorted, Steve." Pasco stood. "I'd better get on. Thanks for the whisky, and take care of that arm."

Steve raised his good arm in acknowledgement. "You'll tell me if you get any more, won't you?"

Pasco nodded. "You want to come to watch the Pirates again? Selwyn's getting jumpy about his A Levels; doesn't reckon he can take Saturdays off. So his ticket's going to waste."

"That would be great, but at least let me pay—"

Pasco raised both hands with palms open towards Steve in rejection. "Hang on to your money," he said. Then added, with the frankness Steve was coming to accept, "From what you tell me, you need it."

"True, but that—"

"Don't worry about it. I'll see you in The Miners at twelve, and I'll try not to shout too much this time."

TEN

Taff Evans had joined Steve again for lunch. He asked how his shoulder was getting on and reluctantly accepted that Steve would not be helping with the rugby coaching "for a week or two", which Steve reckoned was a considerable underestimate. Taff seemed to feel that their rugby involvement was as firm a bond of friendship as any man could expect. He asked Steve frankly about his move to Cornwall, and Steve found it surprisingly easy to tell him.

Taff was sympathetic to matrimonial problems; he was on the second Mrs Evans, he explained. "Got married too young, boy: big mistake. Expensive, too."

Steve could certainly identify with that. "I need to try and bolster my income, Taff," he explained, "but I'm not sure how."

"Not easy."

"I had thought of trying to get some private coaching work."

Taff looked sceptical. "Not in this part of Cornwall. That might be a goer in the yachting belt but down here if anyone's got any spare cash they're more likely to blow it on a Sky dish."

"I suppose so," Steve accepted. "I knew it would be hard to find anything."

"Especially this time of year," Pasco elaborated. "It's only cutting cauliflower and picking daffodils now, and nobody fancies that: the unemployed down here would rather surf than do that, and I don't blame them." He laughed and pointed at Steve's arm. "Not that you'd be much good with that shoulder. More chance in the summer, of course; holiday time. There's always bar work and the like; if you're not too proud, that is."

Steve smiled. "I can't afford to be proud, Taff, but I doubt I'll be here for the summer holidays."

"Of course, I'd forgotten: you're maternity cover for poor old Rachel, aren't you?"

"Yes. But why 'poor'?"

"Out of her depth, boy. Too sensitive by half. We won't see her again." Taff stood up and made to clear his plate away. "I reckon they'll ask you to carry on. That's if you want to."

As Taff moved away, Steve remembered that Pasco had said much the same thing. When Taff had gone Steve took a letter out of his jacket pocket and reread it. If anyone had been watching they would have assumed the contents were welcome to the reader, as Steve smiled and on occasion even laughed. Hannah had managed to make the account of her week upbeat. Her description of some of her classmates amused him, and her account of attending someone's eighteenth birthday party captured all the noise and chaos and unfulfilled romantic expectations of such occasions. She had liked the music and mentioned tracks by bands 'you will never have heard of, Dad'. She assured him she had drunk only Coke, but the exclamation mark at the end of that assurance made him suspect she was teasing. That changed his mood. He put the letter down and felt the familiar sense of loss again. He was not there to be a part of her life. He told himself again that all the clichés were true: only when something is taken from you do you belatedly recognise its worth.

Like a dog shaking water off its coat, Steve flexed his shoulders and forced himself to sit up straight, not just to ease his aching collarbone, but to shed his incipient melancholia. He resumed reading and began to feel more cheerful again. Hannah had picked up on the more positive tone of his recent letter to her, in which he had told her about Pasco and his new car. She told him he was clearly becoming 'proper Cornish' and perhaps he should apply to be an extra in Poldark, which, she told him, her mother still watched avidly. That was the only mention of Linda apart from the assurance that she was well. Steve reflected that his daughter would be a strong contender in the tact and diplomacy stakes.

He was smiling at that conclusion when he became aware of Taff returning. He quickly folded the letter, put it back in his pocket and looked up inquiringly.

"Don't know if it's of any interest, boy, but Bill Rogers has just put a notice up in the staffroom."

Steve barely knew Bill Rogers. They had exchanged the occasional pleasantry but beyond that he knew only what Taff had quickly told him in the staffroom. Bill was head of the Further Education Department, responsible for running the various evening classes the academy offered. Taff was brusquely dismissive of them: "A few art sessions; a bit of pottery; some keep-fit stuff for oldies. Nothing too exciting. No call for it in these parts, you see." He implied this low-key profile suited Bill, who, he explained, was near retirement and "a nice enough old boy but lazy as hell".

Bill certainly seemed to be taking his ease when Steve found him in the stationery store, the overview of which seemed to be within his remit. Bill had cleared enough space to accommodate a comfortable armchair and a small, rickety coffee table upon which rested a chipped tin mug half filled with tea and a plate bearing a couple of chocolate digestives. "Just catching up with a bit of paperwork," he explained as he beckoned Steve in and hastily folded away the newspaper he had been reading.

Steve nodded sympathetically. "If this is a bad time—"

"No." Bill looked studiously at his watch. "I've got a few minutes yet. Take a seat." He waved a hand vaguely at the spartan furnishings of shelves and trestle tables piled high with packets of copy paper, ring binders and assorted exercise books.Steve carefully cleared a space so that he could perch precariously on the edge of a table.

"So what are you after?" Bill asked. "I'm out of laminating sheets at the moment but—"

"No," Steve cut in quickly, "it's about the notice in the staffroom; the evening class."

"Ah, I see. Are you interested?"

Steve tried not to seem overeager. "I could be. I thought perhaps you might give me a few more details."

Bill looked reflective. "To be frank with you, Steve..." He paused. "It is Steve, isn't it?"

When Steve nodded in confirmation, Bill pressed on.

"I could do without this. I've got enough on my plate already."

"So I believe," Steve lied.

"But no getting out of it; a directive from County Hall, you see. There's still this EU money sloshing about and they're frantic to use it up before the tap gets turned off."

"EU money?" Steve asked.

"Yes – some initiative from Brussels, they tell me. Part of closer European cultural integration. A bit rich when you think we shall be unintegrating PDQ." Bill chuckled at the silliness of it all.

"But in the meantime?" Steve encouraged.

"In the meantime we have to play ball. The mandarins have identified this area as having a high concentration of non-English-speaking residents. And they don't just mean the Cornish." Bill laughed at his own joke, and Steve joined in dutifully. "Those working in what they call the hospitality industry, and of course on the land."

"So the class is aimed at them?"

"Yes – those who, to use the politically correct phrase, do not have English as a first language." Bill paused. "We used to call them foreigners."

"I know. I did a course. TEFL. They called it English for Foreigners in those days."

Bill looked quite animated now. "You did a course? Excellent."

"It was in my first couple of years teaching. Money was a bit tight so I did some evening-class work."

Bill was now leaning forward in his chair. "So you are telling me, Steve, that you have a qualification in this field and some experience?"

"It was nearly twenty years ago," Steve admitted.

Bill did not see that as a problem. He had clearly moved on. "It would cut out all the paperwork. We will have your references on file here, and your DBS checks." He looked at Steve. "Do you still have the TEFL diploma?"

"I think I've got it at home somewhere."

"Excellent. If you bring that in I can sew this up. No need to waste time and money on advertising." Bill had now assumed that Steve had accepted the position. He pulled a scuffed leather briefcase from under his chair and rummaged in it to find the relevant papers, which he briefly consulted. "The course runs for two sessions of two hours twice a week. Starts in a fortnight and ends in late July." He looked up at Steve. "That all right for you? Remuneration as per FE hourly rates and mileage allowance."

Dazed, Steve confirmed that it was but then expressed a doubt. "But will enough people turn up to make it viable?"

"I think so. County Hall is pulling out all the stops. Flyers in all the supermarkets; local papers; stuff on the radio."

Steve felt immediately nervous. "Serious business, then."

"Money from Brussels, you see. Play the game on this one and they can hold out the begging bowl for more; make hay while the sun still shines."

"Maybe, but will the punters turn up? After a long day busting a gut in some cabbage field, why would you feel like going back to school?"

"It's free," Bill said, as if that was sufficient explanation.

"Even so—"

"And," Bill paused dramatically, "and, if they complete the course they get a certificate of attendance and a proficiency grading."

"Is that such a big deal?"

"Think about it, Steve. Who knows when the Brexit door will slam? After that, no more free movement. They're going to need a work permit or some such; so many points to qualify."

Steve was beginning to understand. "And some evidence of competence in English will help."

Bill smiled. "Spot on."

The sudden, jarring clamour of an electric bell pronounced the end of lunchtime. Steve eased himself off his perch on the table. "Must go. Year 9."

Bill nodded sympathetically. "Hard luck." He bent and rummaged again in his briefcase. "I'll keep you in the picture. Registration is online so we'll soon have some idea about numbers."

"Online?" Steve said doubtfully. "Will that work?"

Bill laughed. "They may cut cauliflower or pick daffs but they've all got smartphones."

Steve moved towards the door whilst Bill remained seated. Steve made to hold the door open but Bill showed no indication of moving, still fumbling in his briefcase. He looked up and became aware of Steve holding the door.

"Oh, I've got a free." He waved airily at the stacked shelves. "Catching up with the paperwork."

As Steve closed the door he glimpsed Bill unfolding his newspaper.

ELEVEN

Pasco was halfway through his pint by the time an apologetic Steve joined him.

"Sorry, I got stuck with some stuff online; didn't realise the time."

"Working on Saturdays? You and Selwyn both."

Steve gratefully swallowed some ale. "I'm trying to get my head round this new job. Well, possible new job."

Pasco frowned. "You leaving Trengrouse? Already?"

"No, nothing like that. Evening classes." Steve explained the situation.

"Well, the extra cash will be handy. Hard work, though, I dare say."

Steve put down his glass, now nearly empty. "Very. It's all changed since I last did this stuff. Then it was just a bit of a chat; conversation practice." He smiled ruefully at the memory.

"And now?" Pasco asked.

"It's all digital now."

"What's that mean?"

"The internet. Working online."

"I'll take your word for that." Pasco pointed at Steve's glass. "Sup up – you look as if you could do with another."

Steve made only half-hearted protests and drained his glass as instructed. Pasco walked back to the bar and Steve relaxed back into his chair. He could almost regard The Miners as his local now. He had been greeted cheerily by the throng at the bar and Sam had quizzed him on the likely outcome of the afternoon's match. He could not deny that he felt contented – happy would be overdoing it, but he could settle for contentment.

Pasco put down the pints. They raised their glasses to one another.

"You know your way around a computer, then, Steve. I can just about manage my phone!"

"Not as much as a ten-year-old, but I get by."

Pasco looked thoughtful. "Might be handy."

Steve felt a moment of guilt. In the past few days he had been so absorbed in the prospect of the evening class that he had put Pasco's concerns about Trevalwith to the back of his mind. Now he switched on. "Do I take it you've made progress? I remember you were trying to get hold of one of your old rugby mates."

"Keith Rowe," Pasco reminded him. "Useful outside centre in his day."

"And now?"

"Now he's got his own business. He's a draughtsman. Done some drawings for me; a couple of extensions I worked on."

Steve could not see yet where this was going. "How does—"

"Before he set up his own business he worked for the council. In the planning office."

"I see." Steve was not sure quite what he could see, however.

Pasco dropped his voice and leaned closer. "I just wanted to check a few things out. See what he could remember about Penpol."

"And their projects?"

"Right."

"And could he? Remember anything?"

"Couldn't stop him once he started. When he was working for the council he knew there was something fishy going on. He tried poking about a bit but was more or less warned off."

Steve looked doubtful. "That sounds pretty heavy."

"I don't mean he was threatened or anything, but it was made clear to him that he should just concentrate on the routine stuff he was given; not rock any boats."

"Penpol's boat in particular?"

"Correct. They were well in with the council – still are, Keith reckons. They got all sorts of stuff going on all over the county. Housing, mostly; new builds." Pasco sighed.

"But?" Steve knew there must be more.

"Penpol always play the same game. Start with large-scale plans, knowing they haven't got a cat's chance in hell of getting permission; so they give it a few months and come back with something toned down, saying they've taken on board all the objections, listened to all the concerns of local residents and the environmental lot and so on. If it goes to a public inquiry they wheel out all the experts; professors of this and that to kiss the inspector's arse, and of course they have the best lawyers to drive through all the loopholes. They must have splashed out big money to get that crew on board." Pasco sat back, wearied from his explanation, and drank thirstily from his glass.

"It must be worth it," Steve suggested.

"Big time. They build high-end stuff. Nothing you or I could buy; they haven't got the likes of us in mind."

"Who, then?"

"People who can fork out a spare half a million from petty cash, or someone selling up in London who can retire down here and still have some change."

"And they get away with it? Get permission?"

"Not all the time, but enough to make it worth the effort. Sometimes they have to play the affordable housing card."

"What?" Steve asked.

"Do a deal with the council. Agree to include properties affordable to local people in any new development."

"Well, that's good, isn't it?" Steve protested.

Pasco laughed at the notion. He leaned closer. "How well do you know St Ives, Steve?"

Steve was surprised by this change of direction. "Not well."

"Very fashionable these days; lots of art galleries and poncy shops selling rip-off tat to tourists. Can't hardly breathe there in the summer, and can't park your car any time of the year."

Steve grinned. "You make it sound really attractive."

Pasco shrugged. "No accounting for taste. It seems to be the place to be – people want to live there; houses go for stupid prices."

"How do Penpol come into this?"

"A couple of years ago they bought an old hotel just outside the town; it was falling down so they picked it up cheap because no one thought you could get permission to build on the site."

"But Penpol did?"

Pasco smiled in encouragement. "You're catching on quick, Steve. Yes, Penpol did, because they struck a deal with the council to include some affordable homes in the development."

"And did they?"

"Two ground-floor one-bedroom flats with a view of the car park. The other ten apartments had balconies and sea views. And the two 'affordable' ones were not affordable to any normal young couple working down here. They had played another card: the viability assessment one."

"What's that?"

"Convinced the council that any more affordable units would have a negative impact on their profit margin." Pasco pushed away his empty glass. "That's one of their favourite tricks."

Steve frowned in disbelief. "But how did they get away with it?"

"That's what Keith wondered. The deal is supposed to be thirty per cent affordable units."

"Did he find out?"

"No. If anybody knew, they weren't saying. But he had his suspicions."

"Which were?"

"The planning guys don't make the big decisions, Steve, they can only make recommendations to the council, but the council don't have to follow them. That really pissed Keith off; it was why he got out and went on his own. He didn't see the point of telling the council what the right action was, only for them to ignore it."

"I suppose that's democracy for you," Steve offered.

"I'd say that's corruption for you."

"Is that what Keith thought?"

"Could never prove it, of course, but that's the only thing that made sense of it to him."

"Was he saying Penpol were bribing councillors? That seems pretty full on."

"Nothing so obvious; nothing you could ever go public with." Pasco got to his feet. "Look at the time, Steve." He gestured to the station clock above the bar. "We'd better push on or we'll miss the kick-off."

The atmosphere in the beer tent was much more subdued than it had been on Steve's previous visit. There was a distinct lack of fervour in the voices of those vowing to defend Bishop Trelawny, and the bar staff had time to lean on their counter and chat to each other as their customers drifted away early. The Pirates had lost a game they were expected to win, and gloom was all around. Pasco was unusually quiet. Even during the match he had restricted himself to a few despairing appeals to his vanquished team, and afterwards he sipped glumly at his pint, acknowledging the greetings of friends with scarcely more than a nod. Steve had not seen him in this mood before, and doubted it was just a result of the match. When he finished his beer Pasco declined the offer of a refill, telling Steve he had better get home to Tamsin.

In the car on the way back Pasco apologised "for being such a wet blanket". Steve tried to make light of it, sensing that this was not the time to ask questions. Pasco did eventually force himself into counterfeit jauntiness and his parting remark was to explain that he was just feeling a bit under the weather; probably getting "another bloody cold". Steve doubted that that was the real cause of his friend's melancholy.

TWELVE

The weather on Sunday had now reverted to default mode. Steve recalled an oft-quoted verdict on British weather that it was of two kinds: light grey or dark grey. Cornwall added another dimension to the dark grey: mizzle, not quite fog and not quite rain, mixed with a sharp wind which failed to disperse the fog or blow away the rain. The weatherman on Radio Kernow, with whom Steve was beginning to form a love-hate relationship, had described it as "Western Ocean weather", as if that excused it.

As Steve sat in front of his laptop on the kitchen table, the bleakness outside did not bother him unduly. He had plenty to do on this alleged day of rest which made it easy to accept internment in the hovel, although as he looked around at the results of his new determined housekeeping regime he told himself that he must stop thinking of it as 'the hovel'. After a glass of wine or two in the evening he could almost admit it was cosy.

His first task was to plough through another batch of GCSE coursework. This time he had tried to challenge the apathy of the class by inviting them to consider how Shakespeare presents attitudes towards love in Romeo and Juliet. They had made faces of disbelief when he had given them the assignment. The rugby captain, who had so recently inflicted the damage on Steve's still-aching shoulder, had glared at him as if he would like to do it again, and then groaned and buried his head in his hands. Steve had felt some sympathy. He could scarcely credit that this brawny Cornish lad had much grasp of the concept of Elizabethan ardour, but the coy glances he often attracted from some of the more nubile girls in the class suggested he might have some experience of its twenty-first-century manifestation. It took Steve nearly two hours to wade through the scholarly dissertations so obviously culled from the archives of virtual knowledge At least he derived some pleasure from the thought that it had probably been as much of a chore for them to trawl the internet for the appropriate words as it was for him to read them. Thankfully, he scribbled some encouraging platitude on the last script and pushed the pile to one side. Coffee time.

Sipping his brew of instant, Steve debated which of his next two tasks he should tackle first, and decided he would indulge himself by putting pleasure before duty. So he wrote to Hannah. At least he had something positive to tell her, and he recounted his meeting with Bill Rogers and the possibility of taking on the evening classes, which he was viewing with a mixture of nervousness and enthusiasm. He confessed that he didn't know whether he would be disappointed or relieved if they never happened. He also described his recent rugby outing with Pasco and tried to capture for her the drastic change of mood defeat had triggered in the beer tent. He kept the tone light, hoping to amuse her, but was reminded uncomfortably of Pasco's dejection which he was fairly certain had not been caused solely by the rugby result. He made no mention of this to Hannah but instead told her how much he had enjoyed her last letter with the pen portraits of her school friends; he told her she clearly had a gift for writing, and joked that he should know as he had just spent two hours reading the efforts of those who did not. After a dutiful inquiry after Linda's health he concluded by telling Hannah how much he loved her. He wanted to add how much he missed her but he always held back from that; unwilling to self-indulgently unload onto her the sadness of their separation.

He risked a brief foray into the Western Ocean miasma to post Hannah's letter, and this burst of activity was sufficient to galvanise him into opening a tin of tomato soup for lunch. In a moment of pure hedonism he allowed himself the indulgence of a glass of wine from a bottle selected purely on the grounds of price rather than quality. The label advised him that it was a product of several European countries. Steve could live with that; he told himself he had always been a good European. He did have to accept that the wine tasted slightly of Dettol but that did not prevent him risking a second glass. Guiltily, he pondered whether he was in danger of drinking too much. He could never remember what the government's precise recommendations were in terms of weekly units (how the hell could you raise a 'unit of cheer' in salutation?), but he suspected that he exceeded the quota. He could perhaps blame Pasco for his decadence. They must have polished off a good few units in their whisky-fuelled musings, and there were the Saturday pints in The Miners. Steve remembered a glum Pasco's recent uncharacteristic, subdued abstinence and wondered if he would ever work that out. He admitted to himself that he hoped Pasco might tell him one day.

The second glass of Dettol was beginning to make Steve feel drowsy, and it took an act of will to rouse himself sufficiently to return to his laptop. Although the evening classes had yet to be confirmed he disciplined himself to do some preparatory work. There were dozens of online sites inviting subscribers to discover the secrets of teaching English to non-native speakers ('foreigners' had been so much less of a mouthful), but by judicious foraging amongst the free samples Steve was able, in a couple of hours, to assemble enough material to map out several lesson plans. The concentration involved in these acts of piracy, combined with the lingering effects of the plonk, induced a headache. Blinking away the dancing floaters in his strained eyeballs, he found the energy to fill the electric kettle. At least the descending darkness outside was obliterating the mizzle. He pulled the kitchen curtain across to complete the exclusion of the feeble light of the lingering day.

He felt pleased with his day's work, and he could still look forward to a gourmet supper of sausage and instant mash, with possibly yet another glass of his wine of uncertain provenance. After that there might be something of passing interest on the box, but he would not be holding his breath. In this twilight time his choice of viewing would be limited to inane quiz shows or soporific nature programmes with presenters who looked as if they would be more at home in city wine bars, floundering instead in muddy bogs feigning enthusiasm for honking geese or elusive otters. The boiling kettle claimed his attention and, having made his tea, he went back to the table and diffidently picked up his Sunday paper. He was not sure why he bothered with one. He could confidently predict the contents. There would be exclusive revelations of the transgressions of politicians who had been caught with trousers down or a hand in the till. Recently, too, there had been a spate of anguished disclosures from middle-aged actresses cataloguing multiple acts of inappropriate behaviour by loathsome media moguls; a phenomenon which Steve had heard Taff Evans, who was defiantly unwoke, describe as "the Not You Too brigade". Banishing such cynicism, Steve flipped quickly through harrowing accounts of persistent hostilities in the Middle East and the dissipation of the ozone layer, to find the sports pages. This was usually the only section of the paper he trusted. There wasn't much you could do to distort the football results, but beyond that he found the ranting of ageing pundits banging on about imagined glories and claiming it was all so much better in their day rather wearisome. Although there were still volumes of inserts and supplements to contend with, Steve lacked the will to tackle them. They were mostly absorbed with the glossy lives and habitats of celebrities (Celebrated by whom and for what? he wondered), which presumably resonated with about fifty people who lived in Islington. In his present circumstances he might just as well read about life on Mars. However, he had recently taken to studying one section of the paper which in the past he had reserved to light the fire: the financial pages. His besetting worries over money had made him desperate enough to look for advice on how to maximise his pitiful savings and where he might get a minuscule percentage point more by switching accounts. Invariably, he ended up more confused than enlightened. The advice offered seemed to be fashioned for those with many spare thousands to play with, and various suggestions as to how he might 'enlarge his portfolio' were frankly risible. Today he was told it was a good time to get into the Pacific Rim. Where the hell was that, for God's sake?

Steve started to screw the paper up in frustration when a headline caught his eye. 'Penpol offers share bonus'. He unscrewed the paper and flattened it out. He could not make much sense of the article beyond the fact that Penpol were doing rather well for themselves and their shareholders. With nothing much else requiring his attention, Steve's curiosity made him turn to his laptop and ask Google to search for Penpol Investments Limited.

THIRTEEN

Bill Rogers found Steve in the staffroom, where he was snatching a quick coffee in the mid-morning break. Scrabbling about in his shabby briefcase, he produced a single sheet of typed paper which he handed to Steve. "Signing up well. These are the definites. Only a few places left and I'm pretty sure we'll fill those," he paused and affected nonchalance, "after my radio spot."

Steve was alarmed. "Radio?"

"Yes. They want to interview me."

For a moment Steve envisaged Bill on the Today programme, talking to the nation.

"Mandy Trewellard."

Steve relaxed. "Oh."

"Just to fill them in on the course; get the word out there. Bit of a pain, really," Bill played the martyr role, "with everything else on my plate."

"It must be difficult," Steve agreed with feigned sympathy.

"But there you are." Bill shrugged. "County Hall are insistent." He took on the air of a man for whom this was just another burden of command.

"So when are you on?"

"Not sure yet. They'll be in touch. It'll mean taking time

off, I'm afraid." Bill found it impossible to conceal a smile of satisfaction.

"Shame." Steve entered into the spirit of the game.

Bill closed his briefcase. "I'll let you know final numbers in due course." With that, he nodded at Steve and left the staffroom.

Steve studied the list. There were a dozen or so names on it. A few he could guess were Spanish or Portuguese, but he stared blankly at the rest, which he could not begin to allocate to any particular nation.

Taff Evans approached, clutching a mug of tea. "What you got there, boy?"

Steve told him and showed him the list of names. Taff studied them for a moment and then laughed.

"What's funny, Taff?"

"I reckon you got a team for the Winter Olympics there, boy."

"What?"

Taff jabbed a finger at the names. "Never saw so many 'ski's' in all my life."

The confirmation that the classes were going ahead concentrated Steve's mind over the next few days. He sat up late preparing his material: creating worksheets and video clips and devising role-play scenarios. It was time-consuming and exhausting but he had to admit he was quite enjoying it. It was different; a change from the treadmill of Ofsted-haunted outcomes and evaluations and assessments. Perhaps it had come at the right time for him; a distraction, possibly, but also (and he was wary of the much-abused word) a challenge. His self-esteem had taken a battering when Linda dropped her bombshell. Like so much else in his life in the past few years, he had taken not only his marriage but also his work for granted. Life had become stale; he could see that now. Linda was right. He'd heard people talking about losing their mojo and never been quite sure what that meant, but whatever it was, he was sure his had been eroded by his acquiescence to the humdrum. Now at least he had a shift of focus; he was not constantly looking at the world through the prism of self-pity. Working on ideas for the evening class had kindled within him an enthusiasm for teaching which had lain dormant for too long, and his involvement with Pasco had brought not only the balm of friendship but also a heightening of interest in the activities of Penpol Investments. He had news for Pasco on that front, which he looked forward to imparting over their Saturday pint at The Miners.

Mandy Trewellard was working hard to interest her listeners in how to cook cauliflower in ten different ways. By the time she had completed her task, with a suggestion of cauliflower Wellington, the traffic light at the roadworks had changed to green and Steve was able to drive slowly past the red-and-white cones which demarcated an empty lane of tarmac on which no work was taking place, nor had been for several days. A board at the end of the bollards carried a telephone number to contact for information. Steve had no doubt that anyone naive enough to try that would be answered, if at all, by a recorded message apologising for an exceptional level of calls and suggesting a visit to the website. He was distracted enough by this train of thought to be oblivious to Mandy Trewellard droning on in the background until a familiar voice jolted him into full concentration.

"Yes, Mandy," Bill Rogers was saying, "we are certainly excited about this, and of course proud that Trengrouse has been chosen as one of the venues for this initiative."

Steve was fully alert as Mandy dutifully plugged on. "You say this is a groundbreaking experiment?"

Bill was happy to concede that. "And long overdue, Mandy. We need to do all we can to help our foreig..." he corrected himself just in time, "our European friends and partners here in Cornwall to feel fully engaged with their local community, and of course fluency in English has an important part to play in that."

Mandy agreed. "Of course. And you say there has been a good response from the... urm..." She hesitated, looking for an acceptable term.

Bill came to her rescue. "From those who do not have English as a first language. Yes; very encouraging. In fact, such has been the response that we might need to lay on more classes."

"And this starts next Tuesday, you say?"

"Indeed; we're keenly looking forward to it."

"So just to recap: next Tuesday at 7pm at Trengrouse Academy?"

"Correct."

"Well, good luck with that, Bill." Mandy was ready to sign off. "I hope you will enjoy teaching it as much as the students will enjoy learning from it."

Bill laughed. "Kind of you to say that, Mandy." He paused. "Unfortunately, much as I would love to, I have previous commitments which prevent me from actually teaching the class myself; a shame, but it can't be helped. However, we are very fortunate at Trengrouse to be able to call on a staff member with considerable experience and expertise in this field."

"That's great. Thank you, Bill." She paused. "I don't know how it is where you are, but it looks a bit drizzly out of my window. Let's get an update on Cornwall's weather..."

Steve was too stunned by Bill's comments to take in what the weatherman was saying, and he forced himself to concentrate on his driving just in time to avoid demolishing yet another set of cones planted on the road ahead.

The toad-in-the-hole was perfectly acceptable to Steve, although Taff was grumbling that it was more hole than toad. He was in a bad mood because he had spent the morning having to rearrange his cricket fixtures for the summer term. He looked at the crossed-out and underlined list on the table in front of him. "One day cancelled and you have to shuffle the whole bloody lot about."

Steve was barely listening, still preoccupied with his thoughts on the imminent challenge of the evening class, but he felt he should show some concern for Taff's problems. "So what's been cancelled, Taff?"

"The Thursday we were due to play Truro. That's a big game for us and now I've got to try to fit it in somewhere else."

"Why is it cancelled?"

"Local bloody elections! We're a polling station." Taff shook his head in disbelief. "Complete waste of time if you ask me; only about three people vote and get to choose between Tosser A and Wanker B."

Steve laughed. "People chained themselves to railings to get the right to do that."

Taff was unrepentant and continued muttering to himself as he scribbled on his fixture list. Steve resumed finishing off his meal but was distracted again, this time by Bill Rogers looming over him with papers in his hand.

"Sorry to interrupt your lunch but I've got the final numbers here." He plonked himself down on the bench next to Steve.

"Heard you on the radio, Bill – very impressive," Steve said, trying not to be distracted by a wink from Taff.

"It seemed to go quite well. County Hall are happy."

"You'll need an agent soon, Bill," Taff said without looking up from his fixture list.

Steve pressed on hastily. "The final list, you say?"

Bill handed it over. "A full house." He stood up. "Must get on; busy day."

Taff now stopped his jottings and looked with exaggerated sympathy at Bill. "It's all go, isn't it?"

Bill nodded vaguely and wandered off.

Taff laughed. "Gone to put the kettle on, I expect." He stretched across the table and picked up the list Bill had delivered. He studied it for a few seconds before handing it to Steve. "Not all '–ski'ers now; you seem to have picked up a few '–escu's as well."

FOURTEEN

This time Pasco bought the pasties. He handed one to Steve and took a hefty bite out of his own. Steve thanked him and protested that he had wanted to pay.

Pasco waved away the protest and gulped down his mouthful of beef, potato and swede. "Least I could do, after last time. Not much company, was I?"

Steve understood. "Well, they had been expected to win."

"Not the rugby. I can handle that." Pasco laughed. "Tamsin keeps telling me it's only a game, but she puts it a bit stronger than that."

"She's a brave woman, your wife," Steve teased.

Pasco put his pasty down and frowned; his mood had changed. "She's more than that, Steve. She can read me like a book. She knew I was fretting over something; getting all worked up." He sighed. "Can't keep nothing from her."

"The Penpol business?" Steve asked.

"Yes. I was letting it get to me."

"And you told her."

"No need, really; she guessed. I had been going on about it a bit at home."

"And what did she say?"

"Told me to forget about it. No point getting in a state about it. Not unless..."

"Unless what?" Steve demanded.

"Unless I could do something about it," Pasco picked up his pasty, "which I can't." He sat back and munched reflectively. "She's dead right, of course. I've got to put it out of my mind."

Steve was curious. "What put it in there in the first place?"

Pasco smiled at him. "You did."

"Me?" Steve could not conceal his astonishment.

"Talking to you; explaining how things are down here. I never do that with my regular mates." Pasco gestured towards the crowd at the bar. "We don't do serious stuff; just take the piss and have a laugh. But you're a bit different."

"How?"

Pasco grinned. "Well, you've got a brain for a start."

Steve laughed dismissively. "Lot of good that does me. I can't do anything useful, like buy a car for example."

"Don't put yourself down, mate. You listen, and you understand."

"What do I understand, Pasco?"

"I told you about my dad; never told anyone that, not even Tamsin. And you get it about what's going on down here. You listened to me rabbiting on about it. And when you told me about Hannah it got me thinking about Selwyn."

"About Hannah?"

"How you miss her." Pasco took a sip from his pint. "Selwyn will be leaving soon."

"And you'll miss him?"

Pasco put down his glass. "Never really thought about it, I suppose. I knew he would go off to college, of course, but after that..." He shrugged.

"Hopefully he'll get a decent job. He's a bright lad, you say," Steve offered reassuringly.

"I dare say, but not down here unless he's very lucky."

"Does he want to stay down here?"

"He doesn't talk much about what he wants; keeps it all buttoned up." Pasco smiled. "A bit like his dad."

Steve laughed. "Of course."

"But just thinking about it got me steamed up. No young people down here can afford a house; they've got no choice whether to stay or go. They get married, their only choice is to shack up with Mum and Dad. That's what me and Tamsin did; lived with her mum. A couple of years of that was no bloody joke for anyone. Not with the baby." Pasco frowned at the memory.

"What happened? Did you inherit your parents' house?"

Pasco took a few seconds to reply. "My dad died a few months after my mum. I reckon he missed her too much. When he was nearly gone he showed me his will; asked me to understand."

"Understand what?"

"He wanted me to sell the house, but only to someone born in the village."

"Still, at least you could use the money to buy your own, I suppose."

Pasco smiled bleakly. "I hadn't finished, Steve. He wanted me to sell the house and donate all the proceeds to the Methodist Chapel."

Steve looked at him in astonishment. "How did you feel about that?"

"Choked. I hadn't seen that coming; at least not at the time."

"But later?"

"When I could think clearly I could see that it was my dad all over. He'd worked his guts out to buy that house;

nobody gave him anything. Why should I expect something for nothing?"

"Did he say that?"

"Not in so many words but that's what he believed." Pasco smiled reflectively. "Another one of his favourite sermons."

"What?"

"The one about labouring in the vineyard. You remember that?"

Steve laughed. "I'm afraid I didn't have your exposure to the Scriptures, Pasco."

"It never really seemed fair to me," Pasco elaborated. "The workers who stuck at it all day got the same as the ones who put in half a shift. I thought they'd been ripped off, and I told Dad so. He laughed and then explained what the real point of it was."

"You'll have to enlighten me, I'm afraid."

Pasco seemed to be concentrating in order to remember the words which he now recited carefully. "'The master said to them, "Am I not allowed to do what I choose with what belongs to me? Do you begrudge my generosity?"' Or something like that."

Steve raised his arms in mock surrender. "You never cease to amaze me, Pasco."

Pasco smiled. "So that's what he did with the house."

"And you didn't begrudge him that?" Steve echoed the word from the parable.

"Not when I'd calmed down and thought about it. Just sold the house like he wanted and gave the Chapel the money." Pasco grinned. "They were well pleased. I reckon that's the only reason they can still keep going."

"But you did manage to buy your own house eventually?"

"By labouring bloody hard in the vineyard: twenty-four seven. Tamsin took any work she could get until Selwyn came along. Just scraped enough for a deposit. You could do that then." Pasco sighed. "Not any more, of course; no chance."

"For the likes of Selwyn?" Steve said tentatively.

"I won't be giving my house to the Methodists, Steve, but I'm not planning to pop my clogs for a few years yet, so that's Selwyn stuffed. He'll have to move away whether he wants to or not, unless he plans to carry on living with his mum and dad, which I doubt; especially when he meets the right girl."

"No sign of that yet?" Steve asked.

"No, thank God. He's too wrapped up in his rugby and his books. There have been a few loitering about but nothing serious." Pasco drained his glass.

Steve got up and reached for Pasco's empty glass. "Time for another?"

"Why not? No rugby today and I'm a bit parched; been talking too much. I promise not to rattle on. Just don't mention the price of houses, or jobs, or bloody Penpol, or anything likely to set me off."

Steve made no move to the bar, but stood with the two empty glasses in his hands and looked at Pasco thoughtfully. "You quite sure you're all done with Penpol, Pasco?"

Pasco stared at him. "What you saying, Steve?"

"It's just... I did some digging around online. Interesting."

"About Penpol?"

"Yes. More than meets the eye there, Pasco."

Pasco groaned. "I told Tamsin I'd forget it." He paused. "But I suppose it wouldn't do any harm if I pop round sometime to have a quick look."

Steve had nothing against badgers, or anything very much for them, come to that. He had felt fleeting sympathy for the odd dead one he had glimpsed flattened on the roadside, of course, but that was about the extent of his actual involvement with the species. Now, a half-hour into Wild Britain, he was suffering from a surfeit of badger. He found it hard to share the commentator's hushed enthusiasm for the black-and-white-striped denizens of the woodland underworld who were either entering or leaving their setts, or rootling about outside a bit before repeating the sequence. That was the problem with British wildlife: it was neither very wild nor very lively. The New Forest, where the badgers were being filmed, was hardly the Serengeti. Now, if a pride of lions or a stampeding herd of wildebeest suddenly burst out of the Hampshire undergrowth, that would be something to get excited about. As it was, Steve expected that the rest of the programme would invite him to become enraptured by the adventures of a dormouse or a crested newt. He felt guilty that he could not raise himself to that level of interest, but salved his conscience by not switching the television off; rather, pressing the mute button on the remote control so that the badgers trundled about in silence in their moonlit glade. He found their inaudible monochrome meanderings curiously soothing; almost balletic, like the therapeutic goldfish in the dentist's waiting room.

He knew that early Sunday evening viewing was unlikely to raise the heart rate but he lacked the energy to do anything but slump. It had been a long day. The usual marking chore ('How does Dickens portray Scrooge's redemption?') had been particularly onerous because there didn't seem to be a model online answer to copy, which had presented his class with a severe challenge to their literary and grammatical skills; a challenge which many had not overcome, but their brave struggles had delayed Steve in a protracted quest to make any sense of what they had written. That had taken most of the morning. A cold sausage roll had not done much for his flagging energy levels, but in the afternoon he forced himself to press on with preparing material for the evening class. Working from the list Bill had given him, he prepared name badges for the class so that at least he would be able to identify a student without having to attempt pronunciation of intimidatingly unfamiliar forenames and surnames. He worked on a simple questionnaire for the first session which asked for basic biographical details and information on work and leisure interests, although he was doubtful that leisure would be a concept familiar to those working in the sorts of jobs he guessed his class were engaged in. Still, he needed to set the ball rolling. He presumed there would be a wide range of linguistic skill, and so had arduously compiled a list of online dictionaries which he trusted was comprehensive enough to cater for the needs of the various nationalities represented. Spanish and Portuguese looked likely and he was fairly certain Poland and Romania were represented, and he had thrown in the Baltic States and Bulgaria for good measure. Hopefully, that should do it. Finally he had assembled some video footage of a busy railway station and devised some simple questions to be answered while watching it. Bill had organised the use of Trengrouse's language lab, so with access to individual screens Steve expected people to be able to work at their own pace.

The afternoon had faded into dusk by the time Steve sat back from his laptop. He had made himself a cup of tea and then written his weekly letter to Hannah. He had described his preparations for the evening class and told her that she would be impressed with his research into the surnames of Eastern Europe. Did she know that in Romanian, '–escu' means 'son of', and in Polish the suffix '–ski' indicates possession? He joked that in Polish she would be called Hannah Miltonska. He found it heartening that he could write with a sense of anticipation and enthusiasm.

By the time he came back from posting the letter it was nearly dark. He told himself he would have to sort out some supper, but he postponed that chore and succumbed instead to the lure of the sofa and the badgers. They moved in their silent, ghostly formations across the television screen until Steve roused himself sufficiently to extinguish them.

Steve could cook; there had been a time when he'd quite enjoyed it. If Linda had been late back from work he'd turned his hand to getting food on the table, often with Hannah as his cheerful assistant. It had been fun; the two of them laughing as they tried to follow the instructions of Mary Berry or Delia Smith or some other kitchen goddess. Steve sighed as he remembered, and distracted himself from the memory by foraging in the fridge for some quick-fix fodder. There was no pleasure in cooking for himself; food was just fuel these days. He found the energy to put together an omelette accompanied by some shrivelling mushrooms and a handful of frozen peas. He summoned up enough willpower to forgo the wine. There had been yet another polemic in the Sunday paper warning of the fearful consequences of overindulgence. He really must try to cut back.

Steve cleared away his plate and reconciled himself to an evening of British rubbish on the box. He really ought to read a book or find himself a hobby but he reckoned he was overexposed to literature in his daily round and he could not see himself settling down to an evening of fretwork or fitting a ship into a bottle. He was old enough to remember being taught carpentry as a schoolboy (before it was supplanted by the mysteries of 'design technology'), and his teacher had soon recognised that Steve with hammer and chisel in hand was a danger to himself and the rest of the class. Wisely, he had suggested that Steve bring a book with him to the carpentry lesson and read quietly at the back. Glancing listlessly at the

TV schedules, Steve was forcing himself to choose between another episode of an apparently endless saga chronicling the vicissitudes of life in an Edwardian stately home, and a reality show (about as real as Peter Pan) following several has-been celebrities on a journey of self-discovery in an Indian ashram.

He was still confronting this Hobson's choice when the doorbell rang. Pasco stood outside with a bottle in hand. "Is this a good time for you? Tamsin's gone to visit her mum so I thought I could nip out." He tapped the side of his nose conspiratorially.

Steve remembered their earlier conversation at The Miners. "Good timing; you saved me from brain death."

Pasco closed the door behind him and proffered the bottle. "My shout. I remember finishing yours off."

Steve's protests were overridden and he produced two glasses whilst Pasco put the whisky down on the table. They sat and Pasco poured them each a liberal measure. Steve found no difficulty in forgoing his short-lived commitment to abstinence as they raised their glasses to each other.

Pasco savoured the whisky slowly before putting down his glass. "I'm just interested, you see. I know I can't do nothing but it would be good to know what's going on. That is, if there is anything going on."

"Information is power," Steve offered. " I think Stalin said that."

"Did he? I'll take your word for it." Pasco took another sip. "So what information have you got on Penpol?"

Steve gestured to his laptop, still powered up on the table. He moved his fingers over the touch bar and the screen was filled with an image of an elegant apartment building sited above a beach of purest white sand lapped by a tranquil cobalt sea.

"Blimey." Pasco whistled in admiration. "Where the hell is it?"

"The Seychelles. One of Penpol's newest developments."

Pasco shook his head in incredulity. "I didn't know they were into all that."

Steve summoned a succession of photographs onto the screen: similar prestigious developments in a variety of distant exotic locations. "Worldwide; they follow the money. Where the big spenders go, Penpol goes too."

"Where did you get all these pictures from?"

Steve smiled. "Easy. Their website. They like to advertise."

"So it's all legitimate and above board," Pasco said glumly.

"What we see here is. How they got there might be another matter."

"What do you mean?"

Steve gestured towards the screen. "A lot of their developments are in places with pretty lax regulations and governments that are not always, shall we say, of proven fiscal probity."

Pasco smiled. "You've got a way with words, Steve. You mean they can be bought."

"There are plenty of bloggers out there who believe so."

"But nothing you can prove?"

"Penpol are too clever for that. There are no smoking guns. There are offshore accounts, subsidiary companies, phantom companies, front companies, and so on. It would be like shovelling smoke trying to trace any illicit payments."

Pasco poured himself another whisky and swilled it reflectively around his glass. "I don't get it, Steve."

"Get what?"

"If Penpol are big, worldwide, why are they bothering with Cornwall?"

Steve nodded. "I wondered that too. Then I looked a bit more closely at where their major projects were," he sipped his drink slowly, "and it sort of made sense." He put down his glass and looked pensively at the glossy images frozen on-screen.

"What sort of sense?" Pasco asked impatiently.

"I think it's a question of balancing risk. The plus side of investing in what they politely call 'the developing world' is that you can sometimes get away with shortcuts. No tedious red tape; no endless delays for public inquiries; no deferrals to the environmental lobby; no stringent compliance with building regulations. And if you do run into problems then there is usually a way round them."

Pasco mimed rubbing notes between his thumb and forefinger. "Friends in high places."

"Low friends in high places," Steve added by way of qualification.

"I get all that, but what's the downside?"

"Instability. Some of these countries are very fragile democracies; some not democracies at all. One corrupt general disposes of another corrupt general and suddenly the rules change; new snouts in the trough. Or a popular uprising kicks out the government you have been cosying up to and suddenly you have new names on the payroll. And of course, there is always religion."

"Religion?" Pasco looked baffled. "What's that got to do with anything?"

"In at least two of Penpol's resorts, Islamic fundamentalists have taken over. They're not very big on bikinis and alcohol so Penpol takes a hit; you can't bribe Allah."

"My heart bleeds for them," Pasco said cheerfully.

"So Penpol needs to cover its back; to diversify. Invest in countries with stable governments. The projects might be less spectacular and the process more tedious than they are used to but they are tax deductible and the returns are secure. So they have major involvement in Western Europe, from Mediterranean holiday villages to farms in Cornwall."

"Farms? I didn't know they were into that too."

"They're into everything. In the last few years they have bought into British agriculture big time." Steve gestured towards the laptop. "It's all on there. They boast about it; 'revitalising the sector'."

Pasco looked confused. "And are they? Revitalising farming? Not much sign of it down here."

Steve explained. "What they seem to do is buy out small farmers who are struggling to survive and, where possible, consolidate their land into large-scale agricultural units. Economies of scale, they call it."

Pasco considered all this in silence. When he spoke, it was with bemusement. "And you found all this stuff on that thing?" He pointed.

"Whole world out there, Pasco."

"So Selwyn keeps telling me. Maybe I should listen."

"Clearly Penpol feel they have nothing to hide."

Pasco grunted. "Perhaps because it's too well hidden."

Steve tweaked the touch bar and the pictures were replaced by text. "All open and above board – transparency," he said ironically. "Look, they even disclosed the names of the board members for Penpol South-West Holdings." He indicated the screen and Pasco craned forward to look at the list. "I see your friend is one of them," Steve said, pointing at a name.

"Giles bloody Penhaul," Pasco growled. "Of course. So that's how he made all that money in London."

Steve took another nip of his drink, but Pasco seemed fixated on the screen. At last he sat back and turned to Steve.

"Would you credit it?" he laughed.

"Credit what?"

Pasco seemed galvanised. He pushed away his empty glass and got to his feet. "I'd better go before Tamsin gets back." He stood briefly at the door. "Thanks for all that, Steve, I owe you."

Steve shrugged. "I enjoyed it. Something different. Anyway, I only pushed a few buttons."

"You certainly just pushed one for me, Steve," Pasco said, looking back at the laptop, and he smiled as he closed the door behind him.

FIFTEEN

"My name is Maria and I am coming from Lisboa." Then she corrected herself hastily and replaced her sibilant pronunciation of her country's capital city with the hard consonants of English. "Lisbon." She smiled apologetically at Steve, who smiled back and silently clapped his hands in encouragement. Emboldened, Maria resumed reading from the biographical questionnaire Steve had given the class when they had assembled. "I am working in care home in Camborne with old persons. I like." She addressed the last two questions. "I think English weather is not good. When time, I will go to movies." She sat down and grinned bashfully as, prompted by Steve, the class applauded her efforts.

Steve stood up. "Thank you, Maria; very good." He pointed at the clock on the wall and, remembering to articulate slowly, said, "We are going to take a break now for ten minutes." He held up two outstretched palms to reinforce the time allocation. "There is tea and coffee for you next to the boiler. Help yourselves." He tried a joke. "And if you are feeling brave, you could try the biscuits."

Some stared blankly at him in response to that, or looked in puzzlement at each other, but a few laughed. With only one hour of his first session completed, Steve was already aware of the wide divergence of competence in English in his group. He congratulated himself on anticipating this and creating programmes they could follow at appropriate levels of comprehension. He felt more relaxed now; less awkward and stilted than when he had introduced himself and completed the formalities of registration. He strolled over to the trestle tables which the Trengrouse kitchen ladies had dutifully set up for him earlier in the day, complete with a note reminding him to switch on the boiler. He noticed that those who had come in groups stood protectively together, and those who had come alone stood in nervous isolation. He caught snatches of low conversation in unrecognisable tongues and decided to force the pace.

"Right, ladies and gentlemen," he said with a cheerfully raised voice. "Rule Number One. Here, we speak only English."

Some of those who clearly had not been doing so smiled sheepishly.

"So now I would like you to find someone you do not know and introduce yourself in the English way. Do you know what I mean by 'the English way'?"

No one offered an explanation.

Steve contorted his features into a near-manic grin to show he was being jocular. "You will shake hands in a very serious way and make some remark about the weather. Look, I will demonstrate." He advanced on Maria, who stepped back a pace in some alarm but Steve was not to be deterred. He stretched out his hand for her to shake, which she took timidly. "Good evening, Maria," Steve thundered. "My name is Steven Milton. Do you think the rain will stop?" He released Maria's hand and looked at the startled students.

No one spoke for a few seconds, until one clapped in appreciation of Steve's performance. Steve smiled at her gratefully. He remembered she had come with two others – a young man and a thin girl who looked like an adolescent but whose application form declared her to be twenty – all of them still wearing their outdoor protective clothing.

Still smiling at Steve, the woman turned to face a small, dark-skinned young man who Steve recollected was a bar worker called Ricardo. "Good evening. My name is Eva Albescu," her accent was only slight, "and I do not think it will ever stop raining."

This broke the ice, and the rest of the coffee break passed in relatively animated greetings and giggling until Steve announced that it was time to return to their iPads for the second half of the session. He took his cup back to the trestle table and, as he put it down, found himself next to Eva, who was doing the same. He nodded in recognition.

"Thank you. That was very helpful; you set the ball rolling." He realised as soon as the words were out of his mouth that she would wonder what the hell he was talking about. He tried to explain. "What I mean is—"

She smiled at him. "An idiom. Not literal."

Steve stared at her in astonishment. "You know about idioms?"

"I think I did. Once. But to use another one, I have gone a bit rusty."

Steve tried hard not to gawp. "But why are you here?"

Eva raised her eyebrows. "You do not want me to be?" She feigned dismay.

"No, no, of course not. But what I mean is," he tried to compose his thoughts, "this course is pretty basic; you might find the evening a bit boring."

"Not as boring as every other evening."

Steve laughed. "Well, that's something, I suppose."

"And the certificate. I could need it."

"I'm sure that won't be a problem." Steve smiled at her and, holding her gaze for a moment, registered, rather disturbingly, that she was remarkably attractive. He reproved himself immediately. What on earth was he thinking of?

He turned away and became aware of the rest of the class now sitting at their desks, looking expectantly towards him. He cleared his throat and strode briskly back to his dais. "Right. Now let's listen to the rest of the personal statements."

SIXTEEN

Bishop Trelawny was in safe hands on Saturday afternoon. The Pirates were back to their winning ways, and Steve was on his second pint and hoarse from singing. He felt relaxed in the easy camaraderie of the beer tent; no longer, he dared to acknowledge, an outsider. Pasco's friends included him in their banter and Taff Evans had raised his tankard in recognition from a noisy group at the far end of the tent. Steve had nearly choked on his drink when a meaty hand had thumped him on the back in warm greeting. He had turned, spluttering, to be confronted by the looming presence of Desi Hosken, sweating profusely with his salesman's tie askew and his rumpled suit bearing traces of spilt beer and the crumbs of a fugitive pasty. Above the singing and shouted conversations, Steve could just about make out that Desi was asking how the car was going. Rather than attempt speech, Steve responded with a pantomime smile and two raised thumbs. Desi had beamed, clapped him boisterously on his still-painful shoulder, and plunged his way back towards the bar.

Pasco was in a much more buoyant mood than on their last visit. Steve was not sure that this was just because the Pirates had won. He and Pasco had met at The Miners in what was becoming a pre-match habit, and there too Pasco had been cheerful company. He'd surprised Steve by insisting that he didn't want to think about "bloody Penpol" before the match; it might spoil it. He did, however, say, before pressing on to other topics, that if Steve didn't mind, after the game he would like him to check something out "on that computer thing of yours". Steve said he had no problem with that and, suppressing his curiosity, managed not to press for more details.

Before they had left The Miners it was Steve who did most of the talking. Pasco wanted to know how his evening classes had gone, and laughed at some of Steve's accounts of trying to cope with the Trengrouse Tuesday and Thursday House of Babel. Steve confessed that, in spite of the problems, he had quite enjoyed his first two sessions. He explained to Pasco that not only did his class speak different languages but they were a mix of social backgrounds and cultures: Eastern European field workers alongside care home assistants, bar staff, a bus driver and even a nightclub bouncer.

Pasco had picked up on that. "Are they still called bouncers?"

Steve raised his hands in mock horror. "Forgive me. On his form it said, 'Professional door supervisor'. I had to ask him what that meant."

Pasco grinned. "And he said, 'Bouncer'?"

"Correct."

"I don't envy you, Steve. Must be a nightmare; all those different languages, different jobs..."

"Not only that; there's big differences in ability. Some are barely literate—"

"Like me, you mean?" Pasco interrupted.

"Not a bit like you, Pasco," Steve continued, "and some are clearly pretty bright." He paused reflectively. "In fact, there's one who's way ahead of the rest."

"What's he do?"

"Not 'he', Pasco. And she is a field worker."

Pasco did not seem surprised. "You get that down here. Some of them come over from those Eastern places with degrees and top qualifications and take shitty jobs down here which none of the locals can be arsed to do. We'd be stuffed without them."

"I know why they have to do it, of course, but it seems such a waste."

"It is. Tamsin's got an Albanian girl works in the school kitchen. She's got a degree in chemistry. Can you believe it? There's no work at home so she ends up in Cornwall peeling sprouts and washing dirty saucepans; sends the money back to her family. That's crazy, isn't it?"

Shaking his head at the nonsense of it all, Pasco stood and walked over to the bar to order their pasties. Steve watched him go but, unbidden, his thoughts were elsewhere. Their conversation had stirred his curiosity about Eva Albescu. After their brief interaction over the coffee table he had paid particular attention to her biographical address to the class but it had told him little. It seemed to him that she made an effort not to speak too fluently, presumably to avoid disparaging the halting efforts of others. Her name he knew already, and he learnt only that she came from a small town about fifty miles from Bucharest, that she was in England as an agricultural worker, that she was not a fan of British football, and that she liked reading. He may have imagined it but he thought she'd flashed him a quick smile at that admission. During the second class he'd made a conscious effort not to let himself be distracted by her presence, and confined himself to offering his congratulations on the ease with which she had mastered the assignments he had set her. He'd told her he would produce something more challenging for the next session, and she had said she would look forward to it, again with that soft half-smile and a crinkle of her almond eyes.

Steve was still remembering that look when Pasco plonked his pasty down in front of him. "Better get that down you; we're running late."

Steve poured hot water over the granules and gave the mixture a perfunctory stir. He held up the milk bottle in invitation.

Pasco shook his head. "Black. That third pint was probably a mistake."

Steve handed over the coffee and then carried his own to join Pasco at the kitchen table. They sat silently for a few moments, sipping at their drinks. Steve drained the last of his and put down his cup and looked inquiringly at Pasco. He pointed at his laptop, booted up and displaying its icon-festooned screen. "Right, Pasco, what is it you wanted me to look at?"

"I've been checking out some stuff."

"Online?" Steve asked in surprise.

"As if! No, at The Miners." Pasco put down his cup and wiped a hand across his lips. "There was a darts match on Wednesday."

Steve was puzzled. "I didn't know you were a darts man."

Pasco smiled. "I'm not, but Tommy Williams is."

Steve groaned in mock despair. "Let me guess: another ghost from your rugby past?"

"Tommy is no bloody ghost. Unless you get ghosts over twenty stone, built like a brick shithouse. I tell you; he was some player in his time." Pasco grinned at the memory.

"And now?"

"Builder. Doing very well for himself, always got work."

Steve waited for more detail but none was forthcoming.

Pasco seemed to have moved on. "Those names you showed me; can we have another look?"

Steve had to think for a moment but then remembered. "The board members?"

Pasco nodded.

Steve turned to the laptop and, with a few clicks, summoned the list of names.

Pasco leaned closer to the screen and then sat back, satisfied with what he had seen. "Just double-checking but it's her all right." He looked at Steve and then jabbed at a name on the screen. "Widow Gilbert."

Steve peered at the name Pasco had pointed to. "'Mrs A. Gilbert.' That mean something to you, Pasco?"

"Alice Gilbert. Or 'Slack Alice' as she is better known." Pasco laughed.

"You've lost me now," Steve protested.

Pasco turned away from the screen and switched his attention to Steve. "Alice Gilbert is the widow of Henry Gilbert; he built up a big building business in St Ives. Nice enough bloke; he gave me bits of work. Keeled over about five years ago; Alice was too much for him, they reckoned. She's going on fifty but dresses like twenty; keeps herself in good nick; put herself about a bit for a year or two after Henry snuffed it," he paused, "before Willie Walton came along."

"Who is Willie Walton?"

"Wee Willie Walton." Pasco leaned towards Steve, and when he spoke it was slowly and with emphasis. "Councillor Wee Willie Walton." He sat back with the authority of a barrister who has just proved his case beyond reasonable doubt.

Steve thought he was beginning to catch the drift. "So this Walton guy and Alice are partners?"

Pasco expressed mock outrage at such a suggestion. "What are you saying, Steve? Councillor Walton is a happily married man." It was only when he laughed that Steve realised that was probably not the case. "He has a wife; a little mousy thing he wheels out for council functions."

"But he and Alice—"

"At it all the time. So Tommy tells me."

"And Tommy knows because…"

"Tommy is a St Ives boy; gets all the gossip. I haven't seen much of Alice for a few years but Tommy stays in touch. Used to work with Henry, so he knows the family."

"Family, you say?"

"Alice and Henry had two sons. They run the business now. Alice sold it to them."

Steve was lost again. "Sold it to them? Her own sons?"

Pasco nodded. "Gets complicated, doesn't it? Tommy reckons it was a funny sort of sale; nobody seems to know what money changed hands." He smiled. "If any!"

"But why would she do that?"

"Legally, the company has nothing to do with her now. Clever."

"I think I'm missing something here, Pasco," Steve admitted.

Pasco now seemed to have moved onto another track. "Can you look up Stennack Construction on that thing?" He jerked his head towards the laptop.

This was making little sense to Steve, but once Pasco has spelt out 'Stennack' for him he found the website easily enough. He clicked on 'About Us' and showed the Pasco the result. "What are we looking for?"

"Any names? Who's the boss?"

Steve clicked on another link and after a few seconds had a name for Pasco. "It says here that the managing director is a Louise Hicks. Does that mean anything?"

It clearly did to Pasco. "Tommy was right, then. Louise Hicks is shacked up with one of the Gilbert brothers."

"His wife?"

"No. They've been together a few years but not married; nothing official, that would spoil things."

"Now I'm completely lost." Steve held out his hands, palms uppermost in the gesture of helplessness.

"That's how they like it. Hard to follow; to make any connections."

"But you can?"

"I think so, but it's all wheels within wheels." Pasco looked around. "You got a bit of paper?"

Steve rummaged until he found a recent communication from Sausage & Mash. "You can use the back of this." He pushed the envelope towards Pasco, and with it a ballpoint pen from his jacket pocket. Pasco took both and began to write carefully and slowly. Steve watched closely and saw that he was writing names and connecting them with arrows.

"Alice connects with Walton, but not in any official way."

Steve was catching up fast. "So he doesn't have to declare an interest in any application from Penpol."

Pasco then pointed to the arrow linking Alice with Stennack Constructions. "And she has no legal connection with Stennack because her sons are not the registered owners because they put all that onto Louise Hicks. Crafty."

"But how does Stennack fit into all this?"

"Sorry, I should have said. They get big contracts when the council give Penpol the green light." With his finger, Pasco tracked the arrow linking Stennack with Penpol and Alice Gilbert. To further clarify the situation, he underscored the links between Councillor Walton, Alice, Penpol and Stennack. He looked at Steve. "You get it?"

"I think so, but of course you could never go public with any of this. That must be the pain of it."

Pasco agreed wearily. "They'd sue the arse off you. All their smart lawyers."

Steve looked at Pasco's diagram again. "Councillor Walton is the key, really. Take him out and all the dominos fall."

"No chance of that. They love him up Bodmin way; vote him in year after year."

"Why is he so popular?"

"Says all the right things. Puts his name to a few fancy projects." Pasco shook his head disbelievingly. "Even got a cycle path named in his honour: the Walton Way."

"A populist, then?"

"Whatever. He's always on local telly telling people what they want to hear. Kick the French out of our fishing grounds (that always goes down well); improve the train service; create more jobs for Cornish youngsters. That sort of stuff."

"Nothing wrong with some of that, you have to admit," Steve suggested.

"Course not. He can talk the talk but he does bugger all about it. He's been on the housing committee for years and what have we got to show for it? You seen many new council estates going up in these parts?" Whilst Steve pondered that, Pasco answered his own question passionately with a raised voice. "Of course not. When Maggie Thatcher sold off all those houses, what happened to the money the council got to build new ones? Where did that all go? That was the only sort of housing ordinary folk could afford. That's what the council should have been doing. Instead you have Councillor Walton and the like pissing about with crooks like Penpol." He sat back, exhausted from his outburst. After a few seconds of recovery he smiled sheepishly at Steve. "Sorry; got a bit steamed up."

"Don't worry. I get it. It's very frustrating, knowing what's wrong and not being able to do anything about it."

Pasco agreed. "It is. But like Tamsin says, I just have to let it go."

"Stop tilting at windmills?"

"I don't know about bloody windmills, but forget about Councillor Walton—"

Steve had a flash of recall and interrupted Pasco in full flow. "Sorry, but something's just come to me." He turned to the laptop and scrolled down several pages before stopping at one with a photograph filling the screen. He bent closer to examine it. "I thought I'd seen the name somewhere," he said, leaning back and gesturing to Pasco to look.

Pasco peered uncertainly at the screen. "What am I looking for?"

Steve explained. "This is one of Penpol's publicity shots. A new development on the Costa del Sol. High-end holiday apartments."

Pasco looked more closely. "I can see that. And a line of blokes looking at them and... bloody hell. It's him!" He pointed at a diminutive figure in Bermuda shorts, dark glasses and a floppy panama hat, standing with others looking upwards at the half-built high-rise apartment block. "Can't mistake him, not with those little legs. What the hell's he doing there?"

Steve read from the explanatory PR text. "'In Spain, Penpol hosts a fact-finding visit for south-west councillors at their newest development.' It lists the councillors, and representing Cornwall is..." He left the rest to Pasco.

"Councillor bloody Walton. Fact-finding, my arse! A freebie; a piss-up in the sun." Pasco sighed in exasperation. "Doesn't change nothing, Steve. It's all kosher; council business. We know what's really going on but there's sod all we can do about it." He stood up wearily and shrugged. "Like Tamsin said, better just forget about it."

Steve decided to risk it. "Is that what your dad would have done, Pasco? Just let it go?"

For a moment Pasco stared at him, his look hard and challenging. Then he raised his hands in mock surrender and smiled briefly. "Not fair, Steve. I can't take this lot on. Like in rugby, sometimes the other side is just too big and strong."

"But I'm sure that never stopped you giving it a go, Pasco."

SEVENTEEN

"I would like to have stamps. You have stamps?" Ivan the huge Bulgarian bouncer was concentrating hard on the shopping list Steve had given him.

Maria from Lisbon concentrated equally hard on her list and, after a few seconds' deliberation, decided, "Yes, I have stamps."

Throughout the room, similar transactions were being conducted. Steve had divided the group into shopkeepers and shoppers and given each a list of items they either stocked or wanted to purchase. The exercise was proving noisy but good-humoured as he moved from table to table to encourage and advise. He was pleased with how the class members were beginning to relax and interact; he could see how, for some, their time at Trengrouse was as much a break from social isolation as a language lesson. And where's the harm in that? he asked himself.

One student was not doing any shopping. He looked to a quiet corner of the room where Eva sat chewing the end of her pen and frowning as she studied the task Steve had set her. He knew it would be hard. He doubted if any of his GCSE set would be able to cope. He had butchered a page from a novel, removing all punctuation and quotation marks and leaving only text with descriptive prose undelineated from dialogue. It was Eva's task to reassemble it correctly. Leaving the haggling shoppers for a moment, he crossed over to her. She saw him coming and mimed a face of despair.

Steve grinned. "How are you getting on?"

Eva groaned. "This is very hard. I am too slow."

Steve leant over her shoulder to look at her work. He was conscious of her closeness and as she turned her head inquiringly to anticipate his comments he looked again at those eyes; many times in novels he had read descriptions of female characters with almond-shaped eyes without ever quite being able to visualise the reality. Now he got it. Eva's eyes were wider than they were round, and of a warm-toned brown. Now they narrowed questioningly.

"So, it is not good?"

Steve hastily regained his composure and picked up her work. He straightened up and studied what she had written for a few moments, then put the paper back on the table in front of her. "This is excellent." He pointed out a particular line. "But I think perhaps you should have a capital letter here; a start of a new sentence—"

"Of course!" Eva slapped her forehead in exasperation and corrected the error. "That was stupid of me."

"Not at all," Steve protested. "This is very impressive. Really."

Eva looked at him gratefully and smiled. "It was kind of you to do this for me."

Steve sensed the start of a blush and looked away hastily. "I think the shopping exercise might have been a bit wasted on you. You are way beyond that."

"I don't know; I am not half the way finished with this," she said, pointing.

The decibel level was rising from the retail role players. Steve smiled at Eva. "I think someone is trying to short-change Ivan."

She laughed. "Not a good idea."

"I'd better get back to them." He paused. "I could go through this with you at the end, if you don't need to rush off."

"If you don't mind; I have time. The bus will not come until ten."

"Bus?" It occurred to Steve that he had little idea of how his class travelled to Trengrouse.

"Yes. Before, I had a lift in the car with Luka and Elena."

Steve had noted that they were not present when he'd completed the register. "But not tonight. Are they not well?"

Eva shook her head. "A big football match on the television. Manchester United. Luka is a fan."

Steve shrugged. "Well, I can't compete with Manchester United." The noise was increasing. "So I'll go through that with you when we finish."

Eva nodded and picked up her pen and, brow furrowed, bent her head over the jumbled text.

Steve turned away and moved towards the rest of the class. "Now then, Ivan, what seems to be the problem?"

The last group left with cheerful shouted goodbyes to Steve. He waved them off, telling them he looked forward to seeing them next time, and he meant it. He was enjoying the experience; more confident now and feeding off their obvious enthusiasm. He told himself he must be doing something right. The clacking of footsteps down the lino-floored corridor soon faded and the brief silence was broken by a loud sigh. Eva slapped her pen down noisily on the table in front of her and picked up the paper she had been working on. She studied it, frowning, as Steve walked over to her.

"Have you finished?" he inquired.

She looked up at him and smiled ruefully. "It is finished but it is not right; many mistakes, I think."

"Let's have a look." Steve pulled up a chair and sat next to Eva.

She put down her work between them and he checked it slowly, marking with his pen where corrections were needed. She watched him intently. When he had finished she registered gloomily the alterations he had made. She looked at him apologetically.

"I am sorry."

He turned to her to reassure her. For a moment they were face to face; disconcertingly close for Steve, who registered not just those compelling eyes but the high cheekbones, the wide mouth, and the olive skin astonishingly not degraded by exposure to the Cornish elements. For a brief moment he was lost, but he quickly forced himself to concentrate on the corrected text. He leaned back in his chair and shifted it a few inches away from Eva, who was now absorbed in studying her work.

"No need to be sorry. These are only minor slip-ups. I'll show you."

For the next few minutes Steve went through the exercise with her. When he pointed out a mistake Eva would groan in self-reproach and shake her head in exasperation at her errors. When they had finished he congratulated her on her achievement; told her how impressed he was. She did not seem convinced, and told him she needed to work more on her English but it was difficult; she must read more: proper serious books. She did not elaborate on the difficulties, and Steve was uncertain whether she was referring to the language or her circumstances. He felt it would not be appropriate to delve further, and anyway, she was hurriedly gathering her stuff together and looking at her watch. He remembered that she had to catch the bus. He knew from his register that Eva had given an address in Penzance. Surely there could be no harm in offering her a lift?

"Look, Eva, it's a bit late to be hanging around for a bus, in the cold. I could give you a lift." He paused nervously. "If you wanted, that is."

She looked at him in surprise and after a pause said, "No thank you; it would be too much trouble for you."

"It's no trouble. I have to go through Penzance. But of course..." Steve shrugged and made to pick up his briefcase.

Eva approached him. "If you are really sure it is no problem for you, then thank you. Yes." She laughed rather nervously, as if to defuse sensed tension. "The bus is always late anyway."

They did not talk much in the car. Steve could not entirely shake off a nagging guilt that he could be thought guilty of inappropriate (what a much-used word that was these days) conduct. He had been teaching long enough to know the moral quagmire that had sucked some of his colleagues down into professional oblivion after dalliances with seductive pupils. Inexcusable behaviour, of course, and rightly punished, but he could not always suppress a flicker of sympathy for those who lacked the willpower to spurn temptations which were never far away. More stupid than wicked, he sometimes allowed. The fact that these thoughts were churning around in his head now was ridiculous, he told himself. He was merely offering a charitable lift home to a mature adult. There was no law in the land against that, and the fact that he found her disturbingly attractive was beside the point. He reproved himself for even acknowledging the fact. He knew nothing about her or – what was the phrase they used? – her 'domestic circumstances', and he certainly wasn't going to ask; that would be inappropriate. So, as they drove towards Penzance, he carefully confined his remarks to bland observations on the weather (of course) and the progress of the language class. Eva said little. Steve wondered if she shared his nervousness or was merely bored, and feared the latter.

However, at one point in the journey she obviously recognised the landscape they were driving through and peered out through the window at the dark fields. "I have worked here," she said. "Daffodils."

Steve had known that that was her work from her talk to the class on her first evening. "Hard work, I imagine," he said sympathetically.

"Not so bad as cutting the cauliflower. That is dangerous."

"Dangerous?" He expressed surprise.

"Yes. They give you this big knife. If you make a mistake it does not cut the cauliflower but the..." She paused, seeking a word. "The tend... how do you say?" She frowned impatiently and pointed at her wrist.

"Tendons?" Steve offered with a churning of the stomach.

"Yes, tendons. That is very bad. They must go to hospital. An operation. Then they cannot work, so they must go home."

"Do they get compensation? Money?"

Eva laughed without humour. "No. The boss says it is their own fault."

Steve felt the guilt of the privileged. "That can't be right."

Eva looked at him. Then she chose her words carefully. "There is much that is not right. But we do it. We just work. We cannot change anything. Nobody makes us do it; we chose to come here, for the money..." She broke off and looked out of the window again.

Steve said little for the rest of the journey. He sensed Eva had retreated into the bleak landscape of her own thoughts. When they reached the outskirts of Penzance, she directed him to a steep, narrow road that climbed up behind the town. It was lined with three-storeyed Victorian houses which all seemed to have seen better days. Many were clearly in multiple occupation and the narrow front gardens had long given up any pretence of cultivation. The only crops now seemed to be padlocked bicycles, wheelie bins, miscellaneous discarded kitchen appliances, and the odd battered pram. Eva indicated her house and Steve parked outside with the engine still running. The house was in darkness except for the flickering glow of a television screen in a downstairs room. By its light Steve could distinguish several figures huddled in front of it.

Eva sighed. "The football. The men will still be watching it. That is all they watch."

Steve could not suppress his curiosity. "Are there many men?"

"Seven, and just three of us women. We share a room."

Steve looked at her. "Three of you? Quite a crowd."

Eva shrugged. "It's not so bad. All we want to do is sleep after the work. Nobody has much time to do anything else." She corrected herself and laughed. "Except, of course, for the football. And it is much better than the caravans."

Steve would have liked to have asked more but she was already opening the car door. He decided on impulse to throw caution to the wind. "Look, Eva, you said you wanted to read more English classics?"

She looked at him inquiringly. "I should, but—"

"I've got a lot of stuff at home. If you like, I could pick out a few suitable ones for you." He hoped he had managed to keep his tone casual.

"That would be very kind. I will try to find the time," she broke off and looked at the house, "and the place to look at them. It is not always easy here."

Steve sensed an opportunity. "I have your number on the register. Perhaps I could contact you to see if you have some suitable time I could bring the books round?" He continued hastily. "That would give you a chance to look at them before next week."

Eva nodded. "That would be very nice. But not if it is too much trouble."

Steve was quick to reassure her, and to go for broke. "And if you think it's a good idea, perhaps we could go somewhere quiet for a coffee?" He felt he should leave no doubt as to his purpose in making such a proposition. "That way we could discuss which of the books you want to read." He broke off awkwardly, aware of Eva looking at him in what seemed a half-amused way. He floundered on. "Only if you think it's a good idea, of course."

"Yes, Steve. I think it is a very good idea." She opened the door fully and stepped out onto the road. She turned and waved. "Goodnight, and thank you."

Steve was barely aware of the rest of his journey. He felt quite stupidly happy. He even whistled to himself. She had called him 'Steve'. The voice of spoilsport reason told him not to read too much into that – after all, the rest of the class called him Steve, as he had requested, but until a few minutes ago Eva had persisted with the formal 'Mr Milton'. On top of that, she had agreed to go on a date with him. That odd expression 'giddy with pleasure' now made sense as he forced himself to concentrate on the road ahead. With that came the cold douche of reason again. Of course it wasn't a date; not in the adolescent sense of the word – it was merely an extension of his academic responsibilities; extracurricular work. He must not delude himself into thinking that it was anything more; he should put such frivolous nonsense out of his mind. But despite his best efforts he could not prevent fragments of delusion filtering through the enforced austerity of his thoughts as he drove home.

EIGHTEEN

Steve switched off his mobile. He had just broken his own rule. He had phoned Hannah. After the call he wondered if his months of self-imposed restraint had been a mistake; it had been so good to talk to her. But he reflected that he had been right not to cross that bridge until now. If they had spoken early in his banishment it would have been hard to contain his depression; to feign cheerfulness; to sound jaunty and optimistic. All of which had been possible without simulation a few moments ago. She had picked up on his mood and asked him teasingly if he had been drinking. He'd assured her that it was a bit early for that but he would certainly be raising a glass in celebration later, in anticipation of her visit.

That was the news that had prompted his call. Arriving home from work, he had found Hannah's weekly letter on the mat. Reading it over his cup of tea, he'd had to reread the last paragraph to make sure he had not missed something, but it was clear enough. Hannah would like to spend a week of the Easter holidays with him, 'if it's not too much trouble'. That sparked a memory of his recent conversation with Eva. Why did people assume that pleasing him might be trouble? He had been so elated at Hannah's request that he had phoned her immediately. Fearful of possible problems, he had asked her if she had checked it out with her mother. Hannah put his mind at rest. Her visit to Cornwall would fit in with Linda's plans for a week in Corfu "with a friend". Steve made no comment on that, and silently applauded Hannah's tact. They discussed travel arrangements, and Steve advised her to bring plenty of wet-weather gear and warned her that it would probably rain all the time. She only laughed at that, and reassured him that she had plenty of revision to be getting on with, so the weather would not be a problem.

He also hoped she would not be bored. "It's not the most exciting place in the world and you won't exactly be staying at the Ritz."

Hannah had spoken quite forcibly then. "Dad! It's you I want to see. I don't care about anything else."

Steve had needed to compose himself before replying. "Nor me."

There had been a long pause before Hannah broke it cheerfully. "And I can't wait to meet your friend Pasco. He sounds something else."

That mention of Pasco had stirred thoughts which had been sidling in and out of Steve's thoughts of late. Thoughts which initially he had dismissed as pure fantasy, but which refused to disappear. Indeed, these apparently random musings had coalesced into an idea and then a vague plan, even a strategy. To put it to Pasco would require an act of courage on Steve's part and the likely reaction would, he allowed, probably be somewhere between disbelief and derision. The presumption of it might threaten their friendship. Should he risk that, or should he echo Tamsin's advice to Pasco to stop fretting over things he couldn't do anything about? But the point was, Steve told himself, that there was just the very slightest chance that something could be done. He dwelt for a moment on the problematic conundrum of the human condition: Is it worse to regret the things you did or didn't do? Unsure how that particular philosophical query helped his present dilemma, he put it out of his mind and opened up his laptop. Some research was needed.

"Do Americans drink as much as they eat?" Steve put the question to Eva as he carried the bucket-sized coffee cups across to the table where she sat with a pile of books in front of her.

She laughed at his query. They were beginning to relax in each other's company. When he'd picked her up he had gabbled nervously and she had said little. Part of his agitation was a reaction to how striking she looked. Before he had only seen her in her work attire, and now the transformation was startling. She wore fitted black jeans which accentuated her long, slender legs, and a simple white top. Her dark hair framed an unblemished face free of any make-up. When she looked up at Steve to take her coffee, her wide smile and the slight crinkling of her compelling eyes almost made him drop his own.

"Thank you," she said. Then she turned to look at the books he had selected. "I think I would like to borrow A Tale of Two Cities and the Graham Greene. If that is possible?"

"Of course." Steve forced himself to concentrate; to remember the presumed purpose of the occasion. "I think Dickens reads as well today as he did in the nineteenth century. His prose is timeless." He hoped that hadn't sounded too pompous.

Eva was looking thoughtfully at an open page. When she spoke it was as if to voice an inner dialogue. "It will be hard, this Dickens. After ten years."

Steve was confused and waited for more, but Eva only looked up from the book, held his gaze for a moment, and then looked away uncertainly with a slight shake of her head.

Steve broke the silence. "You have studied Dickens before?"

Eva closed the book and gave him her full attention. She took a deep breath and let it out slowly as if releasing some inner tension. Her tone was now almost confessional. "At university in Bucharest. I was studying English literature; to be a teacher." She managed a half-smile. "Like you."

She seemed to be debating whether to continue. Steve said nothing; he accepted that it was her choice if she wanted to tell him more. He was faintly aware of the low murmurs of conversation from the few other customers and the hissing and gasping of the coffee machine, but his attention was fully on Eva.

She looked at him questioningly. "So now you must be thinking what am I doing working in the fields."

"It did cross my mind." Steve hoped his tone was as far from inquisitorial as he could manage.

Eva seemed to appreciate that. "It is not such a mystery." She looked directly and almost challengingly at him. "I had a baby."

Steve tried to conceal his surprise. "Ah. I see."

"In my second year. It was a mistake. You understand?"

"Yes. It happens." He was aware of how lame his words must sound.

"The man, he wanted me not to have the baby. To..." She broke off and looked away.

Steve filled the silence. "But you?"

"I could not do it. Kill my child."

"So how did you manage?"

Eva was more composed now. "I left the university. I went home and had the baby. A little girl; a beautiful daughter."

Steve was fearful of asking his next question. "And what happened?"

Eva smiled at him. "Nothing happened. She is at home with my mother." She reached for her shoulder bag which she had put down beside her chair, and took from it a small wallet. She opened the wallet and showed Steve a photograph held behind a clear plastic window. It showed the face of a smiling, dark-haired child; a child so distinctly like her mother.

"She's lovely. What's her name?"

"Anya. Soon she will be ten." Eva folded the wallet and put it back in her bag, then turned back to Steve. "So now you know why I could not be a teacher."

"You couldn't carry on with your studying? Not at home?"

She shook her head. "We had no money."

"Your father was—"

"Dead. Since I was a little girl."

"I'm sorry."

She sighed. "He was a good man; a clever man. He was a teacher too. In the local school."

"It must have been very hard for you."

"At that time it was very difficult in Romania. The revolution; much violence."

Steve had some memory of those events; he even recalled the name of the deposed tyrant. "Ceauşescu?" he asked.

Eva grimaced in disgust. "He was a monster." She paused. "He killed my father."

Steve was aghast. "Killed him?"

"Not with his own hands, but he was responsible. At home my father was a teacher in the school; everybody loved him. But he was too brave."

"In what way?"

"He spoke against the government; he organised protests. My mother begged him to stop; she knew it was dangerous."

"But he didn't?" Steve asked softly.

"No. He told her he had no choice. So they came for him."
Eva was not far from tears. "They put him in prison; they beat
him. For many months he suffered."

"That must have been terrible."

"I think he would have died there, but the revolution
came. He was freed."

"Good."

"Not so good. He was weak and in pain all the time. He
was too ill to go back to the school."

"Poor man."

"They gave him a little pension but the country had no
money. My mother had to support us all: my father, my young
brother and me."

"How did she manage that?"

"She was a nurse in the hospital. Working all day and
then cooking and cleaning and looking after my father."

"She sounds a strong lady."

Eva smiled. "Very strong. She is still very strong."

"Is she still nursing?" asked Steve in some surprise.

"No. She finished two years ago. Now she looks after
Anya."

Steve began to join up the dots. "So that meant you could
come and work in England."

"Yes. Before, we had to share Anya. I took her to school
and in the evening looked after her until my mother came
home. Then I went to work."

"What work was that?"

Eva frowned. "Nothing good. It is a small town; no real
jobs. I worked in a bar. Many stupid men." She shuddered.
"Some trying always to touch you."

"Horrible."

"So when my brother found out about the work in England
and decided to come, I thought it must be better than what

I was doing. My mother was retired so she would look after Anya and I could send money home. I could get four times more than I was paid in that bar. So I came with him."

"But had to leave your daughter."

Eva nodded slowly. "That is not easy. I speak on the phone, see her too, but it is not the same."

Steve could certainly understand that.

"I went home for Christmas. It was good but sad too, when I must leave."

Steve could offer no consoling comment. He noticed that their half-drunk coffee had gone cold. He gestured at the cups. "Can I get you another coffee?"

"No thank you. I should go." She pointed at the books and smiled. "I must study."

Steve got to his feet and gathered together the surplus literature. "Don't overdo it. You've been working all day."

She shrugged that off. "But not with the brain; this is different." She picked up her two chosen books and stood for a moment in thought. "My father would be pleased that I am studying again. He did not live long enough to see me win the scholarship to university, but as a little girl I remember him telling me always that I must read." Then her face grew solemn. "But perhaps it is good he did not live long enough to see how I left the university."

Steve felt no comment of his would be appropriate.

"When she's down here," Pasco said, "you must come and have a meal with us. Tamsin's been nagging me to ask you; wants to check out my new drinking partner."

"Hope she doesn't think I'm leading you astray."

Pasco laughed. "That happened years ago."

Steve sat back contentedly. The Miners was buzzing. Sam had enlisted a young girl to help, and she was flat out serving the rapidly diminishing mound of pasties to the noisy crowd milling around the bar. "What's going on, Pasco? Why the party?"

"John and Mary's golden wedding." Pasco pointed out an elderly couple sitting at a table with packages and celebratory cards strewn in front of them. "This is just a warm-up. They're having a posh meal over in Penzance tonight. I reckon Giles will be paying for that."

Steve remembered. "Giles? Giles Penhaul?"

"The same." Pasco frowned briefly, then looked at Steve in a change of mood. "So, you must be dead chuffed. Hannah coming down?"

"Yes. I just hope it all goes off all right."

Pasco grinned. "You worry too much, Steve. Why shouldn't it go off OK?"

"It's been a few months. She might have changed."

Pasco shook his head in mock wonder. "Changed? Why should she have changed? She's your daughter; you're her dad. That hasn't changed."

Steve accepted the reassurance. "I know. I'm being stupid."

Pasco seemed to reflect for a moment before he spoke. "I'll tell you what, Steve. I know someone who has changed."

"Who?" Steve asked.

"You, mate."

Steve stared at him. "Me?"

"If you don't mind me saying so, you were a right miserable sod when I first met you. Not a happy bunny."

Steve groaned. "Was it that bad?"

"I knew why, of course. I suppose it takes time."

"And now?"

Pasco laughed. "Now you're in danger of looking happy. Things must be looking up."

Steve hesitated. He had always been wary of agonising self-appraisal but Pasco seemed to have an inbuilt detector of fake emotions. Tell him the truth or tell him nothing, Steve warned himself. He abandoned caution. "I do feel more positive about things, I suppose." For a moment he held back from more and opted for banality. "Must be the better weather."

Pasco was not to be deflected. "I think it's a bit more than the weather, Steve." He leaned forward in anticipation.

"Well, things are going OK at work, I am getting to know a few more people, and of course I have met you."

Pasco held up his hands apologetically. "Not all good news, then."

They both laughed.

Steve pressed on. "No, I mean that. You sorted out my car, got me back into rugby—"

"And bored the arse off you with all that Penpol crap."

"Far from it. I got involved; gave me something to think about." Steve continued with his checklist. "And of course there is Hannah to look forward to, and..." Now he stopped. That would be too much.

Pasco would not let him off the hook. "And what, Steve?"

Steve wished he had never started on his confessional; he could not expect Pasco to react like a priest. "This is going to sound really pathetic but I went on a sort of date." He slumped back in embarrassment, anticipating Pasco's mirth, but none was forthcoming.

"Good for you. Who is she?"

Steve was surprised by the relaxed inquiry. "One of my students."

Now Pasco was animated. "Christ, Steve, that's a bit dangerous."

Steve was quick to clear up the misapprehension. "Not a schoolgirl! One of my language class."

Pasco relaxed. "Oh, good." He thought for a moment. "Let me guess: the brainy one you told me about?"

"Yes, as it so happens."

"Go all right, did it?"

Steve brushed the question aside. "It wasn't really a date, you understand. We discussed books," he hesitated, "amongst other things."

Pasco stood up. "I'll believe you." He indicated the table where the Penhauls, greeting well-wishers, were sitting with their cards and presents. "I'd better go and pay my respects."

Steve stood too. "I'll get another round."

Pasco was some time talking to the Penhauls. Steve could hear occasional bursts of laughter punctuating the general conversational hum. Pasco's absence gave him a chance to reflect on his recent soul-baring. At least Pasco had had the decency not to mock, but perhaps he should have done so. It might have cleared Eva out of Steve's thoughts, which, since the coffee encounter, had the unsettling pattern of frequently calling her to remembrance. He had to reprove himself when this happened; chastise himself for behaving like an immature schoolboy. He knew more about her now but she knew nothing of him beyond his role as her teacher. She had asked for no details of his private life. For all he knew, she might have him down as a happily married man with four children. When he considered that, he berated himself again. What possible interest could it be to her what his personal circumstances were? He was her teacher; end of story. And yet... and yet... to revert to the old cliché, he could not put her entirely out of his mind.

Pasco returned to the table in a surprisingly thoughtful mood. He nodded his thanks to Steve as he drank slowly from his glass, then he put it down after a couple of mouthfuls and frowned. "I tried. I told Tamsin I would and I have. Until just now."

Steve was lost. "Until what just now?"

Pasco was defensive. "I didn't bring it up. I just congratulated them. He was the one." He raised his glass again and drank.

Steve put his own glass down firmly. "Pasco, what are you talking about?"

"He remembered me asking him about those sheds at Trevalwith. Didn't know nothing about them."

"The new sheds? I remember you asking."

"That got him curious; so he asked Giles."

"Who said what?"

"That they were 'necessary dormitory accommodation for his farmworkers'." Pasco shook his head in wonder.

Steve was still lost. "And are they?"

"He doesn't have any bloody farmworkers; just a manager and a bit of casual labour. Perhaps a week or two in the year he'll bring in a coachload of the foreign lot to cut the broccoli or harvest the spuds; that's it."

"Surely it wouldn't be worth building accommodation for them?"

"Course not. They're all out in caravans somewhere anyway."

"It doesn't make sense, then."

"That's what old John says. Doesn't understand the boy."

"But you do?" Steve guessed.

"I think so." Pasco put down his glass and leaned across the table. He looked around before lowering his voice to not much more than a whisper. "If you're a farmer you can more or less build what you like on your land if it's for agricultural purposes. You could put up the Taj Mahal in your farmyard as long as you said you were going to put pigs in it."

Steve considered this. "So Giles could put up those sheds, claiming they were necessary for the running of the farm."

"Correct. And no one was likely to object since Penpol had so reasonably withdrawn their application to build holiday homes there."

"But how does building sheds benefit Giles? It looks like pointless expense."

"Quite. For a year or two it will be. But they play the waiting game."

"Then what?"

"If I'm guessing right, he'll apply for change of use. Conversion of existing farm buildings into dwellings. 'In the same footprint', as they put it."

"Will they get away with it?"

"They're in with a shout. They've done that sort of thing before, and with a nod and a wink from the likes of Willie Walton..." Pasco left his sentence unfinished, then sat back and shrugged resignedly. "As Tamsin says, nothing we can do about it."

There was a lengthy silence whilst Steve gathered himself. The idea that had been forming in his mind now needed expression. He would risk it. He looked steadily at Pasco, who slowly registered his scrutiny and sat back up straight with a look of puzzlement.

"Actually, Pasco," Steve said with some force, "there is something we might do about it."

NINETEEN

The class was already assembled by the time Steve arrived. He had been delayed by the foul weather. Traffic had moved slowly as a gale-force wind drove sheets of rain into windscreens, and then there had been a frustrating wait at the perpetual roadworks, where the rain seemed to have incapacitated the temporary traffic lights whose function was replicated by a policeman in a yellow high-visibility jacket who, Steve fretted, seemed to show disproportionate partiality to the oncoming lines of traffic. His humour had not been helped by having to dash in the rain from Trengrouse's car park to the classroom while trying to prevent his papers from being soaked to a pulp by the rain or torn away by the wind. The umbrella with which he had planned to shelter them had been instantly blown inside out as soon as he'd stepped out of the car.

He was conscious of cutting a pitiable figure as he entered the room with water dripping from his now-tulip-shaped brolly, but the class were too busy drying themselves out to notice. Anoraks and soggy hats were placed over radiators, and water had pooled under the boots of those who had come straight from the fields. In spite of their soaked state the mood of the students was cheerful; pointing at one another to compare who was the more bedraggled, and laughing at what the Cornish weather had done to them. Steve entered into the spirit of the occasion by making a theatrical event of bending his umbrella back into its correct shape. He even earned a round of applause when, after a protracted struggle, he held the tamed beast aloft in triumph. Then a few comments on the Cornish weather further raised spirits, and Steve was able to hand out the still faintly legible worksheets to the class and see them settle at their workstations.

The room quietened as heads bowed in concentration. Steve was pleased to see that all but one booth was occupied. In spite of the dreadful weather, his motley crew had turned out. He tried not to feel flattered as he had a day or so ago when Bill Rogers had bumbled up to him and said he was getting "very positive feedback" and County Hall were pleased. Steve smiled at the memory and held his smile for Eva, who stood rather shyly by her table with the two borrowed books under her arm. She had obviously come with Luka and Elena straight from work, but even in her damp work overalls Steve was unsettled by how attractive she looked. He disciplined himself to remember where he was and what he was supposed to be doing. He indicated that she should take herself off to a quiet empty table at the far end of the room, and held up both hands to indicate that he would be with her in ten minutes.

In those minutes Steve checked on the progress of the others. He had prepared tasks of varying degrees of difficulty, and he checked to make sure everyone was coping. Happy that they were, he went over to Eva. He had prepared a list of questions for her to answer to test her comprehension of the two books she had asked to borrow. He wondered whether she would have found the time to read much of them, and was impressed when she told him that she had got through them both. He gave her the questions to work on and said he would catch up with her at the coffee break. She smiled up at him and then bent her head to study the worksheet.

Although only English was allowed there was no scarcity of conversation above the chinking of coffee cups. Steve mingled. He asked Luka how Manchester United were getting on and listened patiently to the lengthy reply, and tried to ignore Elena, who he now knew was Luka's girlfriend, miming exaggerated yawns behind his back. Two unshaven and weather-beaten Latvian car washers quizzed Steve about the relative strengths of various English beers, although why they thought he might be an expert in the matter was a little disturbing. Whilst muttering vaguely about the respective merits of lager and bitter, he caught a glimpse of Ivan hovering attentively over Maria and delicately passing her a biscuit. Steve wondered if an unlikely romance might be developing there. Glancing at his watch, he saw that the ten minutes were nearly up. Excusing himself to the Latvians, who were now arguing with one another in slow, formal English over which was their favourite vodka, he moved away from the coffee drinkers to the table where Eva still sat, working on her assignment.

"No coffee for you?" he asked.

"No thank you. I must finish this." She gestured at the answers she was penning to Steve's questions.

Steve looked at what she had written. After a few moments he had seen enough to be able to turn to Eva and congratulate her. "This looks really good. You must have worked hard."

She looked pleased. "Thank you. It was not easy to start with but it got better. I looked forward to the reading, after my work."

Steve smiled. "I don't know how you find the energy after a day's physical work. I couldn't."

She shook her head. "But you are working with your mind, your brain."

He tried to make light of that. "I'm not sure about that. Some of my pupils—"

Eva was insistent. "But for me it is just my body. When I am working my mind is dead. So to read these books I can be alive. You understand me?" She looked at Steve earnestly, as if willing him to comprehend.

"Yes. I think so. I understand." Steve held her gaze for a few seconds, feeling that he wanted to say more; to prolong the moment, but he knew that would be dangerous. He smiled jauntily and changed the subject. "If you would like, I could bring you round some more books to choose from."

She nodded. "Thank you. That would be good."

He tried to affect nonchalance. "And perhaps we could have coffee again?" He paused briefly and then quickly moved on to clarify his intentions. "Just to discuss the books."

Eva's smile, Steve decided, was enigmatic. "Yes. That would be nice; to discuss the books." He half wondered if she might be teasing him.

For the rest of the evening he was kept busy, going through the work of the other students and then directing a role-play session with the participants acting as either passengers or railway officials negotiating the various route options and fares for a trip to London. By the end of that he felt quite exhausted, but the class seemed to have enjoyed it. The rain was still lashing at the windows as the session came to an end. Steve said he hoped to see them all again next time and told them how well they were all doing. There was then a hiatus as wet-weather gear was dragged off the radiators and struggled into before taking on the tempest outside. Steve quietly observed Ivan chivalrously holding out Maria's overcoat and bending low so that she could wriggle into it. He was still smiling at that as the room began to empty. He looked to see if Eva was still working and felt a flicker of disappointment that she was no longer there, but then remembered she had come with Luka and Elena and would not want to hold them up. People were calling out their goodbyes now, and Steve raised a hand in acknowledgement. He moved to his desk and began to gather his papers together.

"Goodbye, Steve." It was Luka calling from the doorway. His passengers were still getting their outdoor clothing on. Elena did up a last zip, waved goodbye and followed him.

Eva was the last to leave. She was tying the laces of her boots. She finished and stood up straight, but didn't follow the others immediately. She rummaged in a pocket and produced some sort of headgear. Carefully she pulled the balaclava down over her head until it rested just above her eyes, then she stood and looked at Steve. "Goodbye," she said, and, pulling the balaclava down fully, turned and walked away.

Steve could not move. In the few seconds she had looked at him he had travelled back in his memory to that night which had seemed, until now, to belong to the distant past. Now the past had come to life. The woman in the car; the one who had driven away after speaking a few words of English. PC Basset's alleged foreign field worker. Above all, the woman in the balaclava.

Steve was not sure how long he stood there, motionless. His mind was a swirl of confusion. People spoke of their world crashing down about them, and that was how he felt. He barely remembered leaving the building, and it required a real effort of will to focus on his driving as the car splashed through the rain to carry him to a home which seemed, that night, particularly cold and cheerless.

TWENTY

Steve was finding it hard to concentrate on the information he was compiling for Pasco. He was expecting him any minute now and was uncertain how the meeting would go. Pasco's immediate response to Steve's proposition had been a mixture of shock and incredulity. It had taken all of Steve's persuasive powers to get him to at least think about it for a few days. Tonight Pasco would reveal the outcome of those thoughts. Steve was not hopeful. Perhaps it had been a hare-brained idea. Perhaps he had misread Pasco. It seemed he might not be a good judge of character. That depressing reflection dragged his thoughts back to Eva. Had he completely misjudged her or was his imagination in overdrive? Was she the driver of the stolen car? If she was, that suggested criminal conspiracy. Was anything she had told him about herself true? How could he ever find out? Should he just push it all out of his mind and treat her as just another class member? After all, by the time the summer holidays came round the course would be finished and she would go and take her guilty secrets with her. That, of course, presumed that she had been driving the car and had any guilty secrets. It was all hopeless, and most hopeless of all was why Steve was so desperate to know the truth about Eva Albescu.

His distracted thoughts were dispelled by a rap on the door. He let Pasco in. There was no whisky this time; Pasco was unsmiling, and sat down and fixed Steve with an accusatory stare.

"You were serious, weren't you?" His tone was challenging.

"Never more so." Steve held Pasco's stare.

Pasco was the first to look away. "I thought you were joking at the start."

"It's no joke, Pasco – you could do this."

Pasco turned back to look at Steve and allowed himself a wry smile. "Councillor Pasco. I can't see it somehow."

"Why not?" Steve insisted. "At least give it a go. What have you got to lose?"

"What?! Make a fool of myself; give everyone a laugh. And what about my work?"

"Councillors don't have to give up their employment, and if you were elected perhaps you could take on a bit of extra help."

Pasco laughed. "'If I was elected.' Look out for flying pigs."

Steve held up a restraining hand. "Hang on. Think about it rationally." He used his fingers to enumerate Pasco's qualities. "You are well known in this place, you have a real concern for local issues, you are not afraid to speak your mind, and most of all you are honest. Beyond corruption." He sat back. "I rest my case."

"Even if all that was true, Steve, what about the rest of it?"

"What 'rest of it'?"

Pasco shrugged. "I don't know. Meetings, committees, writing stuff. I'd be useless at all that. All those educated people. I left school at sixteen, remember."

Steve shook his head. "None of that is important; it's not a problem. What is important is that you would be doing what you think is right; what you think matters to people. People who so easily get forgotten."

Pasco looked as if he was wrestling with some inner conflict. "You really think I could do all that?"

Steve spoke emphatically. "I've only known you a few months, Pasco, but long enough to be certain you could."

"I don't know." Pasco sighed. "But there's Tamsin, of course—"

Steve was sympathetic. "I know, that could be difficult but..."

"What?" Pasco seemed puzzled.

"Getting her used to the idea. Convincing her—"

It was Pasco's turn to interrupt. "What are you on about, boy? It's only because of her that I'm even thinking about it!"

"Sorry?"

"I told her what your idea was."

"And?"

"She said it was about time I got off my arse and did something instead of moaning about other people."

There was a silence at this revelation. Then Steve laughed wryly. "I really must meet your wife; she sounds a remarkable woman."

Pasco laughed too. "She's put up with me for twenty years, so she must be."

The mood was lighter now. Steve shuffled together the papers he had printed out. "I've run off some of the basic information. Procedures. It's not too complicated."

"Hang on! I haven't said yes yet," Pasco protested.

Steve pushed the first sheet across the table. "Oh, I think you have, Pasco."

It took well over an hour for Steve to take Pasco through the steps to stand for the council. There was plenty of time to get the requisite ten registered electors to sign his nomination papers. Steve joked that Pasco could probably get more than that just from the Saturday lunchtime regulars at The Miners. Pasco would be standing as an independent, so without the backing of one of the major political parties he would need an agent to handle all the paperwork and oversee his election campaign. Pasco took fright at that thought, until Steve offered his services, which were gratefully accepted. He explained that Pasco would need to work out and publicise his manifesto, which again provoked alarm, but Steve suggested it was something they could sort out over a 'working lunch' at The Miners, which made them both laugh. With Pasco reconciled to his imminent debut on the political stage, Steve thought the occasion should be marked with a minor celebration. He produced the familiar bottle and two glasses and they toasted the success of the new venture. They relaxed; Pasco had crossed his Rubicon. There was a comfortable silence as they savoured their drinks. Steve felt his thoughts wander again to the uncertainties that blurred his perception of Eva, and he frowned in frustration.

Pasco registered Steve's expression. "You all right? Gone a bit quiet."

Steve regained his composure. "Sorry. Miles away."

Pasco was curious. "How many miles?"

Steve thought to laugh off the question, but then thought again. He needed to talk this through with someone who would not think he was paranoid or delusional. He put down his glass and took a deep breath. "Look, Pasco, you'll probably think I've lost the plot but...."

Pasco did not think he was unhinged. He sat quietly as Steve explained his problem. How the sudden recall of the night of the crash had been triggered by seeing Eva in that balaclava, and how, insofar as he could rely on his memory, the brief words the driver had spoken could have come from her mouth. Pasco had not met Eva and doubted he would be able to identify her as the driver anyway as he had only caught a fleeting glimpse of her that night. He asked Steve what he was going to do, and Steve admitted that he wasn't sure. Was there any point in agonising over it?

"Perhaps I should just forget about it," he said.

"Like I was supposed to forget about Penpol?" Pasco asked.

Steve took the point. "Easier said than done, but what do I gain if I confront her? If it wasn't her she'll be highly offended that I thought it could be—"

"And if it was her?" Pasco demanded.

"If it was her she's hardly likely to admit it, is she? So I'm stuffed whatever I do."

"So why do anything?"

Steve had asked himself that many times. He tried to explain. "This is going to sound pathetic..."

"Try me." Pasco smiled encouragingly.

"I like her. Not just because she's beautiful, which she is, but... I don't know, I thought perhaps there might be a bit more than just the teaching thing." Steve looked uncertainly at Pasco. "Now you know."

Pasco persisted. "Then you can't just leave it, Steve. You've got to ask her and trust yourself to know if she's telling the truth. Risky, but you can't carry on as if everything's normal, and if you just walk away you'll always be fussing about what might have been."

Steve sighed. "Thanks, Pasco. I suppose you're right. I'm due to see her before the next class." He laughed bitterly. "Probably be the last time I will see her, knowing my luck."

TWENTY-ONE

The coffee was turning cold again in the jumbo cups. Eva had been animated talking about the books she was borrowing; asking Steve's opinion on which Thomas Hardy novel he would recommend and questioning whether she would find Virginia Woolf too difficult. Steve had found it hard to assemble his thoughts sufficiently to respond, and had to work really hard to maintain the pretence of interest. He had tried and failed to summon the courage to ask her the questions to which he needed an answer. He had hoped forlornly that an opportunity might naturally present itself when the matter could be raised. Mentally, he had rehearsed a dialogue in which the mood might be light-hearted enough for him to ask in a casual way, "I know this must seem silly, but were you by any chance involved in a car crash a few months ago?", or something similar. But no such opportunity had presented itself and Eva would soon have to leave.

His confusion seemed to communicate itself to her. She closed the book she had been discussing and looked apologetically at him. "I'm sorry. I have been talking too much."

Steve pulled himself together. "No, not at all."

Eva was not to be deflected. She leaned forward and looked directly at him. "You are tired, I think. I must not keep you." She made to stand, but Steve held out a restraining hand and she sat down again and looked at him with some concern.

Steve took a deep breath and looked around to check no one was within earshot. When he spoke he kept his voice down. "You must forgive me, Eva, but there is something I need to ask you."

Her eyes widened questioningly. "What must you ask me, Steve?"

He could think of no tactful preamble. "I need to ask if you were involved in a car crash. Just after Christmas."

He sat back resignedly. He was prepared for responses ranging from bafflement to indignant outrage to stark denial; what he was not prepared for was no response at all. Eva had barely moved, and her features were impassive. The silence seemed eternal before she spoke.

Her voice was low; her question simple. "How did you know?"

Steve felt a wave of depression swamp him but now there was no turning back. "It was my car."

Eva said nothing but there was no hiding the anxiety in her expression. Perhaps aware of it, she looked down at the table and distractedly moved her coffee cup aside.

Steve managed a weak smile. "You could have denied it. I would have believed you."

"But I would know that I had lied." She said this as if it was irrefutable.

"Well, at least no one was hurt; and I got another car," Steve said half-heartedly.

Eva looked at him directly. "I will tell you. It was wrong, what I did, but perhaps you will understand."

"Perhaps."

"The other person in the car. It was my brother, Cristian."

Steve remembered. "Your young brother?"

"Yes. You must know he is not a bad person but it was difficult for him. My father had died when he was just a baby and my mother was working all the time. He had no one to look out for him. School was not good for him. He left as soon as he could but there was no work; only sometimes in the fields. There were other boys the same. Nothing to do, and if they did get some little job there was just drinking with the money."

"Not easy for him."

"Not for my mother too. She worried always about him. When I came home from the university I tried to help; talk to him; find work for him. He did his best but it was hard. Sometimes I asked him to look after Anya and gave him some of my bar money. He was very good with her. But there was no future for him there. You understand?"

"Of course. So that is why he came to England?"

"Yes. The Gang Masters came round to our town to get people to work over here. Cristian and some of his friends decided to try and he was happy here, sending money back to us. He came home for holidays; told us what he was doing and how much money he was making."

"That is how you came here?" Steve asked.

"Yes. Anya was old enough for me to leave her and my mother had retired. Cristian said there was work for me. My mother was pleased for me to come; she said I would look after my brother." Eva paused reflectively. "That was not easy."

"There were problems?"

"Some of the same boys from home were here; his friends. Cristian is not like them, but he tries to show he is a big man." She managed a weary smile at Steve. "You know what I mean?"

"Yes, I see it a lot in teaching. Timid kids trying to prove themselves to the tough ones; often ends in trouble."

Eva sighed. "Cristian was like that. He tried to prove he was a hard man. There were fights and too much drinking, and other things. I tried to speak to him but it was no good. Until it was too late."

"What was too late, Eva?"

"The car; the stupid car. He does not even have a licence!" She raised her voice in exasperation, but lowered it again quickly as one or two other patrons of the coffee shop looked her way. When she spoke again she had regained her composure. "They had gone to Truro; Cristian and two of the others. There was a band he liked. Of course they were drinking and there was some trouble with Cornish boys. They were thrown out. Cristian said they were angry; the fight had not been their fault, he said, and now they had missed the train back. They didn't know what to do. One of the others said it was not a problem; they would steal a car. He said it was easy; he had done it at home. He knew how to get in and how to start the engine. Cristian was too weak, or perhaps too frightened, to try to stop him."

"The old lady's car," Steve told her, "that explains it."

Eva looked at him in surprise. "An old lady?"

"That's what the police said."

Eva was wide-eyed. "The police have found out?"

"They know who it belonged to." He paused. "But not who took it."

"But now you know." She hesitated. "You will tell them?"

Steve recalled the lugubrious PC Basset. "I'm not sure they would be very interested."

Eva was remembering something. "There was a man with a phone. Cristian said he took a photograph."

"Pasco," Steve said.

Eva made little of that. "I could not stop. Cristian would have been arrested. He is scared of the police. In Romania you do not want to be in trouble with police."

Steve thought again of PC Basset. "Not quite the same here, I think, but I can see why he wanted to get away." He thought for a moment. "But you, Eva, what were you doing driving a stolen car?"

Eva looked defeated. "You will not believe me."

Steve looked at her unblinkingly. "Maybe."

Eva spoke slowly and with remorse. "I should have done nothing. But it was my brother." She seemed to be appealing for Steve's understanding. "I was trying to take the car back. I know that sounds stupid but I didn't know what else to do. Cristian was so afraid that the police would come. The other boys said they would burn the car but I knew that was wrong. Cristian remembered where they had taken it from, so I thought if we drove it back there at night-time we would leave it where they found it and there would be no police." She looked down at the table, as if unwilling to register Steve's reaction.

He was unsure of how he felt; what he should say. He settled for the non-committal. "It might have worked. But then I spoiled it for you."

Eva looked up now. She seemed not far from tears. "It was my fault. I am not used to driving any more and it was a car with no gears. I don't know—"

"An automatic," Steve prompted, relieved to fall back on the banal. "It can be difficult until you get used to them."

Eva made an effort to regain some self-possession. "We didn't know what to do," she explained. "Cristian phoned the others. They told us to take the car to the old mine."

"Ding Dong. I went there."

"They came there. They burnt the car. I was frightened of them..." She shuddered remembering her ordeal.

"And then what happened?"

"They took us back to town and Cristian collected his passport. Then they all left."

"Where to?"

"Back to Romania. They were worried the police would come."

For the third time in as many minutes Steve remembered PC Basset. "I don't think they need have worried," he said wryly.

Neither spoke for a few moments. Eva broke the silence. "So what will you do now, Steve?"

Steve was still processing his thoughts. "I don't know, Eva. It's a lot to think about."

Eva stood. "Of course. I understand." She handed Steve back his books. "Maybe I will not need these." Before he could reply, she turned and walked away without a backward glance.

TWENTY-TWO

"So what will you do?"

"Nothing. What can I do? Nobody gains anything if I report this. What would be the point? I can't see Basset alerting Interpol."

"Did you tell her that?" Pasco spoke through a mouthful of pasty.

"No. I should have but I had to think about it. Stupid of me, but it was a lot to take on board at the time."

"More to the point, boy, did you believe her?"

Steve hesitated. "I think so. She couldn't have made a story like that up on the spur of the moment. But I was a bit in shock. I'm not one for rushing in. 'Not spontaneous enough,' Linda was always telling me." He sighed at the memory.

"So you'll tell her you're OK with it all? Everything back to normal?"

"Can anything ever really go back to normal? But we'll see. I'll talk to her at the next class."

There was a sudden commotion at the bar; a scraping of bar stools, and raised voices. Steve turned in some alarm and saw two of the heftier regulars striding towards their table. He clutched his pint in a nervous reflex.

One of the men approaching thrust out a hand. "Well done, Pasco – about bloody time we had someone like you on the council." He pumped Pasco's hand in congratulation. "I'll be happy to sign your forms if you want, and so will Cyril here." He pushed Cyril forward, who also shook Pasco by the hand. The formalities over, they retreated to the bar.

Pasco looked stunned. "What the hell was that all about?"

Steve confessed. "I thought it might be an idea to put the word about that you're prepared to stand." He tried to look innocent. "I might have mentioned it to Sam."

Pasco looked at him admonishingly for a moment and then allowed himself to laugh. "You might turn out to be some agent, Steve." He raised his half-eaten pasty in salutation.

Steve had Jude the Obscure and To the Lighthouse in his briefcase. He had rehearsed in his mind how he would talk to Eva. He would put her mind at rest that her secret was safe with him. The matter was closed; he understood that what she had done was to try to protect her brother. Then he would give her the books, and with any luck they could arrange another coffee date to discuss them. It all sounded so simple, but the nagging voice of experience reminded him of the sad lesson that when you make plans, God laughs. Then doubts flooded in to swamp his optimism. Would she, he wondered, want to keep a distance between them now that their relationship, if you could call it that, had taken a more personal turn? She had shown Steve a vulnerability which she might now regret. Perhaps she had been hurt by his seeming hesitance in expressing his complete acceptance of her version of events. He regretted that now, blaming his besetting caution, but also having to concede that there was still a scintilla of doubt that refused to fade away entirely. How well did he really know her, or she him? He tried not to agonise too much over these unanswerable questions, and told himself not to overdramatise. He would give her the books and take it from there.

He arrived in good time for the class and was able to lay out all his teaching materials for them. As the students drifted in he tried to greet them individually; by now he knew them well enough to personalise the exchanges. Ricardo complained that the bar had been very busy at the weekend but his boss would not hire anyone to help. As Steve sympathised with that, he raised a hand in welcome to his two Latvian alcohol aficionados, whose bleary appearance suggested that they might have been pursuing their research over the weekend. They sat down wearily in front of their screens and Steve made a mental note not to expect too much active participation from that quarter. Maria and Ivan came together, and Steve pretended not to notice that they had entered hand in hand for fear of embarrassing Maria, who, catching his eye, quickly let go of Ivan's massive paw. By now the room was filling up and Steve ticked off the names on his register. There were only three more to come and he felt a nervous tightening in his chest. He reproved himself, and sought distraction in taking the books he had brought for Eva out of his briefcase. He had his back to the door as he heard it push open. He took a deep, calming breath and, with the books in his hand, turned towards the door. Luka and Elena stood there and began taking off their coats. Steve waited for a few seconds and, when they began to move towards their workstations, intercepted them and made a show of checking off their names in his register, whilst anticipating the door opening again and Eva entering.

The hiatus was interrupted by Luka, who pointed at Eva's name on the register. "She will not come tonight," he said.

Steve tried not to betray his concern. "Oh," he said. "Is she not well?"

Luka turned to Elena for support. "She is not here," she said slowly; English still a struggle for her.

Steve tried to be patient; to calm his anxiety. He spoke slowly to Elena. "Yes. Thank you. I see she is not here, but is she unwell? Ill," he added by way of clarification.

Elena shrugged. "I do not know. She is not saying to me."

Luka, who was the more fluent, came to her rescue. "Elena and Eva, they do not work in the same place this week. Speak only in the evening—"

Steve tried not to hurry him, but cut in nervously. "And this evening? You spoke?" He directed his question to Elena.

She shook her head. "No, she is not there." She paused, looking for words that eluded her, then turned for help to Luka.

"She is gone," he said.

"Where?" Steve almost shouted.

"We think home. But she did not say."

"Nothing? She said nothing?"

Luka shrugged. "She left a..." He fumbled for the word. "A... piece of paper for Elena. How do you say?" He looked inquiringly at Steve.

"A note? She left a note?"

Luka agreed. "Yes. That is it. A note." He seemed pleased to have recognised the word, and turned to Elena for approval of his prowess.

Steve resisted the impulse to shake him. "What did the note say?" He was suddenly aware that his evident concern might seem disproportionate. He paused and then held up the register. "I just need to record reasons for absence. That's all." He smiled reassuringly at Luka, who seemed to have grasped very little of that explanation. Steve tried again. "So if I knew what the note said..."

Elena, surprisingly, seemed to have grasped the point. "She says there is a big problem. She cannot stay."

Steve waited for more but nothing was forthcoming. "That is all?"

Elena nodded firmly. "That is all."

Steve stood immobile; shock and dismay anchoring him to the spot. Only the rising noise level from the waiting students forced him to function. With an effort, he turned and fixed them with a rictus smile. He waved Luka and Elena to their places and walked back to his dais. Before addressing the class he slowly put the two novels intended for Eva back into his briefcase.

It was just warm enough to sit outside in the beer garden but not warm enough for Steve to discard his anorak or Pasco his thick woollen sweater. They were the only customers to have ventured out. They sat at a wooden table with slats still soggy from winter moss. The damp parasol drooped unfurled. Some optimistic bird hidden in a tangled shrub offered a sporadic half-hearted attempt at song, providing a counterpoint to the occasional noise of laughter and raised voices drifting from the warmth of the distant bar. Their foray into the garden was driven not by a brave if foolhardy attempt to welcome the first glimmer of Spring, but the search for privacy.

Steve handed Pasco a folder. "It's all in there."

Pasco tested the weight of the folder. "Blimey! Have I got to plough through all this?"

"I'm afraid so. If you want to be a councillor you need to have a grip on what the council actually does." Steve allowed himself a smile. "And before you say, 'Bugger all', you'll find they are responsible for just about everything from collecting the bins to filling in potholes – or failing to."

"I know that, Steve," Pasco protested. "I'm not quite as thick as I look."

Steve laughed. "I should hope not. But the details of how it all works, the various committees with their budgets, how meetings are organised, that sort of thing; it's all in there." He pointed at the folder Pasco was clutching.

Pasco looked doubtful. "I've got to know all that?"

"Yes. If you want people to take you seriously." Steve was conscious that that might seem a touch condescending. He tried to lighten his tone. "Well, you know what I mean."

Pasco did not seem to have taken offence. He had opened the folder and was studying the first page intently. He looked up at Steve. "Just as well there's no rugby."

"Why?"

Pasco closed the folder and held it up. "Looks as if this is what I'll be doing all weekend." He put the folder down resignedly.

Steve hesitated. "Look, Pasco, it's not too late to change your mind. We haven't submitted your papers yet."

Pasco looked at him sharply. "Is that what you think I should do?"

"No. Of course not. I just don't want you to think I'm forcing you into this—"

Pasco held up a hand to stop him. "It's not you, Steve."

There was a lengthy silence before Steve spoke. "Who is it, then?" Then he thought he understood. "Oh, you mean Tamsin?"

Pasco smiled. "No, not Tamsin, dear of her." He paused. "No one living."

Steve absorbed this for a moment. "Your dad?"

"I asked myself what he would have said was the right way."

"I understand."

"I'm glad you do, Steve, because anyone else would think I was barmy." He sighed. "Now look what you've got me into, Dad." He picked up the folder again and looked at Steve. "Must have taken you a long time to put all this together."

Steve shrugged. "It's all online. Anyway, I was glad to have something to do."

"Stop you thinking about Eva, you mean?" Pasco guessed.

"I keep asking myself, Why didn't I just tell her at the time that I believed her?" Steve sighed.

"Because you weren't sure." Pasco hesitated. "And now?"

"Now I'm still not sure. Was she just frightened, or..." Steve looked at Pasco questioningly.

"Or," said Pasco firmly, "she had something to hide. You have to face it. She could have spun you a yarn, Steve. All that stuff about her brother. You don't even know she has a brother, do you? Not really. Sorry to say it, mate, but she could have been stringing you along."

"Don't think I haven't been telling myself that," Steve said wearily. He looked distractedly around the bleak garden. "And now I'll never know."

As if catching the mood of the moment, the valiant bird hidden in the bush ceased its song abruptly. A lengthy silence followed before Pasco attempted to break the dark spell. "You can test me on this."

Steve turned back to look at him. "What?"

"Isn't that what you teachers always say: 'There'll be a test next time'?" He pointed to the folder.

The attempt at humour worked. Steve wagged a cautionary finger. "And detention if you fail!"

"I reckon I'll have a lot of homework before this is over."

"You will. We have to think about your platform and—"

"My what?"

"Your platform; your manifesto."

Pasco did not seem to be following.

"Your political statement – in other words, what your policies are."

Pasco protested. "I don't know about policies Steve. Just things I want to see done different."

"Well, we have to tell people that, if you want them to vote for you."

"And how do we do that?"

"Flyers, press releases, social media..."

"I've still got to work, Steve," Pasco protested. "And I don't know how to do any of that. I'm hopeless at all that stuff you're talking about."

Steve grinned. "That's why you've got an agent. Leave it with me." He remembered something. "There is one bit of good news."

"I'm glad to hear it."

"Frank Harris is standing down. You won't be running against him."

Pasco considered that. "It might help. He's been our councillor for years. Decent enough bloke but not got much energy; anything for a quiet life, if you know what I mean."

"Be no quiet life for anyone if you get in, Pasco."

"Who else is standing, do you know?"

"Not yet. The papers aren't due in for another few weeks."

Pasco smiled. "Old Breock Trevaylor will stand. He always does."

"Who?"

"Cornish nationalist. 'Blow up the Tamar Bridge; burn all second homes.'"

"What?!"

"Well, he probably doesn't say that but I don't suppose he'd mind."

"Do people vote for him?"

" A few."

"But not enough?"

"I think most people know him too well. He likes a drop. When he's had a few he starts shouting at the top of his voice, gabbling away a lot of nonsense; not a word you can recognise. He says he's talking Cornish!"

"Is he?"

"I've asked people who should know."

"And what do they say he's talking?"

"Bollocks!"

Both laughing, and with Pasco clutching his folder, they retreated to the warmth of the pub.

TWENTY-THREE

At one point Steve had almost wrapped himself in the cover as he stretched to lodge one edge of the duvet in its designated corner. It had taken him fully ten minutes of his Sunday morning to finally wrestle the whole downy quilt inside its enclosing home; and then another ten minutes of patting and pulling and punching until the ten-tog beast lay vanquished on his bed. As he sat, panting, at the kitchen table with a restorative cup of tea, he felt a childlike pride in his achievement. He had splashed out on this new bed covering in a fit of unusual extravagance because he didn't want Hannah to think she was visiting a youth hostel. Not that he knew much about youth hostels these days; he had heard rumours that they were now positively luxurious and you didn't even have to pretend not to have a car parked a few hundred yards away to gain admission. He had never been a great fan, even in his qualifying youth. He had found attempting to sleep on a corrugated mattress in a dormitory full of farting hikers with thighs like beer barrels a less than restful experience. No wonder everyone got up at the crack of dawn, heartily keen to embrace the day; it was to escape the horrors of the night.

Steve gratefully pushed those memories away. The Easter holiday would be upon him in a few days. He had taught the last evening class of the term and could not pretend that he was sorry to have a two-week break from that. It was not the fault of the class. They had remained enthusiastic and willing enough, but Steve could not quite dispel the memories of Eva. He had needed to work doubly hard to maintain a cheerful front. It was over a month now since she had left so abruptly. There were still so many unanswered questions. Had she really told him the truth? Was she somehow mixed up with the wild young men she blamed for her brother's problems? How could he even be sure that the man in the car had been her brother? There were no means of knowing. If what Eva had told him was true then Steve cast himself in the unworthy role of doubting Thomas, and indeed when he found himself, unbidden, thinking about her, doubt, confusion and uncertainty blurred his recall.

He told himself, as he had many times, that such introspective agonising was futile. He drained the last of his tea and washed up the cup. That burst of positivity helped to refocus his thoughts. He looked around. He would need to smarten up the kitchen before Hannah's arrival. Possibly he might run to a pair of new curtains for the window, provided they were the sort that required no alteration or complicated fixing. His DIY skills were minimal; another disappointment for Linda, he remembered. However, he had managed the duvet. Hannah could sleep in his bedroom and he would squeeze into the box room, although 'matchbox room' would be a more accurate description. In preparation for his move he had indulged himself by purchasing a bright red woollen rug from a charity shop to replace the festering one. Again he imagined how Linda would be aghast at such execrable taste, but it had only cost a fiver and at the bedside it would at least keep his feet off the bare boards. He moved through to the sitting room and convinced himself that a few vases of fresh flowers would, if not transform the place, at least make it less funereal. The sofa was beginning to sag again as its weight slowly bore down on the Trengrouse textbook, but help was at hand. During a recent post-rugby visit, Pasco had noticed the tilting and offered to reattach the missing castor which Steve had found, on one of his sporadic cleaning forays, wedged inexplicably behind the fridge. Pasco was due soon. Steve needed him to look at the leaflet he had drafted to publicise his election agenda. Nomination papers had been submitted, there had been no shortage of willing signatories, and Steve was registered as Pasco's electoral agent. Pasco himself had worked diligently at his 'homework', as he put it, and, whilst he would deny it to his dying breath, seemed to find some satisfaction, if not pleasure, in negotiating the legislative labyrinth of local government officialese. Steve had warned him that bureaucrats would never use one word if they could find a hundred, and it was hard not to agree with Pasco, who, on one occasion, after labouring through some turgid documents, had turned to him and said in disbelief, "But that's just stating the bleeding obvious!"

As if on cue, Pasco arrived. He carried his toolbox. "I'll fix that wheel for you." He walked into the sitting room and briskly upended the sofa.

Steve hovered uncertainly. "What can I do to help?"

"Put the kettle on," Pasco instructed without looking up.

Steve meekly retreated to the kitchen, and after the sound of a few hammer blows and some muttered curses Pasco joined him and, closing his toolbox, put it down on the table.

"Done," he said. "Got any biscuits?"

Steve managed to find a packet and, deciding that a second cup of tea would not be an overindulgence, joined Pasco at the table. Steve booted up the laptop and scrolled to the page he wanted. An image filled the screen. "What do you think?"

Pasco put down his cup and looked at himself on the screen. "Blimey. Looks like a mugshot. 'Have you seen this man?'"

"It's not that bad," Steve protested. "It makes you look thoughtful."

"Constipated, more like."

"Trust me, it will look fine on the leaflets." Steve scrolled to another page. "I've tried to keep it as simple as possible."

"Simple sounds good to me." Pasco studied the layout.

Steve tracked the individual lines with his finger. "So underneath your picture we just get a brief summary of who you are and what you've done—"

"Most of them know who I am and what I've done: not much."

Steve looked firmly at Pasco. "Look. You've got to stop putting yourself down. If you don't believe in what you're doing, how can you expect anyone to vote for you?"

Pasco looked momentarily abashed. "I hear you, Steve, but," he paused, seeking the right words, "I do believe in what I'm doing; I just don't know if I'm up to it."

"Of course you are." Steve was emphatic. "It's not that complicated." He pointed again at the screen. "That's the point of this. We put one of these through every letter box. It asks people to tell us what's important."

"How do they do that?"

"Facebook; email; Twitter. All that social media stuff. Invite them to participate. To see if they agree with your ideas."

"But I don't do any of that," Pasco protested.

"You will; trust me. It's important you involve them. That's your strength, Pasco. You stand as an independent;

you don't have to tread any party lines. You ask people what matters to them and tell them you'll go for it."

"The four points. You reckon I got that right?"

"Yes. We didn't need any complicated market research. You live with these people, Pasco; you have done all your life. They know you; they talk to you." Steve smiled. "And not just in the pub."

"Talk a lot of nonsense there, I expect."

"I've been with you in town and at the rugby. Everyone has time for you. I know it will embarrass you, Pasco, but you have to face it."

"Face what?"

"People like you!"

Pasco looked unconvinced and moved to change the subject. "Tamsin helped with the list. She picks up a lot of moaning and groaning from her dinner ladies and the parents, and her mum is always bending her ear about there being nothing here for the old folk and so on."

"I see where that came from, then." Steve read from the screen. "'A multi-use community facility with provision for both senior citizens and young people.'"

"That's it. A drop-in centre for older folk in the daytime, with a proper kitchen turning out decent meals at a fair price; somewhere cheerful and comfortable to come to. Get them out of the house."

"Help with social isolation?" Steve asked.

"You can call it that. I call it loneliness. And in the evening the kids could use it." Then, before Steve could find any newly coined nomenclature, "We used to call them youth clubs."

Steve smiled. "Those were the days."

"Buses." Pasco was looking at the screen now. "That's another thing that affects the young and the old. 'Improved public transport facilities.' That's how I've put that. It's all right if you've got a car but a lot of old folk don't drive."

"But they do have bus passes," Steve argued.

"Not much good if there are no bloody buses," Pasco countered. "When the council cut the subsidies the service out here went to pot. Not profitable, they said, but it's a service to the public, not a business. And people tell me that half the time the ones that are still running don't turn up. Some poor old dear stands out in the wind and rain waiting for a bus that never comes. 'Never mind, love, there'll be another one along tomorrow.'"

"And the young people. How does it affect them?"

"I know you haven't been here long, Steve, but you must have noticed this place isn't exactly Swing City, is it? At the weekends the younger kids' centre of social activity is the disused telephone box outside the Co-op. The older ones aren't allowed in the pubs so if they want any entertainment, like the cinema or clubs, they have to take a bus."

Steve guessed. "And there aren't any?"

"Only if you want to be home by eight o'clock."

"So improving public transport is a real issue."

"It is. And so is that." Pasco jabbed at the screen. "We've got to do something about that."

"'Help for the homeless.' That might not be popular, Pasco."

"Popular be buggered. I know what people say: that they're all druggies or alkies or benefit cheats. All that stuff. But you've seen them, Steve, even in a small place like this, living like stray dogs out on the street. That can't be right no matter what they are."

Steve nodded. "So that brings us to the fourth topic; the big one. The one that started all this."

Pasco read from the screen. "'More new council houses at affordable rents.' That's clear enough."

"No one can argue with that, and I'm sure you're right not to have a go at second-home owners. It's pointless."

"I know. We don't like it but we can't stop it. This isn't China." Something amused Pasco. "Anyway, I bet old Breock will bang on about that. He always does."

"In Cornish?" Steve asked, and they both laughed.

Steve closed his laptop. "So I'll run off a few hundred of these and then we can sort out the house calls."

Pasco looked doubtful. "Most of them probably won't read it. If they're like me, that sort of stuff goes straight in the bin."

"Perhaps, but at least it's our chance to tell them what you are fighting for; it will raise your profile."

"Whatever that means." Pasco frowned. "When are we going to do all this? I'll have to sort my work out."

"I thought the Easter holidays. I'm free then; 'teacher's rest'." Steve hesitated. "And I can get someone to help us."

"Who?"

"Hannah."

Pasco looked surprised. "Really? Not much of a holiday for her, is it?"

"She knows about you, Pasco, and your election plans. She offered to help."

"No arm-twisting?"

Steve shook his head. "We speak on the phone now. She thinks what you're doing is "peng,", whatever that means."

Pasco smiled. "I hope I don't disappoint her. When is she coming?"

"A week on Friday."

"Right. Come for a meal Saturday evening. Tamsin's been giving me hell for not asking you before. She's dying to meet you."

Steve smiled. "That's not something I hear very often."

"And if it's all too boring for her, Hannah can talk to Selwyn. He does open his mouth occasionally." Pasco gathered his toolbox and stood. "I tell you one good thing about this election business, Steve."

"What's that?"

"At least it doesn't clash with the rugby season."

TWENTY-FOUR

The train was late. No surprise there, Steve thought, but unfortunately it was only a few minutes late, so Hannah would not be eligible for any sort of refund. A uniformed employee of the railway company, lounging against the wall of the left luggage office (permanently closed for the past ten years as an antiterrorist precaution), volunteered that the delay was the consequence of an incident at Bodmin Parkway. Steve knew that 'incident' was sometimes railway speak for 'some poor soul jumping in front of a train', and was relieved to be offered clarification: there had been cows on the line.

As he paced the platform Steve tried to calm his jangled nerves. It had been months since he had last seen Hannah, on that ill-fated Christmas visit. They had taken to talking on the phone of late, but that was more tantalising than the distanced letter-writing. To hear but not to see was a formula for frustration. Would she have changed? How would they cope with each other's company? Would she miss Linda? How would they spend their time together? Steve had made plans but would Hannah fall in with them? With these churning thoughts, he barely registered the tinny Tannoy announcing the imminent arrival of the Paddington train, but when he looked down the line he saw the approaching carriages, so close to the sea they might have been on the beach, snaking around the last bend into the station. He positioned himself by the exit from the platform. The train juddered to a halt, doors opened and passengers flooded out. There were plenty of them: the Easter invasion of Cornwall. The first wave flowed around Steve. He was aware of backpacks and cameras, slung around the necks, of chattering young people, many of whom might have been Japanese or Chinese, he suspected, but the distinction was of only fleeting interest as he craned to see over the advancing throng. Now the less fleet of foot were trudging towards him: distracted mothers herding small children whilst attempting to juggle assorted items of baggage; a Germanic-looking couple probably in their sixties, but announcing their fitness to the world with stout hiking boots, walking poles and bush hats. Steve wondered if they would relax after their journey with a brisk ten-mile walk along the Coast Path before supper. Then it was the turn of ladies with bulging shopping bags, presumably bringing home the booty after bargain-hunting in Plymouth. But where was Hannah? His anxiety levels were rising now. Had she missed the train? Surely she would have texted him? He walked a few yards down the platform through the thinning crowd.

Then he saw her. She was almost hidden behind a large suitcase which she was struggling to keep off the ground with one hand whilst dragging a much smaller wheeled one behind her. She turned to check the stability of the trailing bag and was unaware of Steve's approach. For a second he had time to wonder with some dismay why his daughter had felt the need to travel with so much stuff.

"Are you sure you can manage that, dear?" The inquiry came from an elderly lady who puffed up alongside Hannah, scraping a large, battered trunk behind her.

"Here, let me." Steve grabbed the handle away from the old lady, who looked at him in some surprise.

"Dad!" Hannah let go of both her cases. She looked at Steve and broke into a wide smile.

Steve released the trunk handle. Simultaneously, Hannah moved towards him. They hugged. Steve felt tears pricking at his eyes which he tried to hide by blinking them away, but when at last he let Hannah go he could see that she had made no attempt to hide hers. They looked smilingly at each other.

"I suppose I could try to find a porter," the old lady muttered hesitantly.

Steve managed to recover his composure. "I don't think they have those any more." He grasped the handle again and also relieved Hannah of her suitcase, trying to ignore the still-niggling pain in his shoulder. "On we go," he said, with more confidence than he felt.

Eventually, when all the other passengers had long dispersed, Steve and Hannah managed to deposit the old lady and her baggage in a taxi. During the lengthy trek along the platform Steve had learned that she was visiting her daughter for a few weeks, that she was a widow, and that she had been waiting too long for a hip operation. Fortunately a taxi had arrived before she could continue articulating the inadequacies of the National Health Service. She did pause long enough to tell Steve how Hannah had been kind enough to help her with her bags. Before she wound up the taxi window she whispered to him, "that's a lovely daughter you've got there."

The smell of fresh coffee brewing was not how the day usually greeted Steve. Hannah must have got up before him. Lying half awake in his cell, he congratulated himself on another recent extravagant purchase: ground coffee and a percolator. Maybe he hadn't stretched to the organic, fair trade, thrice-roasted beans from Machu Picchu but whatever he had got smelt good. He swung his feet out of bed and onto the red rug, and in so doing trod on the radio. Cursing, he picked it up. There was no room for a bedside table in the cubicle that passed for a box room. Out of habit he switched on the radio and then groaned at the sound of Mandy Trewellard interviewing some seriously deranged listener from North Cornwall who had stayed awake all night to count the cars coming into the county. Presumably they were short of entertainment in North Cornwall, Steve concluded, whilst also speculating whether Radio Kernow had any other employees besides Mandy. As if to answer his question she handed over to the ghastly weatherman, which was a cue for protracted mind-numbing banter. When the weatherman had finished chortling at his own wearisome jests he managed to turn his attention to the forecast. He was now in more sombre mood. He could only predict a spell of fine, settled weather. He said this with none of the animation he displayed when threatening the imminent arrival of flood and tempest. He had to confess dolefully that there were no yellow warnings in place, and that winds would be no more than gentle breezes, and temperatures above the seasonal average. That last admission seemed to render him speechless, and he handed back to Mandy with not even the hint of a quip. Steve silenced her immediately and, by standing on the bed, managed to dress.

"Croissants! Where did you find those?" he asked Hannah, who was pouring him a cup of the freshly brewed coffee.

"The bakers." She put the cup down in front of him.

"You've been to the shops already?"

"I've been getting up early at home. Revision. It's a good time for me."

"But you slept OK?"

"Fine, once I got used to the silence." Hannah sat down and helped herself to a croissant.

"What?"

"You remember. Police sirens, trains, buses, ambulances..."

"The city that never sleeps. All that stuff." Steve dipped his croissant into his coffee before beginning to eat it.

Hannah smiled at him. "I'd forgotten you used to do that."

Steve paused guiltily with his croissant inches from his mouth. "Do what?"

"Dunk your croissant. We used to have them on Sunday mornings, didn't we? A treat."

Steve remembered but took no pleasure in the recollection. "So we did," he said softly.

Hannah sensed his unease. "I'm sorry, Dad, that was stupid of me."

"What was?"

"Talking about the past; what we used to do."

Steve refocused. "No. It's me that's being stupid. I suppose I've tried not to think too much about how things used to be. Can be a bit painful sometimes, the past."

"Yes. The land of lost content."

Steve looked at her quizzically. "Housman?"

Hannah nodded. "One of the A Level texts."

"Then you know how it goes on." He paused to recall the lines. "The happy highways where I went and cannot come again. That about says it all, doesn't it?"

Hannah said nothing but her look was one of sympathy.

Steve silently reproached himself for this lapse into self-pity. This would not do. "Right, daughter mine," he said with a conscious attempt at breezy enthusiasm, "that's enough of poetic melancholy." He munched his croissant vigorously. "What would you like to do on this lovely sunny morning?"

"I leave it to you, Dad. You know the area."

"Not as well as I should. The weather was too grim when I first came down and now I seem to spend all my weekends working on Pasco's election stuff; like getting him on Facebook and then showing him how it works. That was a struggle, I can tell you."

"Do you mind all that?"

"No – after all, it was my idea and," he paused guiltily, "I sometimes wonder if I am doing it as much for my sake as his."

"How is that?"

"You know: occupy the mind; find a new focus. Get back a bit of mojo." He laughed. "You see, I've learnt a new word. How cool is that?!"

"I'm impressed, Dad."

"So all of which means, I haven't seen much of the Cornwall you see on the postcards."

"Then it will be a treat for both of us." Hannah got to her feet and carried the breakfast cups and plates across to the sink to wash them up, shushing Steve's protests that he should do it.

Steve looked at Hannah busy at the sink. She had tied her fair hair back in a ponytail. She had inherited Linda's colouring and slim, athletic figure. She wore a simple white T-shirt and stonewashed jeans. Steve remembered a phenomenon described in so many novels: people's hearts swelling with pride. He had always questioned that as an unlikely physiological response, but now he could swear that, as he looked at his daughter, he could feel his heart hammering at the wall of his chest.

Steve congratulated himself on his choice of walk. He had worked out a circular route taking in a stretch of the Coast Path and then returning through fields. There was even a pub conveniently sited at the halfway point. The first section of their walk along the cliffs revealed views to which no postcard could do full justice. There was scarcely any wind to agitate the sea, which splashed lazy, apologetic wavelets against unmoving rocks or reclaimed reluctant shingle from inaccessible sandy coves. Near the shore, in the shallows, sand and waving fronds of seaweed looked to be supporting the translucent water above them. Further out the blue deepened; impenetrable to the eye. Gulls occasionally disrupted the serenity with a reproachful cackle at some imagined slight but there was little man-made intrusion. Once they had left the car park the Easter holiday crowds were soon left behind. Steve joked that the British suffered withdrawal symptoms once out of sight of their car, and tried to shrug off the moral superiority he felt because he was walking and not driving. There were a few other walkers about but they were unobtrusive in the huge space of their surroundings. Steve thought he recognised two of them as the couple from the railway station. The memory was triggered not just by their bush hats and walking poles but by the speed at which they overtook. He and Hannah stood aside to let them power past and they were soon out of sight, striding purposefully ahead with eyes fixed firmly on the path, oblivious to what lay to either side of it. By contrast, Steve had no difficulty in persuading Hannah to take frequent breaks. Not just because he was out of breath, which he sometimes was after a particularly challenging descent followed by an equally steep ascent, but because it seemed almost blasphemous to be in the presence of beauty and not pause to worship it. Anyway, that was what he told Hannah when he needed to pause, and he meant most of it and she was kind enough not to doubt his explanation. She was possessed of the natural fitness of youth, and when they sat with their backs against some sun-warmed rock to gaze in silent wonder at what lay before them she was hardly out of breath, whilst Steve needed a few restorative gulps of oxygen before he could appreciate the view.

Eventually they turned away from the cliffs to trek inland to pick up the field path which would take them back to the car, but there was time for the pub break Steve had promised them. Time for the drink he had been fantasising about for the last thirsty mile. He carried the two glasses out to the beer garden, where Hannah sat at a tree-shaded table. He put the smaller of the glasses down in front of her.

"I've just broken the law for you."

"A half of lager. Where will it all end?" Hannah feigned shock and raised her glass. "Anyway, in a few months I'll be allowed to buy you a pint."

"I'll drink to that." Steve glugged down at least half of his pint and then put down his glass and sat back with a contented exhalation of breath. "That's better." He produced two crumpled bags of crisps from a pocket and, examining them briefly, tossed one to Hannah. "Cheese and onion for you, I recall."

Hannah opened the bag. "And salt and vinegar for you. Am I right?"

"A creature of habit." He munched hungrily on a handful of crisps. "I was nearly tempted to buy us pasties but it's dinner with Pasco tonight, so I resisted. Another time."

"Promises, promises." Hannah ate her crisps more circumspectly, one at a time.

They sat in contented silence. The garden was quiet, with only a few tables occupied. The sun had obviously lured most people to the beaches, and from where they sat they had a seductive view of the shimmering sea.

Hannah screwed up her eyes against the sun. "I don't think I've ever seen the sea this colour." She turned and looked at Steve. "Not even in the Maldives."

Steve was jolted from relaxation by the mention of the Maldives. He had to tell himself that he could not erase from memory or conversation the fact that he had been married to Linda for twenty years and father to Hannah for nearly eighteen. "Ah, the Maldives." He could think of nothing more to say.

"Our last family holiday," Hannah reminded him. She too seemed reluctant to add more.

Steve dared. "Not one of the best."

"No." Hannah smiled ruefully at him. "I think I preferred that wet week in a Welsh tent."

Steve groaned at the memory. "Surely not?"

"The Maldives were lovely, of course, but..." She broke off and looked again at the sea.

"But you knew, didn't you? I have been asking myself that recently. What you knew and when."

Hannah looked back at him. "It wasn't sudden. Just gradual; little things at first."

"What sort of little things?"

Hannah paused in remembrance. "Like holding hands."

"What?"

"I remember that when I was little and you and Mum took me out you used to hold hands. But when I was older I noticed you didn't, and I wondered why."

Steve felt the guilt. "I'd forgotten that. I suppose we got too used to each other."

"And then there was the kissing."

"Kissing?"

"Yes. When you came home from work you used to give me a hug and Mum a kiss; that's when I was small. Later it was just me that got the hug."

Steve looked down and slowly crumpled his crisp packet into a small ball. "You noticed all that?"

"Yes. But I didn't worry about it. I didn't think it meant you were going to split up or anything. I thought maybe that was the way it was with parents. I didn't have anything to compare it with."

"I suppose I thought the same, if I thought about it at all. Just the way it was." He shook his head in disbelief at his insensitivity.

"It wasn't as if you had violent arguments or anything; you just bickered a lot more and didn't seem to do much together. I think Mum missed that." Hannah smiled at Steve. "I'm not blaming you, Dad; in the last few years you always looked a bit... I don't know, worn out." She shook her head. "Sorry, that sounds awful. Tired; you always looked a bit weary. Not that I was surprised: that awful school and the Tube—"

"The bloody Northern Line." Steve groaned.

"But you look much better now." Hannah leaned forward and studied him. "In fact, you look really healthy."

"That's something, I suppose."

She sat back. "Has it been really awful, Dad?"

"Not great. Especially not to begin with. But..." He shrugged. "Life goes on."

"You always sounded so upbeat in your letters."

"I tried."

"I told Mum you were coping. That pleased her."

Steve looked at her in amazement. "She cared?"

It was Hannah's turn to look shocked. "Of course she cared. She doesn't hate you or anything. Why should she? You never did anything horrible to each other. We had good times together; we were happy."

"Yes, until Jason came along." Steve could not keep the bitterness from his voice.

Hannah frowned. "Jason? He wasn't really the reason."

"Not the reason?" Steve looked at her in disbelief. "They were sleeping together."

"I knew that; probably before you did. But Jason was an effect, not a cause."

"I'm not sure I'm following this, Hannah." Steve looked at his daughter in some bewilderment.

"It's a woman thing, Dad." She spoke slowly to make her point. "Mum was over forty. I was going to be leaving home soon. What was her role now?"

"She was my wife. She had a good job. Was her life that bad?"

Hannah shook her head impatiently. "Maybe not, but it's the biological thing. Having children; being a mother. That was over. Just the menopause to face."

"But surely that's life; isn't that just the way things are?"

"For some. But Mum is not one to go down without a fight. She is still very attractive; works hard to keep her looks. You remember?"

"I do."

"So along comes Jason. Just when she's feeling vulnerable, wondering if that's all there is. Of course she's flattered. She feels young again."

"My fault. I should have been more aware."

"Don't keep blaming yourself. It happens. All the time." She sighed. "Jason was just a good shag."

"Hannah!" Steve could not conceal his shock.

"Sorry, Dad." Hannah pulled a mock-contrite face. "Should I go and wash my mouth out?"

There was a lengthy pause. When Steve spoke again it was as if he was seeing his daughter quite differently. "I suppose I still thought of you as a child, Hannah. Another mistake. You knew more about our marriage than your mother and I did. The voice of objective reason."

"And I'll tell you something else objective."

"What's that?"

"Jason and Mum. It's finished."

"But I thought they'd gone to Corfu together?" Steve protested.

"Yes. Mum's idea. She's paying, of course. I think she's giving it one last try."

"But you—"

"It was never going to work, was it? Long term?" Hannah looked questioningly at Steve.

"I don't know. Why not?"

She laughed, but without humour. "Come on, Dad. You know what Mum's like: sparky; clever; restless."

"And Jason?"

"None of the above. Not that I see much of him. Neither has Mum recently. They've definitely cooled off. Corfu isn't going to change that."

"So what will she do?"

"Move on. Mum's good at that. She's very positive; she'll survive."

"I hope so."

Hannah smiled at him. "You mean that, don't you?"

"Of course. Why wouldn't I?"

"Some men would say it serves her right. Payback time."

Steve frowned. "I don't feel that. I try to remember the good times, and there were plenty. We loved each other and we loved you. We were happy. I can't feel bitter about that." He paused and looked away. "But that was then and this is now."

Hannah leaned across the table and put her hand on his. "I know, Dad. But there's always tomorrow."

Steve summoned a smile and gently squeezed her hand.

"Have you finished with them glasses?" The impatient

query came from a harassed-looking young girl standing over them with a tray.

Steve nodded in response and let go of Hannah's hand. She grinned at him as the girl scurried off with her tray.

"Right." Sounding more energetic than he felt, Steve consulted the guidebook they had been following. He stood a little unsteadily on his protesting legs as Hannah sprang up lithely from the table. "We should pick up the path at the next stile."

TWENTY-FIVE

"Delicious." Steve put down his fork on the empty plate. "Strawberry pavlova with clotted cream; what a combination."

"What did you expect? Boiled cabbage and spotted dick?" Tamsin teased.

Steve had guessed that Tamsin would be no shrinking violet. Living with Pasco would keep you on your toes, but the mental picture he had drawn of her bore absolutely no relation to the reality. He had pictured her as a plump, bustling, rosy-cheeked, matronly figure; the archetypal school dinner lady of popular perception. He smiled to himself at the banality of his imagination as he passed his empty plate down to the end of the table where she sat. For a start she was tall: 'willowy' was the word; only an inch or two shorter than her husband. She had that striking Celtic combination of dark hair and blue eyes edged with laughter lines, and she had out-talked Pasco during the meal. She and Hannah, who sat at her right, had clearly hit it off, and now they were chattering and laughing conspiratorially at some muttered aside from Tamsin.

"Any more for anyone?" Pasco held up the bottle. He had been a generous host and Steve was at that stage of feeling that he had probably had enough but surely one more glass wouldn't hurt, so he held it up for Pasco to fill.

There were no other takers. Tamsin had managed a couple of glasses and Hannah had accepted one with a wink at Steve. Selwyn had drunk only water and endured with a weary smile his father's clearly familiar routine of his son not wanting to desecrate the temple of his body. Selwyn certainly looked like an athlete. He was tall, had the same dark hair and blue eyes as his mother, and carried himself with a confident strength. Steve could well believe that he was an outstanding rugby player. He said little during the meal but seemed happy enough to be there. With two such extroverted parents Steve guessed that from an early age Selwyn had decided it was better to observe and not compete. Now he and Hannah were talking quietly as Tamsin piled up the plates at the end of the table.

"I'll put some coffee on," Tamsin said as she got up.

"Let me take some of those." Hannah gathered some plates and followed Tamsin towards the kitchen.

Selwyn said nothing but cleared the rest of the used dishes and, with a slightly abashed look at his father, carried his load to the kitchen, shutting the door behind him.

Pasco laughed. "Well, well. First time for everything."

Steve raised his eyebrows questioningly. "What?"

"Selwyn helping in the kitchen. I wonder why?"

Steve smiled. "They seem to be getting on all right. Less boring than listening to us wrinklies."

They sat in silence for a moment; the silence of contentment that follows good food and several glasses of wine. From the kitchen came muffled voices, the clinking of china and the sporadic running of a tap. Steve sat back contentedly in his chair; the weariness of his over-walked legs soothed, he was convinced, by the red wine coursing through them. "He's a good lad, Pasco." He glanced towards the kitchen. "You must be proud of him."

Pasco tried not to look too pleased. "He'll do." He drank some wine. "To be frank with you, Steve, he's been sorting me out a lot recently."

"How do you mean?"

"The computer stuff. That Facebook thing you got me into."

"He's been helping you?"

"Too right." Pasco pointed a finger at Steve. "Tell you what. He'd make a good teacher."

"God help him," Steve laughed. "So how is it going? Facebook?"

"I think I'm getting the hang of it. But do you know what?"

"What?"

"I'm getting dozens of people wanting to be my 'friend'."

"That's good."

"But I don't know any of them! Bloody ridiculous."

"Never mind. I'm hoping you'll have a proper following after our leaflet drop tomorrow."

Pasco frowned. "Can't say I'm looking forward to that: knocking on people's doors. If it was me I'd tell myself to bugger off," he paused to ponder his words, "if you catch my meaning."

Steve smiled. "I'm sure your natural charm will win them over."

Pasco grunted. "Ha, ha." He drained the last of the wine into their glasses. "You sure Hannah is up for this?"

The wine was definitely making Steve skittish. "Like a coiled spring."

"I thought I'd come round to your place about nine o'clock. We can start from there. That sound OK?"

"How long will it take, do you reckon, to do the whole town?"

"Forever if you let him talk too much!" This from the eavesdropping Tamsin at the open kitchen door, where she stood with coffee pot in hand. Hannah stood behind her with cups balanced on a tray, and Selwyn brought up the rear with a jug of cream. Tamsin put down the coffee pot and looked accusingly at Steve. "Are you really going to make this poor girl spend her Sunday carting leaflets round town?"

Steve hesitated to reply, but Hannah saved him. "Really, Tamsin, it's fine. I did offer."

"Maybe, but in this lovely weather too..." Tamsin shook her head, unconvinced.

Hannah insisted. "Anyway, it will give me a chance to see the town."

Tamsin laughed. "Good luck with that." She arranged cups on saucers and held up the coffee pot. "Black or white?"

The effect on the legs of yesterday's wine and walking made dressing while standing on the bed in the box room hazardous, but Steve managed it with some help from a supporting wall. Not for the first time, he renewed his vow of abstinence. When he made his way gingerly down to the kitchen he found Hannah, in pyjamas, sitting at the table with a cup of tea and the teapot in front of her, humming along to something, inaudible to him, relayed from her phone to her headphones; but seeing him, she switched the music off and unplugged her ears. She studied her father for a few appraising moments and permitted herself a sympathetic smile.

Steve raised a hand in wry acknowledgement. "I know; don't say it. Just look upon your father as a visual aid to the evils of alcohol." He slumped down heavily at the table.

Hannah laughed and poured him a cup of tea. "I didn't make coffee this morning. Pasco will be here any minute."

Steve looked blearily at his watch. "God! Is that the time?" He gulped his tea urgently and then forced himself to his feet. He took a deep breath and shook his head slightly as if to clear it of confusion. "I must get all the stuff together." He groaned at the thought of it.

"Never mind, Dad. You'll feel better outside. It's another lovely day." She pointed to the sunshine flooding through the kitchen windows.

Steve blinked at the light, but then managed to take himself off to the sitting room and, after a few minutes, return, looking slightly more purposeful, with a clutch of plastic bags overflowing with Pasco's leaflets. Hannah had cleared away the teacups and gone upstairs to change. Steve dumped the bags on the table. He looked at the resultant heap despondently, but was distracted by the impatient sound of a car horn from the street. A moment later there was a brisk knocking at the door.

Pasco looked remarkably spry, Steve felt, rather resentfully, as he gestured towards the leaflet mountain. Pasco stood for a moment reading one of the leaflets and seemed satisfied that it said what they had agreed.

"Good morning."

Steve turned to see Selwyn standing in the doorway. "Selwyn. This is a surprise."

"Well, I didn't like to think of Dad carrying all that stuff." Selwyn allowed himself a quick grin. "He's not as young as he used to be."

Steve laughed, more in astonishment than at the comment. Selwyn, it seemed, had a sense of humour. Now that was a surprise.

Pasco feigned indignation. "Watch it. Respect the aged."

Hannah reappeared in the middle of the banter. "Morning..." She broke off in some bemusement. "Oh, hello, Selwyn." She smiled broadly at him.

Steve recognised bashfulness when he saw it, and hastened to change the mood. "Yes, Selwyn's kindly offered to lend a hand. Should speed things up."

Hannah turned her attention from Selwyn. "Right, Dad, how do you want to do this?"

The heat, the hangover and the wobbling legs made Steve only too happy to agree to a break after two hours of street-pounding and door-knocking. Their route had brought them into the town square and there was little resistance to his suggestion that they grab a coffee. The café was empty – most sensible people had opted for the cool of the beach – and Pasco quickly arranged for their drinks to be brought to them at an outside table. Wearily they put down their bags; lighter now, but still half full.

"Here you go." The café proprietor placed a tray on the table, then straightened up and stared at the plastic bags. "What you up to, Pasco?"

Pasco drank a mouthful of coffee before replying. "Raising my profile." He smiled enigmatically.

"Eh?"

Steve hurried to explain. "We're canvassing. For the election."

"Oh yes, I've heard about that." The proprietor patted Pasco on the shoulder. "Good luck. You've got my vote." He beamed and turned back to the café.

"Well, that's one, at least." Pasco put down his cup and wiped his hand across his perspiring brow.

"Two," Hannah offered.

"How do you reckon that?"

"Dad," this addressed to Steve, who was hoping that black coffee would ease his throbbing headache, "you remember the old lady we helped at the station?"

Steve forced himself to focus. "Er, yes; the one with all the luggage. What about her?"

"She was staying at one of the houses we knocked at. Wasn't she, Selwyn?"

Selwyn confirmed this with a nod.

"She recognised me and told her daughter, and the daughter said she would vote for Pasco because we helped her mum."

Pasco laughed. "That's one way of getting elected. Perhaps we should spend more time at the station."

Steve was now beginning to benefit from the restorative effects of caffeine. "I don't think we need to be that desperate." He consulted the photocopies of the electoral register pages he had found at the library. Against each name they had made contact with, he had ticked one of three boxes: 'Probable', 'Possible' or 'Pointless'. "I think it's going quite well." He paused. "Considering."

Pasco managed a wry smile. "Considering most people were at the beach and most of those who were in aren't allowed to vote."

"I couldn't believe how many second homes there were," Hannah said. "It's crazy."

"Welcome to Cornwall," Selwyn muttered.

Hannah persisted. "Our street at home, Dad, in London. How many houses do you think there are?" Even the caffeine could not launch Steve's thought processes on that one, so she answered her own question. "I reckon about a hundred."

Steve had caught up enough to confirm that. "About that, I should think."

"And how many of them are empty for half the year?"

This was clearly a rhetorical question. There was no need for anyone to respond. Pasco shrugged and spread his arms in a gesture of resignation.

Steve was more animated now. "That's why this is important." He jabbed a finger at the bags of leaflets. "We must get on. I tell you, it matters."

Pasco looked at him in surprise. "The half-time pep talk, Steve?"

Steve smiled awkwardly. "Talking of which, when we start again, try not to get involved in too many conversations about rugby."

Hannah and Selwyn laughed, but Pasco looked indignant as he got to his feet and picked up one of the bags. "Well, at least then I know what I'm talking about."

It took another two hours of toil to empty the bags. The midday heat beat down on them as they stood on doorsteps explaining their mission, or merely stuffing leaflets through letter boxes if no one was in. Steve was encouraged that those who were both at home and entitled to vote generally put aside their initial suspicion and hostility when they saw Pasco. Some of them even promised to read the leaflet and respond to it on Facebook. Inevitably there were others who, after a cursory glance at the literature, were keen to quiz Pasco on the Pirates' chances of promotion next season. A few were aggressive at being disturbed at their Sunday lunches, but even they softened after a smiling, winsome apology from Hannah.

As they turned away from the last house and folded up their plastic bags, Steve reflected that on balance it had been worth it. He thought they made a good team. Pasco had offered the reassurance of a familiar and popular local character; Hannah had provided charm; Selwyn clean-cut sobriety. Steve allowed himself to take pleasure in his role as facilitator; a term Hannah had ironically bestowed upon him, to Pasco's amusement. He had at least facilitated moving Pasco on rapidly when doorstep exchanges veered towards rugby. His headache was now merely a dull throb rather than an incessant pounding, and whilst on one level he felt he could murder a pint, on a deeper level he accepted that that would be a catastrophe. He would relax on a salvaged, dilapidated deckchair in what the estate agents had described as a 'charming paved patio area' but which was, in fact, just a backyard. He might attempt to read the Sunday paper but, no doubt, fall asleep with it over his face. This pleasurable anticipation of a lazy afternoon ran through Steve's mind as they trudged back home to pick up Pasco's van, but then a disturbing thought interrupted his reverie: Hannah. He could hardly expect her to sit in the backyard. He would have to brace up and sort out some excursion or other. Much as he loved his daughter, that was not a prospect he savoured in his present somnolent state.

When they reached the cottage (Steve had now upgraded it in his mind from hovel status) he invited Pasco and Selwyn in, but they declined, to his relief. Pasco said Tamsin would have lunch on the table. Selwyn said nothing but seemed to be standing rather awkwardly, looking at the ground, which Steve found rather curious.

"Dad?" Hannah smiled meltingly at her father. "Would you mind terribly if I went to the beach this afternoon?"

Steve tried to stifle his dismay. He did not fancy an afternoon broiling on the sand, but if that was what Hannah wanted he would have to go along with it. "Well, if—"

"Only Selwyn's offered to teach me to surf."

Steve adjusted his reaction quickly. "Yes. Well, that sounds fun." Then he felt that perhaps more parental concern would be fitting. "But won't the water be very cold?"

Hannah turned to Selwyn. "Selwyn says he has an old wetsuit from a few years back that should fit me. Don't you?"

Selwyn raised his head sufficiently to nod.

Steve pretended to give the matter serious thought. "If that's what you want, that's OK by me."

Hannah gave him a hug and then stepped back questioningly. "Of course, if you had something else planned..."

"Nothing that can't keep. You go off and enjoy yourself," Steve said, hoping he wasn't overplaying the martyr role.

Hannah raced into the house to get a towel. Pasco winked at Steve, got into his van and started up the engine. Hannah rushed back outside with her beach gear and clambered into the van with Selwyn. She waved at Steve as they drove off, and he waved back before heading into the cottage in happy search of the precarious deckchair.

TWENTY-SIX

The fine weather persisted and the weatherman grew more depressed as he could only predict more of the same as the days passed. Steve and Hannah settled into a routine. She rose early to put in a couple of hours on her revision. Steve slept in and drifted into consciousness only as the aroma of percolating coffee seeped into his cell. Croissants awaited him in the kitchen and were eaten outside in the backyard, the latter rendered hospitable by the warming sun. After their al fresco breakfast he took Hannah off on some excursion; or 'jaunt', as she put it. It broke new ground for both of them, and Steve accepted that in his early months in Cornwall he had been too sunk in depressed lethargy to show much interest in his surroundings. So, in the space of a few days, the two of them caught up with what Steve called "the edited highlights of Penwith". They spent a morning at the Tate Gallery at St Ives. Steve puzzled over the abstract modern art, seeking to find meaning in its colourful blots and squiggles, but was chided by Hannah, who told him he should surrender to the immersive sensory experience and enjoy, not explain. He thought wryly that that advice could also resonate with his life outside the Tate. They picked their way over the causeway at low tide to visit St Michael's Mount, and climbed the hundreds of steps up to the castle. The ascent reminded Steve that his legs had not yet forgiven him for their recent exertions, but the views over Mount's Bay were more than adequate compensation. At the open-air Minack Theatre, carved out of the granite cliffs above a turquoise sea, they sat on the grassy terrace high above the empty stage and ate the pasties Steve had promised. On another morning he had mapped out a walk over the moors to look at some of the surviving reminders of Cornwall's prehistoric inhabitants: the Merry Maidens, the Men-an-Tol, Lanyon Quoit and others. There was some sense of the eternal to be found in imagining the lives of those who, thousands of years before, had erected these granite memorials for purposes which were now matters of dry speculation amongst antiquarians, or objects of tourist curiosity far removed from what Steve was sure had been a cruel and brutal reality.

"It's so beautiful, but it's a bit frightening too."

"Frightening?" Steve looked at Hannah in surprise.

She gestured with both hands at the empty expanse of moorland. "To think people lived up here; died up here. Built these burial chambers and monuments to gods or spirits we can only guess at. Thousands of years ago." She shivered slightly.

"Is that frightening?"

Hannah looked at him. "Probably just me being silly. But it makes you realise how insignificant we are." She looked around her. "Compared with all this."

"Puts everything into perspective a bit, doesn't it?"

"Probably doesn't do to think about it too much." She followed her own advice and smiled brightly at Steve. "Where are those sandwiches?"

Steve laughed. "From the sublime..." He opened up his rucksack and took out their packet of sandwiches. He looked around. "There are some rocks over there that we can perch on."

From their picnic spot they had a commanding view of the moors falling away to the sea. The breeze sighed gently and larks sang busily above them. There was no need for conversation, so they ate their sandwiches and relaxed in peaceful silence. It would have been tempting to while away the afternoon up there, but they had a schedule. Hannah was due to meet up with Selwyn on the beach at teatime. She had done this every day, and told Steve that her surfing was coming along a bit. Steve had asked no more. If she and Selwyn were enjoying each other's company, that was fine by him. She would soon be eighteen, he told himself. Although this week had brought them closer than perhaps they had ever been, it was the closeness now of two people with different lives but an unbreakable bond of affinity. Hannah was no longer his little girl, no longer dependent on him, but ready to go her own way in the world. That realisation had deepened in the past few days but it did not depress him. It simply had to be. In a sense, it was liberating. He and Linda might have damaged each other but at least their daughter seemed unscathed. He did not need to feel guilty. Hannah would cope perfectly well with whatever lay ahead.

"We'd better be getting back." Steve scrambled inelegantly to his feet.

Hannah stood and, whilst Steve packed away the sandwich wrappings, took a last look at the moorland, now dappled by a sun sidling through a puff of cotton-wool cloud. "What's that over there?"

Steve tracked her pointing finger to the distant silhouette of an engine house. He could not mistake it. "Ding Dong," he said quietly.

"What?"

"Ding Dong Mine." He picked up the rucksack and made to move on.

Hannah did not follow him; she was still gazing with eyes narrowed against the sun at the far-off chimney stack. "Why is it called that? Did people really mine up here? That's hard to believe on a day like today."

Steve explained how the name had come about, and agreed that it was hard to envisage the harsh reality of tin mining in such a setting. "But you can get a sense of what it must have been like, just by being up there; a sort of pervasive memory of hardship."

Hannah looked at him questioningly. "You've been there, then?"

Steve hesitated. In his letters he had not told her anything about the aftermath of the car crash; nothing about the burnt-out stolen vehicle at Ding Dong, and certainly nothing about Eva. At the time he had judged that anything other than the humdrum might have caused concern or raised questions that were best left unanswered. Now he looked at Hannah waiting patiently for his response and knew that this was the right time. He took a deep breath. "Yes, Hannah, I've been there, and I'll tell you why."

As they threaded their way back to the car on paths through heather and bracken, he told her everything. Not just about the fate of the stolen car, but how he had met Eva and allowed himself to imagine that there might be some spark between them, only for it to be extinguished by the revelation of her involvement in the car theft, and her sudden escape back to Romania, presumably because she was afraid that he would involve the police. Hannah listened without interruption, but with barely concealed surprise.

They had almost arrived back at the car when Steve ended his monologue. "So now you know," he concluded with a wary glance at his daughter.

Hannah took several moments of reflection before she spoke. "I'm sorry, Dad."

Steve was puzzled. "About what?"

"Was she pretty?"

"Pretty? I don't know about that." He fumbled for words. "Attractive, certainly."

"Intelligent too?"

"Very. No doubt about that."

Hannah offered a rueful smile. "So she was attractive and intelligent and you were getting on well. Am I right?"

"I suppose you could say that," Steve muttered.

"So it must have been a real bummer when she turned out to be a car thief."

Steve frowned. "I'm not even sure that's true."

"You just have to forget it, Dad; you need to—"

Steve interrupted. "Move on? Is that what you were going to say?"

Hannah laughed. "I suppose I was. Terrible cliché but you know what I mean."

"I do, but it isn't so easy. Not when I don't know; not for certain."

"Know what?"

"Whether she was a car thief or whether what she told me was true." He sighed. "And now I'll never know."

Hannah took his arm as they walked the last few yards to the car. "Never mind, Dad; you'll meet someone, I'm sure."

Steve looked at her. "I'm not sure I'm ready for that, Hannah. Once bitten and all that."

She squeezed his arm reassuringly. "You will. I know it."

Suddenly, Steve laughed, and Hannah looked at him in surprise.

"What's the joke?"

"We are. I'm the father who should be advising his daughter on relationships, not the other way round."

Hannah grinned at that.

Steve released her arm and fumbled for the car keys. As he unlocked the doors he looked at his daughter in mock seriousness. "And talking of relationships, how are you getting on with Selwyn?"

Hannah rolled her eyes in disbelief at such a question, but Steve did not miss her blush.

The week passed all too quickly. The sun stayed out and the days hurried by. In the mornings they took their jaunts, and then Hannah joined Selwyn on the beach and Steve dozed outside in his deckchair, fighting a losing battle to stay alert long enough to concentrate on lesson preparation for his language class. He did not look forward with too much enthusiasm to renewing that struggle, but chided himself that he must put personal feelings aside and not allow his disenchantment to undermine his commitment to his remaining students. It was not their fault that his feelings had taken a battering.

He found more to keep him awake in checking Pasco's Facebook page. As the days passed, there was evidence that the arduous leaflet operation had been worth it. Steve was encouraged by the response, which was largely positive, and pleasantly surprised that Pasco was clearly active on his site, capturing the right easy, friendly tone in his comments to his new 'friends'. Steve guessed that Selwyn was doing a good job in coaching his father in social media etiquette. The election was now only a couple of months away, and Steve reminded himself that when Hannah left he must talk with Pasco about plans to keep the momentum going. That, he worried, might be even more of a challenge than teaching English to foreigners (he allowed himself to use that designation in his private musings).

On the last day of the holiday, Steve and Hannah decided they would organise themselves a farewell dinner. Until then Steve had vetoed any home catering beyond warming up the croissants. Trying not to dwell overmuch on the inroads being made into his shrivelling bank balance, he had insisted on eating out – or at least eating in meals which had been purchased without. So they had taken away an Indian, a Chinese, a very British fish and chips, and an Italian-inspired (if that was not too flattering a term) pizza – a cosmopolitan menu, he had boasted to Hannah. But for her last evening they would push the boat out. Almost literally, because in the morning they had driven to Newlyn to watch the fish being unloaded from the boats and into the market. Hannah had googled an exotic recipe for Dover sole and they had bought two at a price which made Steve wonder if he had personally paid for their transportation from Dover by taxi. However, this was no time for parsimony, and there was a further splurge on organic mushrooms, Cornish new potatoes and local asparagus, clotted cream, and strawberries which were advertised as 'hand-picked', which afforded them some amusement in imagining what other methods might be employed to harvest them. Trying not to display any nervous alarm at the cost, Steve had purchased a bottle of white wine of far greater distinction than the usual plonk he swilled down. They'd carried their booty back home, and now that Hannah had returned from her last afternoon's surfing lesson they prepared their gourmet meal. Laughing, and teasing each other about their comparative cooking skills, reminded Steve of the times he and Hannah had cooked together when she was young. Those were happy memories but he was surprised he did not look back on them wistfully. He looked at her now, her fair hair bleached by the sun, tied back neatly in best kitchen practice, and her face browned by that same sun. She was frowning in concentration as she studied the menu on her phone. She looked up and caught Steve's gaze; then she smiled and raised her glass. Steve raised his in response, and they drank a toast to each other in silent harmony.

With the dishes cleared away and mutual congratulations exchanged on the excellence of their culinary skills, they decided it was still warm enough to take their coffee outside to the backyard; Hannah opting to take a kitchen chair with her rather than risk the deckchair. Steve settled himself into it gingerly. They sat in silence for a while, enjoying the coffee and watching the first stars pricking through the darkening canvas of the sky.

Steve sighed in contentment. "You must never come again, Hannah."

"What?" She looked at her father in astonishment.

Steve laughed at her obvious dismay. "You could never have such perfect weather again. It would be an anticlimax."

Hannah looked relieved. "I was hoping to come in the summer holidays."

"To polish up your surfing, no doubt?" Steve teased.

Hannah made a face at him. "Well, since you asked, Selwyn thinks I should be able to stand up with a bit more practice."

Steve knew just enough about surfing not to take her comment literally. "An achievement beyond A Levels, no doubt."

Hannah frowned at the mention of A Levels. She had told Steve she had the offer of a place at Exeter but needed high grades. "I will be gutted if I don't get into Exeter."

"Is that because of its excellent academic reputation or its relative proximity to the surf?"

Hannah grimaced. "I wish you wouldn't go on about surfing."

Steve held up his hands in mock surrender. "Truce."

They finished their coffee in easy silence which Hannah eventually broke with a slightly hesitant question. "It will be OK, though? To come down in the summer?"

Steve smiled broadly at her. "Of course it will. It would be lovely." Then he paused and his smile faded. "That is, if I am still here."

Hannah looked shocked. "Why wouldn't you be?"

"Well, you know my job is just maternity cover for a year."

"But they'll ask you to stay on, surely? Selwyn says they'd be mad to let you go."

"Selwyn said?"

"That's what his dad told him. You're doing a great job, he said."

Steve managed a wry smile. "Pasco may not be entirely unbiased."

Hannah was looking at her father anxiously now. "But if they ask, you will stay, won't you?"

Steve considered the question. Of course it was something that he had needed to think about recently. He had even started to sift reluctantly through the job vacancies in the Times Educational Supplement; a journal Taff Evans described as "a teacher's weekly ray of hope". Moving again was not a prospect Steve viewed with any pleasure but it might have to be endured.

Hannah interrupted his thoughts. "Would you, Dad? Stay?" she said insistently.

Steve nodded. "Yes. If I was asked, I would."

Hannah looked relieved. "That's good." She smiled at him. "And I'm not saying that because of surfing, before you start."

"Perish the thought."

"It's because you look happy here. You don't look so... I don't know... so down."

"You could be right. Perhaps I'm getting the hang of this Cornish thing."

"And now you're involved with Pasco's election. If he gets in he'll need you to hold his hand."

Steve smiled at that. "There's an image for you."

"You know what I mean. You put him up to this; you can't abandon him."

"That's a bit over the top. Pasco will cope without me if he has to."

"Well, let's hope he doesn't have to." Hannah sat back in her chair and looked up at a sky now black but burnished with stars. Then she looked back at Steve. "Sorry if I went on a bit."

"Don't be. You're only telling me things I have probably been trying to avoid." He exhaled slowly. "It will be decision time soon enough."

"Fingers crossed."

"Hope for the best; prepare for the worst." Steve said that with mock solemnity, and as if to punish his reliance on cliché and melodrama, at that moment his deckchair gave up its pretence at utility and collapsed beneath him. After the initial shock he burst out laughing, and Hannah joined in. They were still laughing as they gathered up the wreckage and retreated to the safety of the kitchen.

TWENTY-SEVEN

The house seemed abandoned without Hannah, and even being able to return to his own bed did little to cheer Steve up. The weather too was now playing its part in dampening spirits as well as the parched earth. The weatherman had recovered his brio and spoke cheerfully of a period of unsettled conditions with frequent heavy showers and strong winds. Steve had a few more days of the holiday left and busied himself with work to fend off depression. It seemed to do the trick and after a while he could look back on Hannah's visit without melancholy. It had been a magical week; not just because of the remarkable weather, but because he had reconnected with his daughter. They had relaxed contentedly in each other's company and he had been able to talk to her about feelings that had churned, unspoken, for months. In return she had offered him a view of his marriage which helped him accept that blame was pointless and that, perhaps, in time he would be able to remember the good times without too painful a sense of loss. He had even told her about Eva, and she had sympathised but urged him to put it behind him and look to the future. "The optimism of youth," Steve had observed. He'd told her that he knew her advice was well intentioned but sometimes life was a bit more complicated. Or was it?

Was he just allowing himself the indulgence of caution and self-doubt?

The questions seemed easier to frame than the answers; hence Steve tried to suppress both by filling his days with preparation for the summer term. In addition to his normal teaching load there was material to assemble for the evening class which involved hours of internet scavenging. Even when that was finished he had to find the time to oversee Pasco's election campaign. This involved monitoring the online responses and discussing with Pasco how to maintain the impetus. They had done this over evening sessions when Pasco called in, still in his painter's overalls, straight from work. He was now reconciled to his new venture and showing signs of the determination to win which, Steve guessed, had motivated him on the rugby field. This new seriousness of purpose was such that they only allowed themselves a small whisky when the evening's business was completed.

Steve had something he needed to run past Pasco and some information he suspected would not be well received. He allowed Pasco a few moments to sit wearily at the kitchen table, his hands still splodged with wayward white emulsion, before pushing across to him a sheet of paper. "See what you think of that."

Pasco took a few moments to scan the text. He put it down and looked doubtfully at Steve. "Do you think they'll print it?"

Steve nodded confidently. "I'm sure they will. You know how desperate they are for news."

Pasco could accept that. "Bugger all in it, most weeks, and what is in it they mostly get wrong."

Steve laughed at Pasco's verdict on the local paper. "Maybe. But they can't get this wrong. They can just print it out."

Pasco looked at the text again. "But is it really news?" he said doubtfully. "Not just electioneering?"

"Not the way I've written it. It's a human interest story."

Pasco read from the paper. "'Rugby legend pitches in.' Blimey, that's a bit over the top, isn't it?"

"Make it short, make it simple and make it up. That's an old crack about journalists. But at least I haven't needed to make it up. You were a rugby star and you are standing for the council because you feel so strongly about what needs putting right." Steve looked at Pasco. "That's all true, isn't it?"

Pasco considered the question. "Well, if you put it like that..."

"I do put it like that. And it will let people know about you if they don't already."

"And you reckon they'll print it?"

"I think so. It's certainly worth trying."

Pasco handed the sheet of paper back to Steve. "If they do, it will cost me."

Steve frowned. "How will it cost you?"

"At The Miners. If they see that they'll take the piss something rotten."

Steve laughed. "Never mind. There's no such thing as bad publicity." But now his mood changed. He frowned at Pasco. "I know who the other candidates are now."

Pasco sat up straight. "Who?"

Steve consulted a notebook. "Breock Trevaylor, of course."

Pasco smiled. "Well, we expected that."

"A lady standing as a Lib Dem. A Rebecca Taylor."

Pasco shook his head. "Never heard of her."

"Well, that's a good sign." Steve looked again at his notes. "Apparently she's a chiropodist."

Pasco considered that. "Someone has to be."

Steve looked seriously at him. "Who do you think is standing for the Tories?"

"Tell me."

Steve paused. "Giles Penhaul."

Pasco took a few seconds to register the news. Then he sat back in his chair. "Well, I'll be buggered."

"So it's personal now."

"I can't let him win, Steve. Knowing what we do; him and Penpol," Pasco said grimly.

Steve tried to be reasonable. "Well, if he was elected he would have to declare an interest in any business involving Penpol."

Pasco scoffed at that. "Do you think that would make any difference? You know how they operate: all wheels within wheels."

"You'll have to make sure he doesn't win, then."

Pasco nodded. "I could take losing to Breock and even the foot lady, but never to Giles Penhaul and all that he stands for."

"I hear you, Pasco, but that's why we need to crack on with all this." Steve gestured at the article for the newspaper. "Giles will have the local party machine working for him."

Pasco groaned. "That's all we need."

Steve smiled with pantomimed glee. "Cheer up. We've got all your emails and Facebook stuff to sort through now." He booted up the laptop as Pasco buried his head in his hands in mock despair.

TWENTY-EIGHT

Steve had prepared himself mentally but he could not pretend it was an unadulterated pleasure to be back at Trengrouse, and he was not alone in his lacklustre feelings. The pupils had the look of briefly escaped prisoners now recaptured. Steve recalled that as a boy he had imagined that his teachers were all agog with delight at the prospect of term restarting. Now he knew differently, and understood that staff and students shared a common fate and carried a similar burden. He took some small comfort from the hope that his burden might be a little lighter this term because his GCSE class would not be present and he would have more free time. They had been granted what was optimistically called 'home study leave'. As he drove in he had recognised some of the class playing an impromptu game of football in the local park; nothing very homely or studious about that.

He used some of his new free time to manage Pasco's online traffic. The paper had printed the article and clearly enough people had read it to connect with the blog Pasco had now set up; or rather, Selwyn had set up on Pasco's behalf. Steve also used some spare time to look for a new job. That was a depressing chore but the term was nearly a week old now and there was no word about making his position permanent. He had gloomily written a note to the head teacher – remembering, of course, not to address it to the headmaster in these gender-sensitive times. He left it with the school secretary; a formidable lady whom Taff Evans swore had been trained in some grim Colditz-like establishment reserved for doctors' receptionists, school secretaries and council functionaries whose graduation was dependent on their ability to deny access to their employers. Taff claimed that if you were run over by a bus outside his local surgery and carried in on a stretcher, broken and bloodied, the first thing you would be asked was whether you had an appointment. Certainly the guardian of the Trengrouse office had displayed not a flicker of interest or emotion when Steve had asked her to pass on his note asking the head to provide a reference for any job application he might make.

As he sat in the staffroom after school, sifting half-heartedly through the vacancies advertised in the Educational Supplement, he was surprised to be joined by Bill Rogers. It was the first session of the term for Steve's language class and he had not bothered to go home before it, but had brewed himself a cup of tea to wash down the flaccid sandwich he had purchased in town. The label declared it was tuna mayonnaise but Steve decided after one bite that anyone claiming the contents had recently been anywhere near a tuna was a poor judge of distance.

"Sorry to disturb you," Bill seemed quite agitated, "but there's a bit of a flap on."

Steve put down his sandwich with no great sense of loss. "Oh, is that why you're in, Bill?" Although Bill was the nominal head of the Further Education Department his was definitely not a hands-on approach. He claimed that he had such complete confidence in his tutors that it would be unprofessional to keep looking over their shoulders. Taff joked that Bill had made a philosophy out of his indolence.

Bill slumped into one of the sagging armchairs. "I had a call this afternoon." He looked nervously at Steve. "County Hall." The memory seemed to increase his agitation. "I tell you, Steve, I could do without all this on top of everything else."

"Everything else?" Steve echoed in genuine confusion.

"Everything else I have on my plate," Bill lamented.

"Of course." Steve hastily reverted to sympathy mode. "So what did County Hall want?"

"There's this new chap in the Education Department. Bit of a Young Turk, it seems. Wants to bring himself up to speed on the FE work here." Bill groaned at the prospect. "That's how he put it. Just wants to have an informal look round, he said, but you know what that means."

"What?"

"Snooping." Bill sank down further in his chair.

"I see. When is this 'snoop' happening?"

Bill sat up as if electrified. "Tonight! I'm sorry I couldn't give you more warning."

Steve shrugged. "Not a problem, Bill. I'll just do my usual thing. He can take it or leave it." His nonchalance was not fabricated. He was doing the best he could for his class, and if the Young Turk was not happy with it he could go back to Istanbul. Steve was a veteran of several Ofsted campaigns and had the mental battle scars to prove it, so he was not going to panic over an informal snoop.

Bill seemed unsure about Steve's attitude. "That's one approach, I suppose."

"Anyway, I shouldn't let it worry you too much. You'll be out of all this soon enough, enjoying your well-deserved pension."

Bill brightened at the thought. "True, very true." He momentarily closed his eyes in anticipation of a life of ease, then regained his concentration. "Nonetheless, I wouldn't like to leave the department with any sort of stain on its reputation."

"I'm sure that won't happen, Bill," Steve said encouragingly.

"I run a pretty tight ship here, as you know, but that's the only way to make sure standards don't slip."

"Indeed," Steve said, managing to keep a straight face.

Bill clambered out of his chair and looked over the top of his spectacles at a piece of paper he was clutching. "In addition to your class this evening there are two art groups, and a creative writing session with Mrs Randall." He seemed momentarily uneasy. "I'd better brief her before this chap pitches up," he muttered, almost to himself.

Steve was interested enough to ask, "Creative writing? That sounds harmless."

"You'd think so, wouldn't you, but she's very keen on creating the right ambience, as she puts it, to stimulate creative thinking."

"That sounds fair enough."

"Quite. But it can involve putting off the lights and playing whale music."

"Ah, I see."

"Not only that – she's not averse to burning joss sticks and the like. The cleaners are always complaining; a funny smell, they say."

Steve wondered about that but thought he would not alarm Bill with his suspicions. "I suppose it might seem a bit odd if you just walk in on the class."

"Indeed. So that's why I'll tell her to keep the lights on and stick to the writing." Bill glanced at his notes again. "The art classes should be no problem."

"Not even the life drawing?" Steve ventured.

Bill permitted himself a smile. "That might cheer him up." He made his way to the door. "So I'll wheel him along as and when?"

Steve nodded. "I'll try not to hold my breath."

The class seemed happy to be back. They greeted him warmly and, as he moved around the room setting up the individual workstations, he could hear them chattering amongst themselves – some fluently, some more haltingly – in their accented English. Steve checked off their names in his register. There was only one he could not confirm as being present. He really should have deleted Eva's name from the list by now. The neat row of crosses marking her absences was an aberration he should surely address. He made now to rule a line through her name, but as he fumbled in his jacket pocket for a red biro there was a tentative knock on the closed classroom door. Heads turned in curiosity as Steve opened the door.

"Sorry to disturb you, Steve." Bill Rogers stepped awkwardly into the room. "This is Martin Wilberforce." He gestured to his companion.

If this was the Young Turk of Bill's designation then Steve had a brief moment to wonder what an old one must look like. Wilberforce was certainly not a commanding physical presence. He was a good foot shorter than Steve, and of indeterminate age. His thinning hair and ashen pallor did him no favours; neither did a pair of John Lennon-style wire-framed National Health spectacles. This all atop a baggy, musty suit which looked as if it had been hand-knitted.

Steve registered all this in the second before he stretched out a hand in breezy greeting. "Steve Milton. Welcome to our class."

Wilberforce offered a damp and feeble response, switching a clipboard to his left hand to do so. He gave Steve a brief nod of recognition before turning expectantly to Bill.

"Mr Wilberforce would like you to carry on as normal and he will observe," Bill intoned, and then looked for confirmation from Wilberforce, who again confined his response to a single nod of the head.

Steve wondered if Wilberforce was capable of speech. Perhaps Bill would perch him on his knee and work him like a ventriloquist's dummy. Trying to hide the smile breaking out at that thought, Steve turned to face his students, who were looking questioningly at the party in the doorway. "Right, ladies and gentlemen. In case we have forgotten over the holiday the correct way to ask a question in English, there are some exercises waiting for you on the iPads. After the coffee break we will be doing some oral role play." He turned now to indicate Bill and Wilberforce. "These two gentlemen will be spending some time with us to see what we do, but they want you to take no notice of them." He raised his eyebrows questioningly. "Isn't that right, gentlemen?"

Bill nodded agitatedly several times but Wilberforce was already busy scribbling on his clipboard.

The class were soon absorbed in their work. Steve moved amongst them, quietly offering advice and encouragement. Bill, after an initial wander about, perched awkwardly on a windowsill, casting nervous glances at Wilberforce, who padded silently from student to student, writing intently all the while. Steve had begun to wonder if the poor chap had lost his vocal cords in some horrible botched operation, so it came as a shock when he was aware that the clipboard had been put aside and Wilberforce was actually in whispered conversation with one of the class and pointing at something on the screen they were both looking at. If that was not astonishing enough, Steve was amazed to see Wilberforce smile and even manage a little laugh. Steve was immediately overcome with remorse at his arrogant presumption. Wilberforce was not distant and hostile; he was simply shy. That diagnosis was confirmed as the hour passed. By the time the coffee break was due the man from County Hall had shed his earlier reticence and was even bantering and chuckling his way around the room; his clipboard put aside.

Over coffee, Wilberforce, with Bill an anxious shadow, mingled easily enough. Whilst Steve was listening to Luka's thoughts on Manchester United's chances of clinching the league title he could see that the car washers had cornered Wilberforce and, from the floating snatches of conversation he caught when Luka paused for breath, seemed to be asking him whether he preferred bottled or draught beer. Steve smiled to himself at the incongruity of that exchange, but was forced to refocus his thoughts by a sudden loud, metallic rapping. Ivan, with a teaspoon grasped firmly in his massive hand, was clearly calling everyone to order, and dutifully the room fell silent. Steve waited in some apprehension for events to unfold. He noticed that the class members were smiling at him; clearly they were party to the drama. Wilberforce stood, with clipboard back in hand and pen poised, whilst Bill nervously chewed a fingernail.

"Ricardo!" Ivan barked out commandingly.

Ricardo emerged from behind the coffee urn. With his hands clasped behind his back, he faced Steve. "I must tell you this." He paused to gather himself to deliver an address he had clearly been rehearsing. "I am now deputy bar manager. The boss says I can do this because my English is much good." He paused again, frowning; perhaps realising that there was something not quite right about those words, but took a deep breath and continued. "I have more pay now.

It is better." He stopped and looked at his classmates, and they responded with smiles, nods and mimed handclaps.

Steve, too, offered his congratulations. "Well done, Ricardo. It's what you deserve for all your hard work." He sought to underline his approval with a formal handshake, but as he extended his right hand, Ricardo, like the proverbial conjuror with his top hat and rabbit, suddenly unclasped his hands from behind his back to reveal a bottle of wine which he placed in Steve's grasp.

Steve clutched the bottle in surprise. "Thank you, Ricardo. But you didn't need—"

"It is very good Rioja," Ricardo said earnestly.

Steve glanced at the label. "Yes, I can see. It's a very kind thought but you did all the work."

"To say thank you." Ricardo performed a small, formal bow and headed back to the security of his classmates, who broke into a round of applause.

Steve felt something was expected of him. He faced his students and they fell silent. "We know how hard Ricardo has worked, and so have all of you, and it just shows what we can achieve together. Thank you so much, all of you." He waved the bottle of Rioja at them. "Now I think we had better get back to that hard work." He said it with a smile but could not suppress a moment of quiet emotion. He reproached himself for his diminished enthusiasm for this work following Eva's departure, vowed to give these students his best shot for the rest of the term, and watched with proprietary affection as they returned to their workstations.

Wilberforce was vigorously polishing his wire glasses with his handkerchief to clear them of steam from the urn. Satisfied with his efforts, he rehung them from his ears. He looked at Steve and repositioned his pen in the top pocket of his shapeless suit. "Most interesting, Mr Milton."

Steve was always wary of 'interesting'. He was not above hiding behind the word himself, typically when asked for an opinion on a work of art or an unfamiliar piece of music. Its use caused no offence and was bland enough to preclude judgement.

Bill looked at his watch. "Perhaps we should move on?" He glanced warningly at Steve. "We have to catch up with Mrs Randall still."

Steve raised his eyebrows in recognition of the signal. Bill held the door open, but before Wilberforce passed through it he turned back to Steve and pointed at the bottle he was still holding.

"Enjoy your Rioja." He then walked out into the corridor.

Bill made to close the door behind them, but found time to flash Steve a quick thumbs up.

TWENTY-NINE

"Do you two want any coffee in there?" Tamsin's inquiry came from the kitchen where she was stuffing Pasco's paint-splattered work clothes into the washing machine. She grumbled quietly to herself, "I thought you were supposed to be painting walls, not yourself."

Pasco smiled at Steve and muttered, "Domestic bliss." Then more loudly, "Yes please, love; it might keep us awake."

Both men were tired after their working day but Steve had insisted that they trawl through the details of Pasco's online contacts. Pasco was reading them off the screen while Steve cross-checked the names with the electoral register. What he was looking for, he told Pasco, was evidence of a positive response from the people they had canvassed.

When the list was complete Steve studied it with a worried frown. He sighed wearily. "Still a lot to do, I'm afraid."

This puzzled Pasco. "If they say they're going to support me that's good, isn't it?"

"It's not them I'm bothered about. It's the ones who aren't there; who haven't been in contact but who we marked as possibles when we did the leaflet drop."

Pasco shrugged. "Couldn't be arsed, I suppose."

"That's the problem. Only about thirty per cent of the electorate turn out in local elections. That's why we have to get back to these people, Pasco, to gee them up; a few extra votes could make all the difference."

Pasco nodded glumly. "I suppose you're right."

"I know I'm right. So this weekend we're on the knocker again." Steve pointed to his list on the table. "Just the waverers. We concentrate on them."

"It will be just the two of us. Selwyn's started his A Levels."

"I know. Hannah told me. She's in the same boat." Steve smiled at Pasco. "I think they keep in touch."

Pasco laughed and pointed an accusing finger at Steve. "And some. The only time he's not got his head in his books is when he's texting your daughter."

Steve held up his hands in mock apology.

"What you two laughing about?" Tamsin demanded as she emerged from the kitchen with two mugs of coffee on a tray. Without waiting for an answer she thrust a pamphlet onto the table in front of Steve. "You seen that? It just came through the letter box."

Steve glanced down. "Yes. Mine came this morning."

"I tell you what, Pasco, he's a damned sight better-looking than you are."

Pasco turned to Steve in feigned dismay. "There's loyalty for you."

Tamsin had picked up the pamphlet again. She studied it closely before tossing it back onto the table. "Mind you, I wouldn't say he's my type. Too smooth by half."

"Which makes me a bit of rough, does it?" Pasco protested.

Tamsin walked behind her husband's chair, ruffled his hair, and fluttered her eyes dramatically. "But a rough diamond, for sure."

Steve smiled at the banter but his mind was on the pamphlet before him. He had never seen Giles Penhaul in the flesh but the photograph showed a conventionally handsome face beneath an immaculately groomed and sleek head of dark hair. The photographer had caught his subject in a concerned, thoughtful pose; his eyes narrowed in receptive sympathy. Underneath the portrait was the legend 'Penhaul: Caring for Cornwall'.

Tamsin had stopped teasing Pasco and had come to look over Steve's shoulder. She spoke derisively. "'Caring for Cornwall'! We all know what he cares about."

Steve was examining the pamphlet in some detail. "This is a very slick job. You have to give him that." He turned to the printed text and studied it for a few moments. "He makes a big deal out of his local roots; born and bred here."

"He was away at that posh boarding school most of the time," Pasco objected, "and since then he's been living in London."

Steve quickly paraphrased the rest of the material. "He talks about his business experience; setting up successful companies. Claims that he will bring professional expertise to his work on the council." He looked pointedly at Pasco and then read verbatim from the leaflet. "'We can no longer entrust council business to well intentioned amateurs.'"

Tamsin roared with laughter at that, and pointed at Pasco. "I think he means you, dear."

"He's some cheeky bugger," Pasco allowed.

Steve finished scanning Penhaul's words. "Then there's the usual stuff: from creating jobs, investing in education and so on, to mending potholes and improving mobile phone coverage."

Pasco was puzzled. "Nothing about housing?"

"Oh yes. I was saving the best till last. A paragraph in capital letters all to itself." Steve read out loud. "'I pledge to work for the creation of many more affordable homes through a productive partnership between the council and the private sector.'"

"We all know what that means. A productive windfall for Penpol and the like, and sod all houses for ordinary folk," Pasco said furiously. "We can't let it go on like that."

"Then you'll have to make sure it doesn't," Tamsin said calmly. "And drink your coffee before it gets cold."

"He's throwing a lot of money at this, Steve. Not just this pamphlet, but I hear he's fitted his Land Rover with a PA system and is driving round town, calling on people to vote for him."

"Fat lot of good that will do him," Tamsin scoffed. "People down here don't like being shouted at."

"Maybe," Pasco admitted, "but he's got money behind him."

Tamsin picked up the empty tray, but before she went back to the kitchen she had a word of encouragement for them. "Then you'll just have to show him that money can't buy everything."

Steve was still feeling the effects of the weekend's canvassing when he trudged into the staffroom at Trengrouse on Monday morning. He hoped all the effort would be worth it. It was so hard to predict how people would react. They had been politely received at most of the addresses he had selected, and when Pasco had said that he hoped the occupants might be able to cast their votes his way no one had said they wouldn't, but then again, not many had promised that they would. Some claimed to be thinking about it, and others smiled affably enough but were clearly anxious to get back to watching television or tending their gardens. Pasco had done his best to remain cheerful but his mood had not been helped by some of the more affluent-looking properties displaying the urbane features of Giles Penhaul in their mullioned windows.

At least the absence of his GCSE class gave Steve a free period to start the day. He really must use it to follow up some of the vacancies he had been looking at in the Educational Supplement. He forced himself to wander over to his pigeonhole to retrieve that well-thumbed journal, but was confronted by a note addressed to him from the school office; no doubt from the bulldog secretary. It informed him that the head wished to see him as soon as possible. Steve sighed wearily. That was all he needed. No doubt this was a consequence of his request for a reference, and he would be asked what steps he had taken to apply for a new job. He looked guiltily at the Supplement. He would say that the matter was in hand; that would hopefully buy him time to get on with it.

Straightening his tie and running a hand over his disordered hair, Steve trailed off to the office. He found it hard to put out of his mind memories of his own schooldays, when a summons to the headmaster's office was enough to strike dread into any delinquent youth. The headmaster of his traditional grammar school had been a figure of grim authority. At morning assembly, after the adolescent boys had growled their unmelodious way through some Ancient & Modern hymn, he would invariably work himself into near-mouth-foaming rage at some individual or collective transgression which, he would proclaim, had tarnished the good name of the school. Retrospectively, Steve had concluded that the man's simmering fury had been stoked over the years by what he must have viewed as an act of betrayal by the political party he had supported all his life when a Tory government had abolished corporal punishment in schools. Unable to thrash unsatisfactory pupils, he had to content himself with bellowing at them.

Steve had to acknowledge that the headmaster – sorry, head teacher – at Trengrouse was not in direct line of descent from the headmaster of his memories. Hubert Strudwick bellowed at no one. There would be no point because he rarely came out of his office. Taff Evans joked that if he ever ventured forth he would need to be on a life support machine. Steve could not remember exchanging more than a cursory nod or muttered 'good morning' with Strudwick on the very rare occasions when he had been sighted outside of his sanctuary. At his interview, Steve now recalled, the head had said little, leaving the questions to the chairman of the governors (or should that be chairperson, or just chair?). Musing on this problem, Steve found himself at the school office, or guardroom as Taff called it. He knocked and entered, and was met with a severe frown from the formidable keeper of the gate. He began to stutter an explanation, but was cut short by a finger pointing him to an inner door with Strudwick's name stencilled on it. There was no accompanying dialogue to the gesture, and indeed the secretary had turned her back on Steve to glower at her computer screen. He crossed the office almost on tiptoe and knocked hesitantly on Strudwick's door. He thought he just made out a faint invitation to enter; so he did.

Strudwick sat behind a long desk with papers and folders piled high along its length, except for a cleared gap in the centre where he sat with only a telephone, a glass of water and a packet of paracetamol in front of him. Taff had also mentioned that Strudwick was a serial hypochondriac, which would explain the tablets and also his reluctance to leave the sanctuary of his office for fear of contagion. This alarm over germs would also explain why the chair to which Steve was now being directed was placed as far away from the desk as the dimensions of the room would allow. He sat on it with his back pressed against the thin partition which sealed Strudwick off from the office and through which Steve could hear the distinctive tapping of a keyboard.

Steve looked expectantly at the head teacher, who was now reaching awkwardly to retrieve a sheet of paper from one of the piles. This gave Steve time, from his distant viewpoint, to study the man whom he had barely registered in the months he had been at Trengrouse. Strudwick was certainly not an impressive presence: tall and thin with a wispy moustache which drooped in sympathy with his sagging shoulders. His long, melancholic face had something equine about it, and his incipient baldness was emphasised rather than disguised by a clumsy comb-over. Steve conjectured that if you met him in the street (unlikely in view of his phobia) you could easily take him to be the archetypal commercial traveller of popular imagination, plodding from one sweet shop (or the like) to another, hoping to interest the proprietors in his suitcase of novelties. Steve tried to control a smile at that thought and direct his attention back to Strudwick. He seemed to have found the document he had been looking for, and he placed it next to the box of tablets in front of him. Then, to Steve's alarm, he bent his head so low over the paper Steve thought he was going to lift it with his teeth. After squinting at it fiercely for a few moments, Strudwick slowly straightened up. He pinched the bridge of his nose between thumb and forefinger and looked at Steve as if surprised that he was still there. Steve sat up straight in expectation.

Strudwick spoke loudly to compensate for the distance his voice had to travel. "They must be tested." His tone was decisive.

Steve felt immediately guilty. He could not recall any required assessment he had neglected of late – he was always quite conscientious in marking work – but it appeared he had transgressed somewhere along the line; hence this summons. Strudwick volunteered no further information, so Steve played for time. "Tested?" he echoed.

Strudwick nodded. "I keep telling them there was glaucoma on my father's side of the family but they pay no attention."

Steve felt instant relief as some sort of comprehension returned. "I see," he said, before realising that that was perhaps not the most tactful response.

Strudwick leaned forward almost conspiratorially. "It seems Mrs Hancock will not be joining us." He sat back with the air of a man who had just passed on a state secret.

Steve was lost again. He looked around to see if there was an unoccupied chair put out for the absentee, but there was no sign of one. But who was Mrs Hancock and why would she not be joining them?

Strudwick offered a clue. He held up the paper he had been scrutinising at such close quarters. "The baby is proving quite a handful."

Again Steve struggled to connect. "The baby, you say?"

"So she will not be rejoining us in September."

Steve finally had his eureka moment. He had forgotten that his predecessor had been a Mrs Hancock. He had become accustomed to everyone calling her 'poor Rachel'. "Ah," he managed.

"Which means we could offer you a permanent position." Strudwick paused. "If you were interested, that is. You may have other plans."

Steve tried not to appear too eager, and paused thoughtfully before replying. "I think I can put those on hold." He chewed his lip as if engaged in agonising internal debate before switching to the confident expression of a man who has just made a positive decision. "Yes. Thank you. I'm happy to accept."

Strudwick managed a watery smile. "That's settled, then." He folded the paper neatly and returned it to the pile.

Steve took this as the sign of the termination of their business. Rising to his feet, he wondered if anything further needed to be said or if he should just slip quietly away. Strudwick now seemed preoccupied with sifting through another pile of papers, so it was presumably safe to leave. Steve made quietly for the door but was halted by a cough from Strudwick, who was now looking at him as if had been absconding with the family silver. Steve looked sheepishly uncertain as to his next move, but then Strudwick waved him back to the recently vacated chair. Steve perched nervously on it.

"There is another matter we need to address." Strudwick waved the papers he was holding in Steve's direction. "Wilberforce has been in touch." He looked inquiringly at Steve. "Did you know he's Dai now?"

Steve was surprised. "I didn't know he was Welsh."

"Welsh?" Now it was Strudwick's turn to look surprised.

"I thought his name was Martin."

"It is. Martin Wilberforce. Now head of DIE. It's an acronym." Strudwick spelt it out for Steve's benefit. "DIE. Diversity, Integration and Equality." He put down the papers and looked at Steve reproachfully.

"Of course. I must have forgotten," Steve muttered.

Strudwick frowned at this admission but seemed prepared to overlook it. "He was most impressed with your language class." Suddenly, he forced his head down to within an inch of the papers he had just discarded. Steve saw his lips moving as he read something to himself. Satisfied, he struggled back into an upright position. "He believes

Trengrouse can be a flagship for the rest of the county." He clearly liked the sound of that. "It is not often that we are described as a flagship."

Steve could certainly believe that. If he'd had to think in maritime terms of Trengrouse it would have been something along the lines of a leaking and rusty tramp steamer. "That's encouraging to hear," he said.

Strudwick nodded and then did his apple-bobbing trick again and hunched over what Steve presumed was a communication from Martin Wilberforce. "He wasn't so complimentary about the rest of the FE classes." He peered even closer at the text and then wearily straightened up again. "'Adequate' is the word he uses, but he would like to see a broader spectrum."

Steve tried to visualise what a broader spectrum of evening classes might look like, but Strudwick carried on.

"You are aware that Bill Rogers is retiring at the end of this term?"

"So I believe."

"Wilberforce sees this as an opportunity to appoint a replacement with, to use his words, 'energy and imagination'."

"Does he?"

"And he suggests you." Strudwick sat back and folded his arms across his chest.

Of all the surprises Steve had faced in the past few minutes, this was the greatest. "Me?" he said in genuine astonishment.

"It is my appointment to make, of course, but I think I would be ill advised to disregard the recommendation of a top man at County Hall." Strudwick looked at Steve in expectation of some response. "Well?"

Steve tried to order his tangled thoughts. "Well, I suppose it is something to consider."

"I really need to know now." Strudwick was even tapping his fingers on his desk. "If you're not interested then I need to put other wheels in motion." He managed to conjure up a tired smile. "Your normal teaching load would, of course, be adjusted to give you time for the FE work, and there would be appropriate salary increases to reflect your new responsibilities."

Steve took a deep breath. "Well, if you have confidence in me—"

Strudwick shrugged. "That is of little import. If Wilberforce thinks you are the man for the job, who am I to disagree?"

"Well, I'll do my best."

Strudwick managed a bleak smile. "I'm sure you will. I suggest you contact Wilberforce to confirm your appointment. He asks that you get in touch as soon as possible if you are taking up the position." He looked at Steve. "Which you are?"

Steve managed to nod his acceptance. "Yes. Thank you."

Strudwick was now nose down to the papers on the desk in front of him. Without unfolding himself, he pushed a sheet across the desk. "Wilberforce's email and telephone details."

Steve got up from his chair and walked across to pick up the paper, but before he could get there Strudwick forced himself upright and let out a strangled cry.

"It's no good! I can't go on like this."

Steve stood transfixed. Strudwick sat motionless, his eyes closed and face screwed up in anguish. Steve tried to recall his first aid training. Should he attempt to put Strudwick in the recovery position? Or was this a mental breakdown? And if it was, Steve had brief seconds to fret, that could mean that his recent promotions would be rescinded. Banishing this solipsism, he edged around the desk. Perhaps he should attempt to check Strudwick's pulse? He reached carefully for a wrist but before he could make contact Strudwick suddenly opened his eyes, but if he was surprised to see Steve looming over him he gave no indication of it. Steve backed carefully away, presuming that the man must be impervious to all but his own crushing inner turmoil.

"I promised her I would try to struggle on for a few more weeks." Strudwick narrowed his eyes, and that seemed to bring Steve into focus. "Surely you can see it's hopeless?"

Steve considered his response, wary of either confirming or challenging Strudwick's desperate, self-damning verdict. "Perhaps with time things will seem better," he suggested.

"Time?" Strudwick was not impressed with the suggestion. "I told her every day was a torment but she just told me to keep going. Can you believe that?"

"I am sure your wife was only—"

"My wife?" Strudwick looked baffled. "What has she got to do with anything?"

Steve looked equally baffled, but fortunately Strudwick did not wait for an answer.

"I told her contact lenses were no answer to glaucoma, and certainly not bifocal ones." To emphasise his point, he screwed his eyes shut again. "Complete agony."

Steve now understood how Newton must have felt when the apple fell from the tree. Suddenly everything made sense. At last he felt confident enough to engage in unambiguous conversation. "I believe they can take a bit of getting used to."

This seemed of little comfort to Strudwick, who was massaging his temples with both hands. "Now I feel a migraine coming on."

"I'm sorry." Steve made for the door. "I mustn't take up any more of your time."

Strudwick somehow found the energy to free one hand to wave a dismissal. "I'll ask Sheila to draw up the new contracts."

For a moment Steve was plunged back into incomprehension. Was Sheila Strudwick's wife? Did she assist with administrative duties?

Strudwick reached for his paracetamol tablets, but paused to point towards the office. "Check with her in a couple of days."

Steve excused his moment of confusion. Sheila? It had not crossed his mind that the Gorgon in the office could possibly bear such a homely and unthreatening name. "Yes. Of course. And thank you again."

Strudwick managed a brief nod before gulping down his tablet, and Steve, releasing tension in a heavy sigh, closed the door quietly behind him and escaped to the office. Sheila (he must try to get his head around that) was still attacking her keyboard and frowning at her computer screen. Fearful of disturbing her, Steve padded softly to the door.

"Congratulations." The voice came from behind him.

Steve turned in surprise to see Sheila looking at him and even offering a smile. She must have sensed his astonishment. She mimed cupping her ear and pointing at the thin dividing partition. Clearly she missed little of what went on in Strudwick's office.

"Getting one of his migraines, is he?"

"It looks like it, I'm afraid."

"Never mind." She smiled more broadly now. "I'll sort him out."

Steve had little doubt that she would.

THIRTY

"That's brilliant news, Dad!"

"I thought you would be pleased. It means your surfing holiday is secure."

Steve could hear Hannah groan at that. He had delayed calling her until he had made contact with Wilberforce to reassure himself that the surreal interview with Strudwick had not been some Kafkaesque nightmare. He now explained the situation to Hannah. Wilberforce had congratulated him on his appointment to run the FE Department, and had set up a meeting for later in the term when he hoped they could do some "blue-sky thinking" about "rolling out" the county-wide language programme ready for September. Steve had caught on to the jargon and assured Wilberforce that he would be "pushing the envelope" on this one. In his own words, he had to accept that it would be bloody hard work, but his new contracts (duly produced by Sheila, with whom he was now on chummy first-name terms) at least promised that his efforts would not be without financial reward.

"Never mind the surfing. I'm really pleased for you. You must be chuffed."

"I suppose I am," Steve allowed. "It's not really sunk in yet; not with the election coming up."

"When is that?"

"Only ten days away. But before that I've got to organise Pasco for a radio interview; a sort of 'meet the candidates' thing."

Hannah laughed. "Tell him not to swear."

Steve sighed. "Please. Don't panic me."

"Selwyn says he's never seen his dad so nervous."

"You keep in touch, then? You and Selwyn?" Steve asked with pretend innocence. He could imagine Hannah's exasperation at the other end of the phone.

"Yes, Dad. We keep in touch. We discuss our A Levels, believe it or not."

"And how are they going?"

"The first ones haven't been too bad."

"Well, hang in there, my girl."

"I'll try."

Steve knew she would. "I'd better let you get on, then." He looked at his watch. "I must go too. Pasco's coming round for his radio rehearsal."

He could hear Hannah laughing at that prospect. "Good luck with that, and congratulations again. I'm really happy for you."

"Thank you, my sweet."

"And I'll tell Mum. She'll be pleased for you too." There was a pause. "It might cheer her up."

"Is there a problem?" Steve asked.

When Hannah spoke it was almost in a whisper. "Corfu. I don't think it went well."

Steve was unsure of his feelings about that. "Oh, I see."

"Anyway," Hannah said at normal volume, "I can't wait for the holidays."

"Me neither." Then he laughed. "But don't expect the same weather."

"It doesn't matter about the weather, Dad. Not when you're in the water."

"Of course; forgive me, I'd forgotten that." A thought came to him. "By the way, when you get here I'll treat you to a new wetsuit. We can't have you trailing around in Selwyn's cast-offs."

Hannah could not keep the pleasure out of her voice. "Will you really?"

"Why not? To celebrate your A Level results."

"We hope," she said cautiously, and then hesitated. "But, Dad, they can be quite expensive."

"I think I might just be able to run to it." Steve smiled. "Thanks to Wilberforce."

Pasco certainly seemed to be showing signs of anxiety when he arrived; his trademark cheerful exuberance now replaced by a worried frown. He slumped at the kitchen table and declined the offer of a drink. "I'll be glad when this is over, Steve, I can tell you. One way or another."

"It'll be worth it. You can do this," Steve said, more cheerfully than he felt as he registered Pasco's dejection.

"I'm not so sure. Giles is pulling out all the stops. He's got posters everywhere and that bloody Land Rover has been driving about all over the place, blaring out his name."

"Noise, Pasco, just noise. All teeth and trousers."

Pasco seemed to perk up a little at this reassurance. "Perhaps. But it can fool people." He shook his head. "What gets me so steamed up is that we know all about him; what he's really after. But we can't say nothing."

Steve quickly agreed. "We can't go there, Pasco. His lawyers would crucify you. We just have to stick to established facts to back up your arguments." He pushed a bulky file across the table. "I've put together some stuff for your radio interview."

Pasco pulled the file towards him warily. "What sort of stuff?"

"Details of the council's budget; what they spent our money on. Some projections of what your plans might cost if they were implemented. That sort of thing."

Pasco looked doubtfully at the file. "Do I have to get my head round all this?"

"Afraid so. Unless you want Giles to show you up as the amateur he implies you are."

That seemed to stiffen Pasco's resolve. He picked up the file with some conviction. "We can't have that."

"Not with Radio Kernow's listeners hanging on your every word."

Pasco laughed. "All twelve of them!"

Steve smiled. "They may not be many, but if they are listening then we can assume that they are the interested ones. The ones likely to vote."

"Fair enough." Pasco banged the table with the file in exasperation. "If only there was a way I could tell them the truth about Giles and all that lot."

"You have to forget that, Pasco." Steve pointed at the file. "We just have to do it with facts and figures."

Pasco nodded glumly. "I know." He tested the weight of the file. "This must have taken some time to put together."

Steve agreed. "A few hours."

Pasco looked impressed. "On top of all that other stuff you've taken on. Congratulations, by the way, mate."

Steve looked at him in surprise. "How did you know about that?"

Pasco grinned. "Selwyn told me as I was coming out."

Steve pondered that for a moment. "Hannah must have told him."

"She'd just texted him with the news."

Steve raised his hands in resignation. "It seems you can't keep any secrets down here."

"Not unless you're Giles bloody Penhaul," Pasco said, slamming down the file.

Steve was in the staffroom, finding it hard to keep awake. He had been up late working on his programme for Wilberforce. It was the distillation of his experience with the class at Trengrouse, and he had structured it to be as user-friendly as he could make it so that other teachers could follow it in their own classes. He had to admit he was pleased with what he had done so far, but all that concentration was sapping his energy. He had just put in another couple of gruelling hours after school whilst he waited for his evening class to assemble. In spite of his weariness he was quite looking forward to it. He had recovered his enthusiasm after Wilberforce's visit. It seemed as if his efforts were appreciated at least. Consoling himself with that thought, he forced himself to his feet and out of the embrace of the staffroom.

He found a quiet table away from the assembling students and marked his register as they appeared. It looked as if he had another good turnout. He put the register aside and strolled over to one of the workstations, where an iPad did not seem to have booted up. He bent to check the settings, and whilst he was reconfiguring them he could hear the chatter by the door.

Luka's voice was raised in protest. "It was a big offside. The referee is blind, I think!"

There was some laughter from the others at his indignation.

Steve smiled at the exchanges as he checked that the screen in front of him was now behaving. Suddenly, he was aware of approaching footsteps.

"Is it too late to come back to the class?"

Steve did not move. He was no longer aware of the chatter; locked in a moment of suspended time. He must be deluded. Forcing himself to focus, he slowly turned around. It was no illusion. "Eva." He could say nothing else. He just looked at her. He wanted to hug her but managed to compose himself. He smiled broadly. "I thought... well, I don't know what I thought."

"I am so sorry. I wanted to tell you, but then..." She paused. "Then I wasn't sure." She broke off awkwardly but looked up at Steve, those bewitching eyes seeming to ask for his understanding.

Steve said nothing but he felt ridiculously happy. Then the growing awareness that the class had fallen silent and were looking at him with curiosity forced him to adjust. "We'll talk in a minute," he whispered to Eva. Then he addressed the others. "If you would move to your places you will find some questions to answer. Once you have started I'll come round to see how you are getting on."

The class dispersed to their accustomed positions. Eva stood awkwardly at Steve's side, unsure of what she should do. He waited a few moments and then ushered her across to the empty table where he had left his register. He indicated to her to sit, but took a minute or two to walk around the room, checking that everyone was coping with their assignment, before joining her at the table with the register between them.

Keeping his voice low, he pointed at the register. "I never did cross your name out."

Eva smiled at him. "That was kind." She leaned forward so that she did not have to raise her voice. "I was afraid that..." But she broke off as if unsure of how to proceed.

"What were you afraid of, Eva?"

"Steve, I have a problem." This was a shout from one of the students.

"Coming." Steve got to his feet and looked at Eva. "This is crazy. Look. You don't need to do any of this stuff – you're way above it – but as you're here and I haven't brought any books for you, why don't you help me?"

"Help you?" Eva looked puzzled.

"Yes. Be my assistant. Go round and check their work for them."

Eva looked aghast. "I could not—"

Before she could finish, Steve clapped his hands to get the attention of the students. They turned away from their screens to look at him expectantly. "You all know Eva." He waved a hand in her direction. "I'm pleased to say that she is now able to rejoin us and I have managed to persuade her to work with me as my teaching assistant. So there will now be two of us here for you." He turned back to Eva, who was looking at him in shock. "Thank you, Eva." Again he addressed the class. "So we will be coming round to see how you are getting on in just a few moments. Please carry on."

The class carried on, seemingly finding nothing untoward in Steve's decision to enlist an assistant. Eva, on the other hand, was looking at him as if he had taken leave of his senses.

He bent and whispered to her. "You'll be fine."

And she was fine. After some initial nervousness, Eva relaxed into her new role. She had an advantage over Steve in that in some cases she could communicate with class members in their own language, having received dispensation from him to breach the English-only rule in the interest of enlightenment.

At the coffee break, Steve congratulated her on her debut. He handed her a mug of caffeine-flavoured hot water. "You see, there's nothing to it, this teaching business."

Eva smiled. "I hope I am helping."

"You are. In fact I'd like you to carry on helping me until the end of term." He sipped his coffee and grimaced at the taste. "That is, if you want to."

"That would be good." Then she frowned. "But my exam..."

Steve laughed. "Don't worry about that. It's in the bag." Then he wondered if that would make sense to Eva.

She must have sensed his uncertainty. "Another idiom. You see, I remember."

Steve remembered too. That now seemed to have happened in another life. So much had happened since, and yet, perversely, they still knew so little about each other. That must change. "Look, Eva, if we are going to work together we need to find time to plan the lessons. And you still have those books to read: the Thomas Hardy and the Virginia Woolf. You remember?"

Eva did not answer straight away, and when she did it was tentatively. "Yes, I remember."

There was a burst of laughter from the coffee urn, where Ricardo was giving his forceful professional opinion of the beverage he had just sampled.

Steve lowered his voice. "This is ridiculous. We have so much to talk about, but not here. Can I take you out for a meal – not just for coffee? We need more time."

Eva smiled, and even teased. "To talk about the work and the books, of course."

Steve could laugh with her now; all his tension seemed to have drained away. "Of course." He grinned. "Amongst other things. So, are you free tomorrow evening?"

Eva feigned surprise. "So soon?"

Steve put on a mock-serious expression. "In the pursuit of knowledge, Miss Albescu, time is of the essence."

THIRTY-ONE

"The percentage of the council's budget available for social housing is in single figures!" Pasco exclaimed.

"Good," Steve prompted. "And how would you fund the provision of hostels for the homeless?"

Pasco thought for a moment and then remembered his lines. "By reducing the travel allowance paid to councillors by ten pence a mile."

"Bit like turkeys voting for Christmas, that one, Pasco. But the punters will like it."

Pasco certainly seemed to have mastered his brief, as Steve had put it. The radio interview was scheduled for the evening before the election; now only four days away. Pasco had called in after work, still in his overalls. "Took me the whole weekend to go through that lot." He smiled ruefully. "Even got Tamsin to test me."

"Tell her she did a good job. Remember, 'Knowledge is power.'"

Pasco laughed. "That's your old friend Stalin again, isn't it?"

Steve looked surprised. "You knew that?"

"Course not. You wrote it on the front page of the folder."

"So I did. I'd forgotten. Sorry; a bit pompous."

"Well, you know what they say. You can take the teacher out of the school—"

"Yes. Thank you," Steve interrupted, and moved to change the subject. "Have you looked at the notes I put together about the radio interview; how to play it?"

Pasco sighed. "'Stay cool and don't lose your rag; don't swear; don't let anyone wind you up.' That about it?"

"Just be yourself," Steve encouraged.

Pasco laughed. "Me? Not getting worked up? No strong language? Putting up with bullshit? Does that sound like me, Steve?"

Steve made soothing gestures by gently waving his hands with palms down. "Easy, boy. Just remember that I'm sure Giles, in particular, will make a big deal of his professional skills, his business background. He wants to paint you as the amateur; he as good as said it. He will try to baffle us with facts and figures, management speak and all that stuff. He's a smooth operator."

Pasco nodded reluctantly. "Oily. Tamsin said, 'Put him on a hill and he'll slide upwards.'"

"Then there's his public-school education. He knows how to present himself. I'm sure he'll be icily polite and try to appear eminently reasonable. It will be hard to rattle him. I dare say he will treat the rest of you like small children who require patient but firm handling."

"I don't know about the foot lady but if he tries that with Breock he could get an earful."

"But that's the point, Pasco. He wants the rest of you to rant and rave. It strengthens his case as the voice of reason; a professional."

"I hear you, Steve," Pasco said gloomily.

"You can do it." Steve paused. "Remember your rugby days."

Pasco looked baffled. "How does that help?"

Steve explained. "From what I hear from the likes of Desi, when opponents tried to wind you up you didn't react. Not until you could sort them out on your terms; wait for the right opportunity."

Pasco shrugged. "Maybe , but nothing illegal."

"Exactly!" Steve exclaimed. "And that's how you deal with Giles. Play him at his own game: calm and in control, but if you get the opportunity then nail him."

"But what opportunity? I reckon he's got all bases covered."

"Possibly. But you never know. If his guard slips for a moment you have to be ready to take him. That's why you have to keep concentrating; keep focused. Don't let him provoke you into any sort of meltdown."

"I'll do my best."

"You'll be fine." Steve stood. "We'll have a final run-through tomorrow evening in case any last-minute stuff comes up."

Pasco nodded and gathered up his folder. When he stood he noticed Steve putting on his jacket and then knotting a tie he had fished out of the pocket. Steve straightened the tie and became aware of Pasco looking at him questioningly. He smiled sheepishly but said nothing.

Pasco broke the silence. "What's with the smart gear? Parents' evening, is it?"

"No... not a parents' evening," Steve said evasively.

"Don't tell me you've got a date?" Pasco probed.

Steve knew that there was no point in attempting to deceive Pasco. He braced himself. "Not really a date; a sort of working dinner, you might say."

Pasco was not to be deflected. "Might I? And what's her name?"

Steve gave up. He faced Pasco unwaveringly. "Eva has come back."

Pasco's mood changed. He was silent for a few moments, and when he spoke it was with none of the teasing banter of before. "That must have come as a surprise," he said quietly.

Steve nodded. "You could say that."

"But a pleasant surprise?" Pasco asked.

Steve considered the question. "I think so. I hope so, anyway."

Pasco's expression was partly of concern and partly of curiosity. "Well. I won't hold you up." He tucked his folder under his arm and gave Steve a wry smile. "I'm sure you have a lot to talk about."

Steve held up the bottle of wine in invitation. Eva nodded her acceptance and Steve poured them each a glass. They had been seated at a quiet table away from a noisy family party who seemed to be celebrating a birthday, with a cake in evidence and the wrappings of opened gifts strewn amidst the cutlery. Several empty wine bottles suggested that everyone was in festive mood. Steve was grateful that the distraction of serving the large family table left him and Eva free from the overly solicitous attention of the waiter. They had been served their wine and their bowls of pasta and their waiter had performed his charade with the phallic pepper pot and Steve had assured him that everything was fine, and he had left them in peace and was now busy making a flamboyant drama out of kissing the hand of an elderly lady at the birthday table.

Steve raised his glass to Eva, who smiled and raised hers in response. They drank a silent toast to each other and then began the hazardous task of transferring the spaghetti in an orderly fashion from plate to mouth. They caught each other concentrating on this awkward manoeuvre, and laughed simultaneously. Steve felt relaxed, which surprised him. He remembered the tension of their last meeting before Eva's sudden departure, and wondered why tonight was different. They had not talked about that, although Steve knew that at some point the elephant would trumpet its presence. Whilst they had waited for the food he had given Eva the books they had talked about, and outlined her role as his teaching assistant. She had to be convinced that he really needed her, and he had assured her that, as the heir elect to Bill Rogers' throne, these decisions were his to make. She had congratulated him on that news, and Steve might have imagined it but she seemed pleased to hear that the promotion meant he would not have to move away.

The spaghetti was finally vanquished. They pushed away their plates and sat back contentedly. Steve topped up their glasses.

"Thank you so much, Steve. It was lovely." Eva looked around the restaurant. "It is very nice here." Then she looked apologetically at Steve. "I should wear a dress, perhaps, but I do not have one here. I did not expect this."

"You look fine, Eva. Better than fine," he said. "You look beautiful." He found himself saying the words unbidden, and instantly wondered if he had overstepped the mark. He smiled nervously at her.

She smiled back, but passed lightly over his compliment. She looked around the room. "This is a big surprise."

"Life is full of surprises, isn't it?" Steve let the question hang between them. The distant chatter from the family table seemed only to accentuate their silence.

Eva looked at him, and then she looked down and fidgeted with her paper napkin. She seemed to be steeling herself. "I tried to tell you. But I couldn't." She broke off and shook her head in exasperation. "Then I thought, Why would he want to know? Why would he be interested in my problems?"

"What problems, Eva?" Steve asked cautiously, perhaps fearful of the answers.

"I didn't have a telephone number. I don't have an address." She looked ruefully at him. "I don't know anything about you, Steve."

"I suppose not," he agreed.

"So when the call came I had no time for messages. Just a quick note for Elena."

Steve remembered. "She told me there was a big problem and you had to leave."

Eva leaned forward and looked hard at him. "What did you think?"

He hesitated and looked away; embarrassed to remember his thoughts. "I didn't know what to think. The car business, your brother... It was a lot to handle."

"You didn't believe me." Eva stated this as a fact, not a question, but there was no resentment in her voice.

"I did," Steve protested. "Well, I certainly wanted to, anyway. But when you just disappeared like that with no explanation I began to imagine all sorts of things."

"That I was running away from the police? Did you think that, Steve?"

He sighed. "I'll be honest; it did cross my mind." He could not deny it, although he was aware that his admission would be hurtful. He wondered if it was the end of any hope of building some sort of relationship with her. He studied her reaction, prepared for her resentment at his apparent lack of trust, but instead was relieved to see her manage a weary smile.

"It was natural. Anyone would have thought it." She laughed, but without much humour. "I think if I had been you I might not have believed me."

"Thank you. That makes me feel better."

"But I believed you when you said you would not tell the police. And you didn't."

"So…"

"So why did I run?"

"Yes."

"I had to." Eva paused. "Anya."

"Your daughter?" Steve was nervous to ask more.

"My mother was a nurse. She recognised it at once. She had to pay for a taxi to take her to the big hospital in Bucharest. That is where she phoned me from. She thought that…" Eva broke off and absently picked up the napkin to dab her eyes. "That it might be too late." She said this softly, her voice breaking and with a note of despair.

Steve was shocked; unsure of what to say. He could only look at Eva helplessly.

After a few moments she took a deep, calming breath and put down the napkin. She was now more composed. "I could not think of anything else but to be with Anya."

"Of course. It must have been terrible for you." He could not bring himself to ask about the outcome.

"They said she was lucky to survive. If my mother had not recognised the meningitis then…" She stopped as if recoiling from a blow.

"But now? She is getting better?" Steve asked.

Eva managed a smile. "She is home now. My mother is looking after her. She will be fine."

Steve sighed with relief. "That's wonderful."

"Yes. Thank you. But it was a bad time." Tears still dampened her eyes.

Instinctively, Steve reached across the table and put his hand on hers. Then she slid her hand out and their fingers entwined. "You must forgive me for doubting you, Eva."

Eva shrugged her shoulders but did not attempt to move her hand away. "It was not your fault. If I could have explained in that note to Elena it would not have been a problem."

"Why couldn't you?"

She frowned. "Elena is not a close friend; we just work together. I was not sure I could tell her my secret."

"Secret?"

"The bosses. They do not know about Anya. They don't like to take on single mothers; they think that always there will be problems with the children. No one knew except my brother, and he said nothing."

"Now I see." Steve paused. Twenty years of teaching English literature invariably provided the words for most occasions. "Oh, what a tangled web we weave, when first we practise to deceive!" He laughed at his own pedantry.

"Sir Walter Scott, I think?" She raised her eyebrows inquiringly.

"You are amazing, Eva!"

They released hands and sat back grinning at each other.

"Dessert? Or coffee?" The waiter had temporarily abandoned fawning over the birthday table. He slid one plate expertly onto the other and stood back awaiting a response.

Steve looked at Eva. She mouthed a silent 'Coffee' back.

"Two coffees, please," was the request that sent the waiter scuttling off.

"So now you know what I was doing. What about you, Steve? What have you been doing?"

Steve explained how much of his time was now taken up with his new plans for Trengrouse's FE Department, and how he was trying to get everything together for a meeting with Wilberforce later in the term.

"You work too hard," Eva chided.

"And you don't?" he countered, to which she could only shrug. "But at least I took a week off at Easter to spend with my daughter."

"Your daughter?" Eva looked surprised.

"Yes. Hannah. She's nearly eighteen now. She's doing her A Levels, but she managed to get down here for a week."

"She does not live with you?"

"No. With her mother in London." He stopped, aware that Eva was wrinkling her brow quizzically. "I'm sorry; as you say, you know nothing about me." He took a breath. "It's not very exciting, I'm afraid."

"Two coffees, sir." The waiter placed the cups theatrically on the table and hovered until Steve assured him several times that they had enjoyed their meal.

As they sipped their coffee, Steve told Eva about his divorce and the move to Cornwall. He admitted he had been pretty miserable at first but now he was beginning to feel that life was improving. He had got more involved with people; begun to regain some confidence. He confessed that he was actually looking forward to the future; it had to be better than the recent past. Eva listened without comment, nodding her understanding. When he told her he was optimistic that things could only improve, she reached out and squeezed his hand in affirmation.

"A refill, sir?" The waiter had sashayed across the room to them and now, without prompting, poured coffee into their cups from an unnecessarily perilous height, just because he could.

"Thank you." Steve winked at Eva as this piece of theatre unfolded. The waiter responded with an extravagant bow and hurried back to brandish his coffee pot over the family party.

Eva drank some coffee and then put down her cup and studied Steve for a few moments before speaking. "So I think you are happy now. Things are better for you."

"Improving, certainly." Then he frowned. "Not quite out of the wood yet." He continued quickly, with a laugh, "Idiom."

Eva joined in the laughter. "But what is so terrible in this wood?"

"The election. Only two days away now." Seeing her bemused look, he realised that he had told her nothing of his involvement with Pasco. He took a sip of coffee. "It's a long story." By the time he had finished his explanation his coffee was cold. Eva had listened intently and asked the occasional question, not only about the complexities of the electoral process but also about Pasco. Steve tried to sum up his friend's character. "He would be the first to admit that he's no intellectual, but in a strange way that's his strength. He has an uncomplicated view of life; a strong belief in right and wrong. Do you understand what I mean?"

Eva nodded. "Sometimes people like that can make us feel guilty. We find excuses not to do things because they're uncomfortable or difficult." She paused, and when she spoke again it was with sadness. "Or dangerous, like it was for my father."

Steve reached for her hand again in reassurance. Neither spoke for a moment; words were redundant. Then their shared silence was suddenly broken by a boisterous, raucous blast of 'Happy Birthday' from the celebrating family. Steve and Eva sat back and smiled at each other, their mood immediately altered by the revellers.

Steve had to raise his voice above the singing. "So you see, Pasco is on a sort of crusade. Fighting for the little guy against the big battalions."

"Like St George against the dragon."

Steve laughed. "Right. With Giles Penhaul and Penpol as the dragon."

Eva looked puzzled. "What?"

"Penpol Investments Limited."

She frowned. "Oh, them." She spoke contemptuously.

He stared at her in surprise. "You know these people?"

"Of course. I work for them."

Steve took time to register this. "You work for Penpol?"

"They own the farms we are taken to. A gangmaster told me. And that is the name on the contracts we have to sign. But I have never seen any of these people. Our foremen and gangmasters, they are like me: Romanian."

"So the only contact you have with your employers is the name on the contracts?"

Eva shrugged. "They call them contracts but they take away more than they give."

Steve was now oblivious to the discordant strains of the birthday choristers. He grasped both of Eva's hands and smiled broadly at her. She looked at him in some puzzlement but made no attempt to free herself from his grip.

"Eva," he said loudly above the singing, "I say it again. You are amazing."

THIRTY-TWO

"We are nearly out of time. So if you would like to make your final points, this is your opportunity," Mandy trilled.

Steve stared intently at the radio, attempting to visualise the scene in the studio. He was gripping his cup of tea so hard his fingers were aching. He flexed them and offered up a silent entreaty to Pasco to hang on in there. So far he had performed well, presenting his case calmly but with conviction, and marshalling the statistical evidence they had worked on. If there was a slight concern it was that he was coming across as almost too composed. Those who knew him would be wondering where his fire and fervour had gone. Steve felt stirrings of guilt; perhaps he had coached Pasco into an uncharacteristic decorum.

"What I say is, Cornwall for the Cornish!" That was all Breock seemed to have to say in his summing-up. He had been saying little more than that since the first exchanges, when Giles Penhaul had forensically demolished his proposals by demonstrating that they were unaffordable, untenable and unworkable. He'd told Breock, more in sorrow than in anger, that his ideas were "economically naive".

The foot lady (Steve could think of her in no other terms since Pasco had complained that he could not get his tongue around 'chiropodist') had conducted herself in an entirely rational and unruffled manner but Steve doubted that her message would have inspired many voters. She had dwelt on the need for electoral reform so that all views could be represented, and expressed hope that after Brexit local fishermen and farmers would seek to maintain strong ties with "our European friends". Steve felt for her. She was obviously reading from the party manual and maybe she had aspirations to be a candidate in the next general election, but he doubted that her sentiments would be echoed by many local voters.

Giles Penhaul performed much as Steve had predicted. He made much of his local connections but also dwelt on his wide business experience which, he implied, gave him the skills to ensure that money was spent prudently and for the benefit of the electorate. "I have listened to the views of the other candidates with great interest," he purred. "I appreciate that we all share the same concerns for this wonderful part of Cornwall."

Steve nearly choked on his tea at that, as Giles oozed on.

"However, we must ask ourselves what our priorities are. I well understand, and indeed admire, Breock's passion for our beloved Cornwall." Giles had used Christian names as an assumed intimacy from the outset. "But we must temper idealism with realism." He said this with dismissive condescension before turning his attention elsewhere. "Rebecca raised some interesting and important issues which certainly need to be addressed at some point and in some other place, but I remain to be convinced that they are at the top of our list of local priorities." He said this with a little, flippant laugh. Then his tone became almost unctuous. "Peter, as we all know, was a much-admired and brilliant rugby player; a true Cornish man."

Steve frowned in anticipation of what might come next.

"In rugby you stick to the rules and the best side wins. Quite a simple concept, really." Giles paused. "If only local government was that simple."

Steve now guessed where this was going.

"Peter and I want the same things. Decent jobs for our young people, care for the elderly, and of course affordable housing. We are in complete agreement on that, but I have to ask: which of us is more likely to achieve those goals? I have one hundred per cent respect for Peter but I hope I do not sound arrogant if I say that I genuinely believe my experience in the world of business makes me better qualified to take on this challenge. Thank you for your patience, Mandy."

Steve groaned. "You smug bugger." He had to concede that Giles had been convincing. He banged his mug on the table. "Come on, Pasco! Now or never""

"That was kind of Mr Penhaul to mention the rugby." Pasco had studiously refused to descend to first-name terms. "I don't know when he had time to watch any matches, being away all the time at school and college and then busy in London, but the thought is appreciated."

Steve raised a triumphant fist. "Good one, Pasco. Right below the belt."

Pasco now had the steel back in his voice. "I agree with Mr Penhaul that we both want the same things, so the difference is which of us is going to fight the harder for them." He paused. "He would tell us that when it comes to building more affordable homes our best hope is to rely on partnership with the private sector. Am I right, Mr Penhaul?"

Pasco was clearly deviating from Mandy's protocol here. "I thought we—" she fluttered nervously.

"It's quite all right, Mandy, I am more than happy to take this," Giles said with soothing magnanimity. "Yes, Peter, you are correct. A robust involvement with private sector partners is the way forward if we are to provide our young people with decent, affordable homes."

"I see." Pasco paused. "I just wanted to be clear on that." He paused again, and Steve could pick up a rustle of papers. "Do you know how many affordable homes were built in this ward by that partnership you were telling us about, in the last year?"

"I don't have the figures to hand." Steve detected the first signs of wariness in Giles.

"Well, I do." Pasco paused. "Eight." He let the figure hang in the air before continuing. "So by my calculations it would take just over twelve years to provide a hundred affordable homes. I agree I don't have your business experience but that seems a bit slow to me."

Giles was blustering now. "You can't take one year's figures in isolation. There may have been special factors at work."

"Oh, there were. Very special. These private companies agreed, as part of their deal with the council, to build four times that amount of affordable housing. But that all got downgraded by a 'viability assessment' – I dare say you'll know all about them, with your business experience."

Mandy tried to stem the tide. "I think—"

The tide rolled on. "Now, let's move on to jobs. You said you would like to see many more decent jobs created, and you would expect to see private capital investment make a major contribution."

"Indeed." Giles clearly felt on safer ground here.

"And by 'decent jobs' we mean permanent, well-paid work with holiday entitlement, sick pay and so on?"

"Of course," said Giles piously.

"Not jobs with Mickey Mouse zero-hours contracts, no sick pay, no holiday pay, no union representation allowed? And rent charged for accommodation not fit to put a pig in?"

"I would not be party to anything like that."

Pasco racked up his voice by a few accusatory decibels. "I am very pleased to hear it because it means you can put a stop to all of that crap which is the standard practice of a large company operating locally of which you are one of the directors."

"This is outrageous!" Giles was shouting now.

Mandy offered no intervention. Clearly she recognised compulsive listening when she heard it.

"Finally, Mr Penhaul, you implied that I am an amateur." There was real passion in Pasco's voice. "I am, and I am proud of it. When I played for Cornwall I didn't go onto the pitch like a sandwich-board man with some sponsor's logo on my back. I played for the love of it and for pride in my county. I wasn't worried about a winning bonus or upsetting some sugar daddy who'd pay my wages if we lost. I was responsible only to myself and my team. I owed nobody anything, and that's how it will be if I am elected to the council." He paused for a moment before adding quietly, "Thank you, Mandy."

Giles was trying to speak, but Mandy drowned him out. "Well, plenty of food for thought there." She then switched to her clumsy link. "And talking of food, we are now going to join Sandra Beckerleg in the Kernow kitchen, who is going to tell us how to prepare a gourmet mackerel supper."

Steve switched off the radio and pumped a celebratory arm into the air. "Pasco, my beauty! You nailed him."

Someone had hung a banner across the top of the bar. It carried the adapted words of a Cornish rugby chant: 'Oggy, Oggy, Pasco'. Friday was usually the busiest night of the week at The Miners but this was something special. Last night had been a late one for Steve and Pasco with the result not declared until midnight, and today Steve had found it hard to keep his eyes open at school, but now adrenaline and euphoria had rejuvenated him. As he waited to wriggle his way through the heaving crowd at the bar, he was able to savour the atmosphere. He found it hard to believe that the journey he had taken with Pasco these past months had brought him to this.

He had expected the vote count to be a nerve-racking trauma, and he still found it hard to grasp how unexpectedly one-sided the contest had been. Having taken the day off from work, he and Pasco had been able to monitor the recorded voters and match their names against their list of possible supporters. As the day wore on they'd allowed themselves to grow cautiously optimistic that most of those who had been sympathetic had actually voted. Steve, anxious to leave no vote uncast, had suggested as the evening fell that they might drive around the town on home visits to try to winkle out the absentees, but Pasco drew the line at that. "I'm not begging to no bugger," was his veto.

In the echoing sports hall where the votes were counted, the candidates had looked on in varying states of concern. Pasco, with Tamsin by his side, looked uncomfortable in his "funeral suit", as he called it, which she had insisted he wear, but managed a studied composure which Steve guessed concealed an inner unease. Breock, no doubt battle-hardened by regular participation in the democratic process, sported a Cornish kilt and sporran from which, at increasingly frequent intervals, he produced a sustaining hip flask. The foot lady had very sensibly brought some knitting with her, and sat quietly working at it. Tamsin had wandered across to talk to her and reported back that she was a really nice lady, and that she had booked a pedicure for next week. Giles had marched in resplendent in country tweeds with a large blue rosette at his buttonhole. His agent trailed dutifully behind him as they paced about the hall, watching the tellers pile up the ballot papers.

It had soon become clear which way the electoral wind was blowing. Pasco had not only swept the board, but left few crumbs for the others. As Steve brought him regular updates on the progress of the vote he visibly relaxed. When the outcome was assured beyond doubt he astonished Tamsin by suddenly hugging her to him. She quickly recovered enough to ruffle his hair and tell him to behave. Breock seemed to take defeat in his well-practised stride, and when Steve saw the foot lady's agent bear the disappointing news to her she merely nodded and carried on knitting. Giles had shown no such equanimity. When it became clear that the tide had gone out and left him stranded, initial incredulity gave way to outrage. Steve watched from a distance as he jabbed an accusing finger at his hapless agent, who finally shrugged with an expression that seemed to be saying, What did you expect? When the returning officer proclaimed Pasco's victory Giles barely managed to contain himself sufficiently to exchange the traditional handshakes with his opponents, and with a final glare at Pasco stamped out of the hall with his agent almost running to keep up with him.

Pasco had made the required speech thanking the officials and then his opponents for their sporting participation. Fortunately Giles had left before that. Pasco then embarrassed Steve by paying particular tribute to his agent, without whom, he admitted to some laughter, he would have been up the creek without a paddle. He concluded with unfeigned emotion that he would do his best for everyone, whether they had voted for him or not.

Breock, now well fortified and elated that he had finished as runner-up, roared a "Hear, hear" to that, and thrust his hip flask at Pasco, who had no hesitation in taking a swig.

"I think you owed him that, my handsome."

Steve was jerked out of his reverie by the bulky figure of Desi Hosken bearing down on him with a pint in one hand and the inevitable pasty in the other, as he cleared his way back from the bar. His jacket had been discarded and his braces were almost at snapping point over his bespattered shirt.

"Owed him?"

"All that pantomime with the car. Quite a performance."

"Oh," Steve said nervously.

Desi laughed loudly. "That's Pasco for you. What he wants, he gets. The council won't know what's hit them." He made to barrel back to his noisy friends, but took a moment to swallow a generous mouthful of pasty. Through spraying food particles, he had one more thought for Steve. "Remember me when you want a new car."

"I will," Steve hastily assured him.

"But don't bring Pasco with you!" Desi roared, scattering the queuing customers like chaff as he scythed his way through them.

Steve was still smiling when he felt a tap on his shoulder. He turned to encounter the swaying, sweating figure of Breock Trevaylor, still in his Cornish kilt. He fixed Steve with bloodshot eyes which gradually seemed to focus. He leaned close, and Steve could smell the whisky on his breath. He spoke in a secretive whisper. "I was runner-up, you know." He swayed back unsteadily and turned to face the packed drinkers. "I was runner-up!" he bellowed.

There was laughter and ironic applause, which seemed to satisfy Breock, who lurched away to find others to regale with his achievement. Someone shouted, "He'll be talking Cornish soon." There were cheers to acknowledge that.

Steve eventually managed to get served by a perspiring Sam, who told him he hadn't pulled so many pints since the

Brexit party. When Steve went to pay, Sam would have none of it. "It's on the house," he shouted, "for what you did for Pasco." As Steve navigated back towards Pasco he was held up by many offering handshakes and congratulations. He had to admit he felt unashamed pleasure at the experience. He could almost convince himself that he was halfway to being 'proper Cornish'.

He found Pasco surrounded by well-wishers. Pasco saw him coming and called out, in the strict tones of a guardian of the law, "Make way, gentlemen, for the supervisor."

Heads turned in surprise which turned to laughter as Steve blushingly raised his pint in acknowledgement. The crowd parted to let him take his place alongside Pasco. They touched pints in greeting.

Pasco smiled. "Hard to believe, isn't it?"

Steve thought about that. "Not really. You deserve this."

The noise in the room suddenly abated. The crowd around Pasco drew back. The reason for the change of mood was soon apparent. Old John Penhaul had entered the bar and was walking slowly towards Pasco as people manoeuvred to let him through. Steve gripped his pint nervously, but Pasco stood quiet and unmoving, his eyes fixed unblinkingly on the old man as he stopped a few feet away from him. The crowd, so boisterous a few seconds earlier, were hushed in tense expectation.

Penhaul broke the silence. "He's my boy, Pasco, and I'll stand by him till the end." He paused. "But he wasn't right for this. I tried to tell him but he wouldn't listen." He held out his hand. "Congratulations."

The noise was suddenly switched on again; tension released in laughter and chatter. Pasco stepped towards the old man and clasped both his hands around the one offered. "Thank you, John. This means a hell of a lot to me."

Penhaul nodded. "Needed saying," he said gruffly.

"I'm sorry if Giles—"

"Don't you worry about him," his father interrupted. "He's already back in London chasing down a few deals."

Pasco smiled at that. "Let me get you a drink."

"Well, just a quick half, perhaps. I told Mary I wouldn't be long."

Pasco began to move towards the bar, only to pause when Penhaul called his name.

"Pasco. I tell you what. If your father could see you now, he'd be a proud man."

THIRTY-THREE

There was no time to dwell on Pasco's election triumph as Steve laboured to put together his language programme for Wilberforce, whom he was scheduled to meet in the last week of term. There was also the challenge of offering the 'broader spectrum' of evening classes Wilberforce had wanted. To this end, in the past few weeks Steve had approached potential tutors to check their willingness to run new courses in addition to the old faithfuls over which Bill Rogers had presided. In the name of breadth he had proposed yoga and Pilates classes, which were relatively mainstream these days, balanced by mindfulness and Buddhist philosophy on one end of the hypothetical see-saw, and motorbike maintenance and kick-boxing on the other.

Eva featured more in Steve's life now. Ostensibly, their time spent together was to work on her integration into the role of teaching assistant. Steve felt guilty that this was an unpaid role but Eva seemed quite happy to help out. She pointed out that she would be coming to the class anyway so helping him was no problem, and anyway, after a day of back-breaking physical labour it was therapeutic to use her mind for a change. She was a natural teacher, patient and encouraging, and Steve had no doubt that if she had not had to leave university prematurely she would have had a successful academic career. When he told her that, she had merely shrugged. "I have Anya," she'd told him. "That is more important." Sometimes they met at the coffee bar where they were now on first-name terms with the staff, and on a couple of evenings they had worked at Steve's, fortified by fish and chips. On the last occasion, before driving her home, he had taken her to The Miners for a drink. She had loved it: her first visit to an English pub. Sam had made a great fuss of her and, in Steve's opinion, had held on to her hand for slightly longer than was strictly necessary when bidding them goodnight.

It was not all work. They had gone to the cinema one evening to see the highly acclaimed work of a director who, according to one critic, was 'working on the edge of what we understand by cinema'. Others had spoken of 'uncompromising social realism' and 'shining a spotlight on issues we can no longer ignore'. After a few slow-paced minutes Steve began to wish someone would shine a spotlight on the celluloid participants. Most scenes were subterranean; filmed with a handheld camera in dingy basements with solitary, naked hanging light bulbs barely illuminating the tormented souls whose lives, it seemed (although the soundtrack was too muffled to be certain), had been wrecked by addiction. The hopelessness of their existence was relieved only by intermittent acts of graphic violence, and more frequent and even more graphic bouts of fornication. Steve felt embarrassed and even nervous that Eva might question his motives in bringing her, albeit unwittingly, to this abundant display of sexual grappling. In the middle of one particularly prolonged and feverish simulated coupling, he dared to glance at her. She caught his eye and, pointing at the screen, raised her eyebrows in mock astonishment and then started giggling. As the scene grew even more bizarre, Steve became infected by her giggles and needed to put his hand over his mouth to suppress them. They spent the rest of the film trying their best not to disgrace themselves with their obvious hilarity, although Steve did catch a muttered word of censure from some film aficionado in the row behind them. It was a relief to walk out of the cinema into the warm dusk and stroll arm in arm down to the seafront, laughing without restraint at the antics they had just witnessed. They stood for a moment, leaning against the railings above the shingle beach. The waves sucked hungrily at the pebbles and the gulls bobbed lazily on the gentle swell. Steve looked smilingly at Eva, and she held his gaze. It seemed the most natural thing in the world to kiss; so they did.

There was no need for jackets in the beer garden this time. The sun shone warmly on holidaying families in shirtsleeves and shorts sitting at the wooden tables; the parents cheerfully swilling pints of lager and the restless children slurping tooth-decaying fizz. Sam's young waitress scurried to and fro bearing platters of chips and armfuls of pasties. Steve and Pasco managed to find an empty bench in the shade away from the worst of the hubbub. They sat back and raised their glasses in a silent toast.

It was their first chance to talk since Pasco's inaugural council meeting. Steve had been burning the midnight oil to finish his project for Wilberforce, whom he was due to meet in a few days, whilst Pasco had been busy breaking in the lad he had taken on to "shin up the ladder", as he put it. This, he hoped, would give him a bit of time for council duties.

"A surgery, Steve. A surgery! That's what Tamsin tells me I should call it."

"Sorry?" Steve queried.

"It's only the spare room with a table and a couple of chairs in it. And, of course, the bleeding laptop."

"You getting on all right with that now?"

"Like Bill Gates." Pasco laughed and started on his pint.

"Selwyn been coaching you?"

"Good as gold. He's finished his exams now so I'm his project."

"How did they go?"

"You know Selwyn. He doesn't say much but I think he did OK."

"Same with Hannah."

"So she will be going to Exeter?"

"It looks like it. And Selwyn to Bristol."

They sat for a moment in reflection; then Pasco turned to look at Steve. "Exeter to Bristol. Just down the road. Handy for them."

"Who knows? Young love and all that. Unpredictable."

Pasco shook his head. "Not those two. They're stickers. I reckon it could last." He grinned at Steve. "How do you fancy me as Hannah's father-in-law?"

Steve closed his eyes in melodramatic alarm. "Please!"

They laughed at the thought and sipped their ale. Pasco put down his glass on the bench beside him and gave Steve a crooked smile. "Anyway, never mind young love – how are things with Eva?"

The tone may have been jocular but Steve had anticipated Pasco's curiosity, although he was unsure how to answer it. How were things with Eva? On the surface, things were great. They were relaxed and happy in each other's company but hand-holding and the occasional chaste kiss were as far as either of them seemed willing to go in physical intimacy. Not because the flesh was unwilling, as Steve could testify, but because the spirit was unsure. There were complications;

uncharted waters. "Things are fine," he said, with as much certainty as he could muster.

Pasco seemed unconvinced. "But just good friends? Is that still it?"

Steve remembered those words. He had used them to fend off Pasco's probing a couple of weeks ago. That was when Pasco had met Eva for the first time. He had insisted that Steve bring her round for supper to thank her for dishing the dirt on Penpol that had helped him win the election. Tamsin had laid on a Cornish supper, as she called it – not, astonishingly, pasties, but baked red mullet with local new potatoes. Eva had been a little tense at first and had said little, but after a glass or two of wine, and picking up on the banter between the others at the table, she had relaxed and joined in the laughter. What really proved to be the icebreaker was Pasco telling her that he had once played rugby against a Romanian team. Eva admitted that she knew that rugby was played in her country but she had no idea about the game. Pasco saw that as an opportunity to enlighten her. With the aid of various kitchen utensils and empty wine glasses, and an apple to represent the ball, he took her through the basics. Tamsin protested on Eva's behalf, but Eva won Pasco's heart by insisting with a smile that she didn't mind and it was really interesting. Tamsin gave up at that point and retreated to the kitchen with the used plates Pasco had not commandeered as visual aids. Steve moved to help her, but before he joined her in the kitchen he had time to see Pasco explaining the offside law to Eva with the help of two bread rolls,

In the kitchen, Tamsin had taken a plate from him and then poked him in the chest with a warning finger. "She's lovely, Steve. Make sure you hang on to her!"

Hang on to her. If only it was that simple.

"Yes, Pasco, just good friends," he reiterated now.

Pasco looked doubtful. "Nothing more?"

"No." Steve looked away from Pasco's scrutiny.

"Why not?"

Coming from anyone else, Steve would have been irritated by this prying into his private life, but he knew that Pasco did not deal in evasions and half-truths. He sighed and tried to explain. "It's difficult. I don't know if I'm ready for another relationship; not yet."

"When, then? Christmas? Next year? Sometime never?"

Steve was floundering. "And it's not just me. Eva has a child."

"I know, she told me; showed me a picture. Lovely little girl."

"Quite. So she will soon need to be with Anya now that she's growing up."

"So? Is that a problem?" Pasco clearly didn't think so.

Steve looked at him in astonishment. "In Romania?"

Pasco shrugged. "Not necessarily." He looked hard at Steve. "Have you thought of that?"

Steve found it hard to admit, even to himself, that his thoughts had sometimes wandered, half formed, in such speculative and challenging directions, and he really didn't feel ready to articulate them to Pasco in a beer garden. "We'll see," he said, and drained his pint as a conclusion to that particular conversation. "Anyway, how was the first council meeting?"

Pasco accepted the change of direction. "Could have been worse. I kept my head down to start with but people were friendly enough. Funny thing is, I knew one or two of them."

Steve smiled. "Let me guess. From your rugby days?"

"Right on," Pasco agreed cheerily.

"So what will you be involved with?"

"I'm on the housing committee. I pushed for it."

"That's good. Where you wanted to be."

"And you know what?"

"What?"

"Who do you think the chairman is?"

"Wee Willie Walton?" Steve guessed.

"None other," Pasco chuckled. "I introduced myself."

"How did that go down?"

"He was a bit wary. Like he'd been warned about me."

"Probably by Giles. All that Penpol business," Steve suggested.

"That's what I reckoned," Pasco agreed. "But anyway, he congratulated me on my election, shook my hand and said he looked forward to having me on the housing committee. Those were his words." He laughed. "But talk about gritted teeth."

"I can imagine."

Pasco was reliving the moment now. "Before I let go of his hand, I said something."

"What was that?" Steve demanded.

"I said – casual, like – 'By the way, I believe we have a mutual friend.'

"'Who's that?' he says.

"'Alice Gilbert,' I say. 'Perhaps you can give her my regards, as they tell me you see a lot of her.'"

Steve clapped his hands. "Brilliant, Pasco."

"Then I let go of his hand and, just to make sure he'd got the point—"

Steve beat him to it. "You winked!"

"And walked away, but just took a quick look back and he was staring after me with his mouth open like a bloody goldfish."

They both laughed loud and long at that; so much so that they drew curious glances from the picnic tables.

Steve stood up and held out a hand for Pasco's empty glass. "My shout, Pasco. You've earned it."

THIRTY-FOUR

The communication was familiar but its arrival was unexpected. Steve had not been pursued by Sausage & Mash for several months now. He didn't think that he had failed to maintain the required payments. Surely they were not going to try to squeeze any more maintenance out of him? Linda was hardly in danger of the workhouse.

Nervously, he carried the brown envelope across to the table where he had been gulping a quick cup of tea when he'd heard the postman stuffing mail through the letter box. He thought gloomily that he had more than enough to contend with given what was going on at work, without this added distraction. He was due to meet Wilberforce after lunch and he still had a few loose ends to tie up before then. This was not shaping up to be a good day. Sighing, he slid the marmalade knife under the envelope flap and withdrew the contents. At least it was only a single sheet this time. He read it twice to ensure that his eyes were not deceiving him. They were not. He was being informed that, due to changing domestic circumstances and Hannah's approaching majority, Ms Robertson (he had almost forgotten Linda's maiden name) had expressed her wish to dispose of their jointly owned property and to divide the proceeds of the sale equitably when all outstanding charges and fees had been disbursed. Steve nearly choked on his tea. Interpreting the mumbo jumbo, he concluded that Linda wanted to sell the house and he would get half of what was left when the mortgage was cleared. He had never imagined that she would want to sell up but he was certainly not going to argue over it.

Suddenly the day seemed to have got much better. He felt positively cheerful, and even whistled jauntily as he washed up his cup. Whilst he did not exactly skip to the car, anyone watching him would certainly have testified that he had a spring in his step.

"You look pleased with yourself," Taff observed as he sat down opposite Steve with a plate piled high with Trengrouse's finest chicken curry.

"Do I? Must be the thought of the holidays. Only two days to go."

"And what's with the suit?" Taff inquired through a mouthful of curry. "Funeral?"

Steve smiled at him. "Nothing so lively. County Hall."

"Ah, yes. I hear they think the sun shines out of your arse up there."

Steve laughed. "You have a way with words, Taff."

"All to do with your foreign lot, is it?"

"As I say, Taff, a way with words."

Taff wolfed down more of his curry and then looked up at Steve thoughtfully. "I'll tell you something, Steve."

"What's that?"

"I was pleased to hear you're staying with us." Taff focused again on his curry.

Steve was pleasantly surprised by this unexpected display of approbation. "Thank you, Taff."

Taff had now almost completed the demolition of his lunch. He slurped down the last mouthful and stood up clutching his empty plate. He looked down at Steve. "So you'll keep Tuesday evenings free, then?"

"What?" Steve asked blankly.

"Tuesday evening. Rugby training. Remember?"

Steve winced. "I do. The shoulder is still sore. I'm not sure I can—"

Taff brushed aside the hesitation. "Not fit. That was the problem. We can sort that."

"We can?" Steve asked nervously.

Taff sat down again and fixed Steve with gimlet eyes. "This is what you do, boyo, in the holidays." He raised one hand and counted off with a finger from the other. "Start the day with a run – say, five K; no need to overdo it. Follow that with weights – say, an hour; and in the afternoon, a couple of hours on the bike." He stood up again. "That should do it."

Steve stared at Taff in open-mouthed shock and then slowly realised Taff was trying hard to suppress laughter. Steve grinned at him. "Taff, you bugger. You had me going there."

"You should have seen your face, boy." Pleased with his performance, Taff made to carry his plate back to a trolley, but found time for one more piece of advice for Steve. "Well, if you can't manage that, at least buy yourself a new pair of boots."

Steve was still smiling at that when Bill Rogers flopped down on the bench opposite him. "It's all fixed for tomorrow, then?" He asked anxiously.

"Yes," Steve assured him. "I checked with Ricardo yesterday. He's reserved the function room for us and will lay on refreshments."

"Good. If you let me have the bill for that, I can settle it out of the FE discretionary fund. A justifiable expense, I'm sure." Bill didn't look entirely convinced that that was the case.

Steve hastened to bolster his resolve. "Absolutely. A chance to give your department the recognition it deserves, and a fitting tribute to the work you've put in over the years, Bill." He hoped he had not gone too far over the top, but Bill seemed comfortable with the accolade.

"And you're quite sure Wilberforce will be there?"

"Yes. He's agreed to present the certificates. I'm seeing him this afternoon to finalise the arrangements." Steve was giving Bill an edited version of the purpose of his meeting with Wilberforce, which was primarily to work on the implementation, county-wide, of his teaching app.

Bill seemed relieved. "You know, Steve, I have to admit, it is pleasing to be appreciated for all the work one has put in over the years."

"Of course, Bill. Long overdue."

"And something else: I can enjoy my retirement knowing that I have passed on to you a well-oiled machine."

"Yes. That is a great comfort to me," Steve said solemnly. "And it is even more comforting to know that if I have any problems I can always pick up the phone for your advice." He hoped that sounded sufficiently humble, but was disconcerted to see Bill frown slightly at the suggestion.

"Of course, if I can help. But to be perfectly frank with you, I'm going to have a lot on my plate in the next few months."

Steve had wondered how long it would be before Bill invoked his overloaded platter. "Really?" he inquired innocently.

Bill sighed. "Betty has big plans for the garden, and word is, the golf club want me on the committee." He shrugged apologetically. "You know me, Steve. I find it hard to say no."

"Well, don't let them burden you too much," Steve murmured solicitously. "Leave time for yourself."

Bill stood and nodded. "I'll try, but..." He shrugged his shoulders in resigned nobility and paused for a moment, contemplating a future of altruistic sacrifice.

Steve brought him back to earth. "So we'll see you tomorrow evening, Bill?"

Martin Wilberforce, Steve noticed, always looked much more relaxed in his office than he had during their first meeting in the Trengrouse classroom. They were on first-name terms now, at Martin's insistence, and looking at him now, leaning back in his swivel chair with tie loosened and jacket discarded, Steve felt almost at ease. Almost. He could not entirely forget that his destiny, if that was not putting it too dramatically, rested on Martin's patronage.

Martin finished polishing his wire spectacles and restored his chair to equilibrium. He pointed to a pile of scrolls on his desk. "I had these made up for the presentation. I hope I've got all the names right."

Steve laughed. "I'm sure you have." He picked up a scroll, unfurled it and studied it for a moment. "This is brilliant. They'll be so proud to get these."

"Good." Martin had now picked up a pen drive. He held it up for Steve to see. "This is really first class, Steve. I've run it past several colleagues and we are all in agreement: terrific potential; groundbreaking."

Steve tried not to smile too broadly. "Thank you."

Martin leaned forward with his elbows on his desk and his eyes fixed on Steve. "I'll need you to set up an induction day for the other teachers in the county who'll be using your programme. Find a date before the start of next term. Let me have costing details. We can set it up here." These instructions were rattled out at speed. When Martin had the wind in his sails, Steve had learned to remain still until the breeze dropped.

"Right," he managed, before he sensed the wind picking up again.

"There is scope for this beyond Cornwall. I have presumed to contact my counterparts in other authorities and they want to come aboard. As you probably know, the government's track record in this area is not impressive but now they want to be seen to be reaching out to minorities and outliers." Martin paused briefly and smiled wryly. "There is an election not too far away. So funds are suddenly available. We are flavour of the month, Steve. How does that feel?"

"Unusual," Steve suggested.

Martin laughed. "Indeed. So it is imperative that we make your programme the benchmark. Focus our resources on it. Blow the trumpet loudly."

Steve felt disorientated by the talk of benchmarks and focusing and blowing trumpets, but hoped he looked thoughtful rather than confused. "I see," he mumbled.

"But we have a problem."

Now Steve was alarmed. "A problem?" he ventured.

Martin twirled his glasses. "It's an outreach issue."

"Ah," Steve managed.

"It's the interface that worries me, to be frank with you."

"That could be a worry," Steve agreed, hoping he would not be asked to elaborate.

Martin leaned forward intently. "How do we touch base with the potential service users?" Fortunately, he did not wait for Steve's response. "We can put the word out on social media, of course, as well as pitching on the usual print and broadcast platforms, but will that reach the target end users?"

Steve thought he had more or less grasped the point. "I agree it's a concern. Some of the people we need to recruit are unlikely to have much exposure to conventional communication channels."

Martin smacked his hand on his desk. "Exactly. There are issues of cultural assimilation to address."

"And language barriers," Steve added more prosaically.

"Indeed. We really need to be proactive in the workplace. Sometimes there is no substitute for interpersonal referencing."

Steve felt his grasp on the conversation loosening. "So how—"

He was grateful that Martin did not allow him to finish a sentence which had no specific destination. "We need an outreach worker. Someone to carry the message to the migrant labour force in the field, so to speak."

"Quite literally in most cases," Steve added.

"Indeed. Someone who can identify with them, and who ideally has some linguistic skills." Martin paused and shook his head. "Not an easy person to find."

Steve was familiar with the expression 'light-bulb moment' but could not recall experiencing one. Until now. He was aware that he must be careful not to rush into too eager a proposition, so he feigned thoughtful reflection before speaking. "Actually, Martin, there is someone who might fill the bill." Then, to make the prize more elusive, he added, "If she'll be interested."

Martin sat up straight. "Who?"

Steve was careful in picking his words. "She came to the language class at the start but it was clear she was far too advanced for it. I gather she studied English literature at university in Bucharest intending to teach, but family difficulties meant she had to abandon that and find work, any work, to support them." He congratulated himself that he had told no lies in this brief résumé of Eva's recent life. "You know how it is – academic qualifications don't put food on the table everywhere. A sad waste."

"But do you think she might be interested?"

"Well, I would have to discuss it with her, of course, but she has been helping me with the class, on a strictly voluntary basis, and there is no doubt that she has real flair as a teacher and bonds well with the students. Being able to speak many of their native languages and knowing from experience what their working conditions are like gives her a unique perspective, I think."

Martin was hooked. "She sounds just the sort of person we need on board. Do you think you can persuade her?"

Steve frowned. "I am not sure what her plans are but I could certainly put it to her."

"The funding is there. We can run to an outreach worker and the pay is not unreasonable; more remunerative than field work, I would guess."

Steve was thinking ahead. "Actually, Martin, you could talk to her yourself. She will be at the awards ceremony tomorrow – perhaps you could find time for an informal chat?"

"Excellent. If she seems suitable we could sort out the paperwork later."

"Fine. I'll tell her."

Martin nodded at that, but then paused. "There is one possible hitch."

Steve tried to sound casual. "Oh? What?"

"As an outreach worker, she would obviously need to be mobile. She could use one of our vans, but of course she needs to be able to drive."

Steve tried to conceal a smile. "I happen to know that she drives."

"Good." Now Martin found a smile. "And of course we'll have to run a CRB check." His smile broadened. "But I don't imagine she has been in any trouble with the police?"

"I don't imagine so!" Steve laughed at the mere suggestion.

Martin began gathering papers together on his desk, signalling an end to the meeting. He held up a file. "I like the look of the new evening-class courses – a much broader spectrum." He flicked through a few pages and then looked thoughtfully at Steve. "I thought I might enrol on one of them."

Steve tried not to sound nervous. "Really? Let me guess – Buddhist philosophy?"

"I was thinking more of kick-boxing."

Steve stared at Martin in amazement and then realised that he was giggling. He had to accept that, for the second time that afternoon, he was being taken for a ride.

THIRTY-FIVE

Steve would meet Eva later at the coffee shop. He had texted her suggesting that they meet before tomorrow's party. He had not mentioned any details of his meeting with Martin but had told her that something important had come up that they needed to discuss. She had replied that she would be there, but couldn't he give her a clue as to what this important matter was? He had responded with 'Wait and see' and three exclamation marks.

Glancing at his watch, Steve calculated that he had an hour to spare before meeting Eva. He had eaten enough of the lunchtime curry to keep hunger at bay, and the imminent prospect of buckets of coffee deterred him from brewing his usual after-school pot of builder's. He reluctantly accepted that he had no excuse to delay a bout of housework. Hannah would be down at the weekend and he would need to move out of his bedroom and renew his acquaintance with the cell, and much as he was looking forward to seeing his daughter again, he was not relishing the prospect of nocturnal claustrophobia. Needs must, he told himself as he plodded upstairs and rummaged around to find clean sheets for the bed in the box room. The effort of making the bed made him think that perhaps Taff had been right to question his fitness. After ten minutes of kneeling and stretching and crawling and cursing he collapsed on the inexpertly made bed, panting and sweating. As he slowly regained some control over his breathing he accepted that a pot of tea might now be very welcome. He was about to lever himself off the bed when he was distracted by a burst of 'I Do Like to Be Beside the Seaside' emanating from his trouser pocket. He fumbled for his phone and for a moment failed to recognise the caller's number. Then it came to him: his old London landline. Why would Hannah be using that? Had she lost her mobile?

"Hannah?" he said, still panting a little.

There was a pause. "No. Not Hannah."

Steve had not heard that voice for nearly a year but it was unmistakable. "Linda." He tried to compose his thoughts but fell back on polite banality. "How are you?"

"I'm well. And you?"

"Yes, fine. Thank you."

There was a pause before Linda continued. "Good. But you sound a bit breathless."

Steve found himself in once-familiar explanatory and apologetic territory. "It's nothing; just a spot of housework." Even as he uttered the words he could imagine Linda's scepticism.

She gave a dry laugh. "Really?" Then her tone changed to the brisk formality he recognised from their last exchanges before their separation. "You got the letter from the solicitors?"

"About the house? Yes."

"I presume that you have no objections?"

"No, though I must say I was a bit surprised."

"Things change, Steve. Time moves on."

"Of course," he agreed hastily.

"Anyway, this is just to let you know I have put it on the market. The estate agent expects a quick sale at the asking price: nearly half a million."

Steve sat down on the bed again in shock. If he had thought about it at all he knew London house prices had soared, but he would never have guessed to those heights.

"Are you still there?" Linda sounded impatient rather than concerned.

"Er, yes, sorry."

"So that price is acceptable to you? The solicitors need to know."

Steve tried to sound unimpressed. "Sounds reasonable."

"Good. I need to hurry things along."

He remembered that she was good at that. "So where will—"

"I'm moving out of London; the company are expanding. They're going multinational and want me to open a new office."

"Really? Somewhere exotic, I hope."

"Cardiff," she said, in a tone which dared him to mock.

"Ah." He felt that was safe enough.

"I've put in an offer on a flat there."

"Oh."

There was a long silence and Steve began to wonder if he should check that the call was still live.

"Hannah will tell you, anyway." Linda eventually broke the silence. "Things didn't work out with Jason."

"I'm sorry," said Steve reflexively.

"Are you?" She paused as if considering the sentiment. When she spoke again her tone was softer. "I think you really are, Steve. That's generous of you."

"I hope it works for you, Linda. Cardiff, a fresh start and all that."

"I'm sure it will." Her tone had regained its confidence. "Hannah tells me you have really taken to the Cornish life."

Steve laughed; the awkwardness gone. "It has its points."

"Good." Linda reverted to business. "I'll let you know when the sale goes through. The solicitors will sort out the financial details."

"Right." Steve thought that for once he might look forward to a communication from Sausage & Mash.

"I'll let you have my new address."

"Thank you," Steve replied, but he was unsure what use he might make of it.

"Hannah will no doubt keep us in touch. Exeter is halfway between Cornwall and Cardiff."

"Of course."

"She will be our go-between, then." There was a pause. "Goodbye, Steve."

The line went dead. Steve looked at the blank screen of his phone and Linda's words echoed in his mind. He wondered if she had used that term deliberately: a go-between. She, like many, was probably familiar with the first few words of the novel of that name: 'The past is a foreign country.' As Steve eased himself out of the box room he could certainly identify with that.

"You come any time. We give you good scrub."

"Full polish. No charge."

The two Latvians beamed at Steve. They looked as if they had recently taken advantage of their own facilities, with hair dampened down slickly and their work dungarees replaced by pressed jeans and dazzling fluorescent shirts. They each clutched their newly acquired scroll in one hand and a generous glass of red wine in the other.

Steve thanked them for their kind offer. Other members of the class had made a point of coming up to him in the course of the evening to proffer thanks, and some had even handed him small gifts. He was genuinely touched. He knew life was not easy for most of them but they were determined to make the most of what it had to offer. He looked around the room and smiled at the obvious enjoyment of the partygoers. Ricardo had done them proud and Steve watched him, resplendent in dinner jacket and bow tie, directing two waitresses towards glasses that needed refilling or plates replenishing. He had briefly explained to Steve that he was no longer just deputy manager, but full manager. His recent and rapid promotion was a consequence of the abrupt departure of his predecessor following, as far as Steve could make out from Ricardo's explanation, an unfortunate incident in the gents' urinals. One of the waitresses topped up Bill Rogers' glass, and he made only a half-hearted effort to deter her. He seemed to be revelling in the occasion. Steve had made a short, tactful speech wishing Bill a happy retirement and paying fulsome tribute to his outstanding work in presiding over the FE Department for so many years. Bill had nodded happily in endorsement of these plaudits, but thankfully Steve had managed to explain to him that, sadly, time would not afford him the opportunity to make a speech in reply. If Bill had been disappointed about that he seemed to have overcome it with the help of several compensatory glasses of the same vintage Rioja Ricardo had presented to Steve on the occasion of Martin Wilberforce's visit to the class. That seemed a long time ago now; so much had changed. Even Wilberforce had become Martin.

With that thought, Steve glanced again at the far corner of the room where Martin and Eva sat in comparative isolation. He tried not to let his curiosity show. Over coffee last night he had briefed her on how much he had told Martin about her. "Just as much as he needs to know," was how he had put it. He'd assured her that he had told no lies and gone into no unnecessary details. She'd smiled rather nervously and then asked if he had said anything about 'them'. Through tact or cowardice, Steve had played a straight bat to that question. "Just that we are friends and, more recently, colleagues." Eva had flashed him a quizzical smile and seemed about to say more, but in the end she'd just nodded as if to indicate that she accepted his description of their relationship.

Steve was distracted from that memory by the looming figure of Ivan, his bulk constrained by the incongruous formality of the club doorman's livery he had put on for the ceremony. Barely reaching his shoulder, Maria stood alongside him, her hand clutched in his. Steve smiled at them; he had been aware for some time of their strengthening bond.

Maria spoke first. "We thank you. For the lessons, for sure." Her English had improved considerably but now she paused, seeking the right words. "And we thank you for us." She looked at Ivan for support and he beamed at Steve.

Steve was not expecting that. "Oh. Thank you. I am happy for you. Both of you."

"I will go to Lisbon." Ivan said this boldly and looked hard at Steve, as if challenging him to deny it.

Steve spoke quickly in reassurance. "Really? I believe it's a very interesting city."

Ivan seemed confused by this response, but Maria, with a nervous giggle, sought to explain. "Ivan will meet my family."

Ivan nodded. "Yes. We will tell them."

Steve was about to ask what the family would be told, but as he looked at Maria and Ivan, so obviously adoring of each other, he knew that the question was unnecessary.

Maria confirmed his assumption. "Then, next year, we will be married."

"Yes," Ivan agreed. "Work hard now; save money."

Steve reacted instinctively. "Congratulations to you both. I'm very happy for you." He thrust out a hand to Ivan, who released Maria's briefly to crush Steve's. Hiding a wince, Steve managed a more decorous handshake with Maria.

"We will have the wedding party here. Ricardo says he will give us a good price."

Steve smiled. "I am sure he will."

"And you will come?" Maria looked hopefully at him.

"Of course. It would be a great pleasure."

Maria smiled widely at that, and Ivan clapped Steve heartily on his still-twinging shoulder. Then he led Maria away, but she glanced back at Steve and gave a small wave of farewell. Steve, trying to ignore his smarting shoulder, watched them go with real affection. You would have needed a heart of stone not to be moved by their optimism; their hope for a future which was bound to be challenging. But – and Steve hoped he was not being mawkish – they had each other. Maybe that would be enough. He hoped so.

He was still smiling when Martin came alongside. He was sifting through papers in his briefcase and, after peering at several, he found what he was looking for. He handed it to Steve. "She asked me to run it past you before she signs; make sure you're happy with it."

Steve had to force his brain to catch up. "She is interested, then?"

"Yes. I am glad to say she is. Just the person we were looking for. Ticks all the boxes."

Steve tried to look ondifferent. "I thought she might suit." He glanced at the form Martin had handed him. "I'll try to find some time to go through this with her."

"If you would. Just a standard contract, really; terms and conditions and so on. For a year initially, but if I'm right about her we shouldn't have a problem extending it."

"Right." Steve thought it prudent to seem detached. "If she signs up I'll get this back to you."

"Good. Hopefully you can persuade her."

Steve smiled. "I'll do my best."

Martin looked around the room. People had begun to drift away and the waitresses were clearing the tables. "First-class evening, Steve. The first of many such occasions, I hope."

"Thank you. And thank you especially for agreeing to present the certificates."

"Least I could do after all your hard work." Martin snapped his briefcase shut. "Must be going." He gestured to the contract Steve was holding. "Look forward to getting that back, and then we can sort out all the other stuff before next term."

Steve could sense his holiday shrinking, but managed to flap Martin a cheerful goodbye with Eva's contract. He looked for her now and saw that she was talking with Luka and Elena. They were amongst the last to leave, and as Steve walked over to them he could see Luka gesturing towards the adjacent public bar from which drifted the unmistakable sounds of a football match on the big screen.

"Only half an hour, Eva. It is a big game."

Elena made a face at him. "It is too long."

Eva shrugged. "It doesn't matter, Elena. I can wait." She noticed Steve's approach and smiled in welcome.

"It's OK, Luka. I can drive Eva home." Then he remembered his manners. "And you too, Elena, if you want."

"Thank you, but I will stay." Elena scowled at Luka. "Otherwise he will drink too much."

Protesting his sobriety, Luka headed off to the public bar with Elena trailing after him in glum resignation.

Steve laughed as he watched them go and then turned to Eva and held up the form Martin had given him. "We have important matters to discuss, I think."

"I liked him, this Martin. He is clever but he is not arrogant. He was easy to talk to."

"Yes," Steve agreed. "I was a bit suspicious of him at first but—"

Before he could finish, Eva laughed. "Yes, I expect you were, Steve."

Steve took his eyes off the road briefly to look at Eva, who smiled teasingly at him. "What you were saying back there. Am I? Suspicious of people?"

"Perhaps a little bit. It's not a fault. You are just careful; sensible."

Steve groaned. "Sensible. What a depressing word."

"Someone has to be."

"Linda hoped I would be more exciting, I think. Spontaneous; dynamic; that sort of thing. Watch it, you stupid bugger!" This expletive exploded suddenly as an impatient tailgater attempted to overtake them on a blind corner, but thought better of it and hung back. Steve regained his calm. "Sorry about that."

Eva laughed and applauded. "You see. Spontaneous."

"It's easier in a car, isn't it? It gives you anonymity. Sometimes you see very respectable-looking drivers mouthing furious obscenities at some wayward motorist."

Eva thought about that. "Perhaps they are showing their true nature."

"So that outburst just then was my true nature, was it?"

"It shows you can let go; just react."

"You sound like Hannah. She told me that. Don't question everything; don't try to rationalise every emotion; just go with the flow." He remembered what had prompted that. "Mind you, she was talking about art."

"Art and life. Perhaps they are not so different."

There was a long silence, and not just because Steve had slowed down to allow the irritating car following them to overtake. As he watched its tail lights disappear he found the courage to risk all. "Eva. One day I would like to go to Romania to meet Anya and your mother." He said it with a dry mouth and waited for her response. He risked a sideways glance and felt he should say more, but all he managed was, "If that's all right with you, of course."

It seemed an eternity before she reacted, and then he felt her hand rest gently just above his knee before imparting a comforting pat. He managed to concentrate on negotiating a roundabout, but found it hard to focus on that when Eva burst out laughing. He turned his head quickly and saw that she was grinning at him broadly. "Of course I don't mind, Steve. It would be wonderful."

Steve relaxed happily and offered silent thanks to Ivan and Maria.

THIRTY-SIX

Any thought that entered your head, any emotion you experienced, any words you uttered, it was a given that the Bard had got there before you. As Steve sat in the backyard snatching a quick tea break he could hardly believe that the summer holidays were slipping away so quickly, and this reflection brought to memory the sonnet in which Shakespeare warns that summer's lease hath all too short a date. That in turn reminded Steve, more prosaically, that his lease on the cottage would soon be due for renewal. However, he had other plans. As Linda had predicted, the sale of the London house had gone through quickly and a cheque had arrived from Sausage & Mash that very morning. Steve calculated that, with the balance of the sale money topped up by a small mortgage (which he could now afford on his increased salary), he could afford to buy a house. The prospect made him nervous but Hannah had bolstered his confidence when he had spoken tentatively to her of his plans. She'd told him it made complete sense: his future was clearly in Cornwall now, so why pay through the nose for a "crap gaff", as she put it so eloquently, when he could afford to buy his own house? She'd reassured him that, as it would not be a second home, he need have no guilt on that front. He marvelled at the ease with which young people went straight for the jugular when confronted with the complexities of life. But he had to admit she was right: it did make sense. He told himself he would visit the estate agent as soon as he could find the time.

Finding time was a problem. Any thought of a summer holiday sitting in the sun and recharging his batteries had long been abandoned. His days were taken up with preparation for the launch of the new course. He had already spent a couple of days at County Hall with Martin working on the details. Eva had been invited to the first meeting and her outreach role clarified. Steve had been apprehensive that she might be too nervous to contribute much, but after some initial wariness she had played a full part in the deliberations. Indeed, she had been confident enough to unpick some of Martin's plans, pointing out that his strategy for advertising the course needed a rethink. It would be a waste of money, she argued, to advertise in the local press or on local radio, as in her experience their potential students neither read one nor listened to the other. The money would be better spent putting flyers in such diverse places as supermarkets with specialist food sections, benefit offices, and charity shops. They would need to be eye-catching, to the point, and translated into several of their target languages. She offered to do the translations, and stressed the importance of an easily accessible multi-language website, as it was through their phones that these people could be reached. Martin had listened intently to what Eva had to say, turning only occasionally to Steve to nod his approval of her suggestions. Steve had been equally impressed, and delighted that Eva now had an opportunity to use the talents she had needed to suppress for so long. As they drove back from the meeting he had congratulated her on her presentation and assured her that Martin had been impressed. Eva had smiled and remarked that she hoped Steve had been equally impressed because she had learnt from her contract that he would be her 'line manager'. Steve laughed; he had been teaching long enough to know that educational bureaucracy had, bizarrely, adopted the language of Ford's of Dagenham. "Do you think you will be able to manage me, Steve?" she had asked him with a giggle and an exaggerated fluttering of her eyes.

Steve smiled at that memory as he finished his tea. Eva was now back in Romania. Once she had signed her contract she had left her job with Penpol. When Steve had asked if she had to give them notice she had laughed and reminded him that she was on a zero-hours contract. The night before she left Steve had taken her to sample a night of Cornish magic in a former Methodist chapel. The unlikely venue was where Hannah worked; Selwyn had fixed them both up with evening work at The Excalibar. He was a washer-up and Hannah – dressed, to her embarrassment, as a Demelza-style serving wench – waited on the bench-seated punters at long wooden tables which were supposed to provide some vague and uncertain historical ambience. With no shortage of unemployed artists in Cornwall, The Excalibar's owner, Georgio, a Greek Cypriot kebab magnate, had enterprisingly commissioned several to paint garish murals on the white chapel walls so that diners were overlooked by eyepatch-clad pirates, sooty tin miners, and smugglers with kegs of brandy on their backs. These colourful figures looked down on the patrons as they were served what Georgio decreed to be a true Cornish feast; so Hannah and her colleagues started the meal by serving a cocktail pasty (two words Steve had never thought could be found together) followed by an indeterminate gruel and then a leg of chicken in a basket with chips whose Cornish association was hard to fathom.

The final carbohydrate load came in the shape of saffron buns and clotted cream; certainly of sound Cornish provenance but uneasy companions. The food was washed down with flagons of Cornish mead; a drink with a deceptively anodyne sweetness that masked a powerful alcoholic thump. However, it relaxed the holidaymakers' inhibitions so that, by the end of the meal, many were singing along boisterously to the eclectic music that had been played throughout. Steve and Eva put all reservations to one side and joined the Glee Club, so that, with the aid of Georgio's thoughtfully provided lyric sheets, they could warble along to snatches of Gilbert and Sullivan's The Pirates of Penzance as well as 'Goin' Up Camborne Hill', and of course avow heartily that twenty thousand Cornish men would know the reason why.

Eva had handed Hannah her phone and persuaded her to take a photo of her and Steve together. Hannah had threatened to pour soup down Steve's neck if he attempted to take a picture of her in her Demelza dress, but happily agreed to Eva's request. "Come on, Dad, put your arm round her," she had insisted. Eva seemed happy with the resultant picture when she showed it to Steve. She'd joked that her mother and Anya would now know what to expect at Christmas, and she would tell them that they were looking at her manager.

"There's still some in the pot if you're thirsty." Steve directed this at Hannah, who had just returned from her afternoon's surfing at the beach. She had changed out of the new wetsuit Steve had treated her to in celebration of her A Level grades, and had wrapped a towel round her after a sand-sluicing shower.

She drained the teapot of its residual brew and carried her cup out to the backyard to sit on the spare deckchair which, with its partner, had replaced their defunct predecessor. "Still working, Dad?" She gestured at the open laptop.

"I've got to finish the new prospectus for the evening classes. On top of everything else," Steve sighed.

"Not looked at any houses yet?"

"I must get round to that. Tomorrow. Definitely."

Hannah smiled. "I'll believe you." She relaxed back in her chair and sipped at her tea.

Steve concentrated on his laptop. From outside came the noise of children playing, dogs barking, and from somewhere music blasted out which the whole street could unfortunately share. The tantalising aroma of grilling steak indicated an early barbecue supper for one of the families who had surged into the second homes as the schools broke up. Steve had acclimatised by now to the crowds, noise and bustle of high summer in Cornwall. At least he didn't have to face daily gridlock on the roads, and by the time the new term started the bucket-and-spade brigade would have retreated. Consoled by that thought, he closed his laptop and looked across at Hannah, who had closed her eyes against the still-warm sun. She looked beautiful, he thought. The days on the beach had deepened her tan and toned her body. He wondered if in years to come she would look back on this as her golden summer; carefree and hopeful. Life was good; the future exciting. He supposed he must have felt like that at her age. He tried to remember.

She seemed to have sensed his appraisal. She opened her eyes and looked at him quizzically. "What are you thinking, Dad?"

Steve always found that an impossible question to answer, but he tried. "Youth."

Hannah sat up and looked hard at him. "What?"

Steve hesitated. "Well, since you ask, I was looking at you dozing there and tying to remember what it was like to be your age. To be to be carefree; young and easy. "

Hannah considered this. "Is that what I am? Young and easy?"

Steve laughed. "I think I'm talking about a golden time when life can just be enjoyed; when you're young and without cares."

"'Enjoy it while you can; before it all gets complicated and messy.' Is that it?"

"I think it probably is."

Hannah pondered this. She looked up at the sun through narrowed eyes. "I know this is a bit of an unreal time. It can't last. Soon it will be back to studying; then looking for a job and God knows what else." She turned and smiled at Steve. "But I won't forget this summer; I know that."

"Good. Carpe diem, eh?"

"And you don't need to translate that for me, Mr Teacher Man!"

Steve raised a hand in innocent protest.

Hannah grew serious. "It's been a good summer for you too, hasn't it? The new job; buying a house, perhaps; Pasco on the council." Then she paused. "And, of course, Eva." She kept her focus on Steve. "Especially Eva."

Steve glanced away. He knew Hannah and Eva had got on well in the brief time they had known each other, but so far his daughter had not asked any questions about their relationship. He had been grateful for that because he was still uncertain of how to respond. "It's early days," he muttered evasively.

"Really, Dad, you are hopeless!" Hannah exclaimed. "She is such a lovely person and she clearly adores you."

"Does she?" His inquiry was genuine.

"Of course she does," Hannah said in exasperation. "Everyone can see it except you." She sat back as if to rest her case.

Steve felt there was nothing for him to say. He fiddled awkwardly with his laptop.

Hannah pushed herself up out of the deckchair and tightened the towel around her. She looked down at Steve. "The young and easy have to go to work now. Demelza calls."

Steve smiled up at her as she made for the kitchen, but she had not finished with him yet.

"Take your own advice, Dad."

"What's that?"

"Carpe diem," she said as she closed the kitchen door.

Steve had decided against the beer garden, although it was a warm and sunny morning. He needed a quiet space to look through the property details he had just collected from the estate agent. The interior of the pub was cool and quiet, in contrast to the shrieks of children rampaging in the garden as their parents slurped their drinks. Sam had looked harassed when he pulled Steve a pint, and when asked how things were going had replied, "Bloody awful", although when he'd opened the till to find change Steve noticed it was bulging with many notes of large denomination. Lowering his voice to a whisper, Sam had told Steve that he was looking forward to the wind and drizzle of November. Before then, he explained, at least he could relax a bit when August was out of the way and the noisy family groups made way for what he called "the aperitif people"; elderly couples who came to the bar in the early evening for a gin and tonic or a small dry sherry and then retired to their holiday lets to doze in front of the television.

Steve was still smiling at that as he carried his drink across to an empty table. He began leafing through the property details. The estate agent had initially greeted him nervously, anticipating a disgruntled tenant's request for urgent repairs or improvements, but once it became clear that Steve was a potential purchaser his manner changed. Uriah Heep would have seemed arrogant in comparison. He assured Steve that he would be unflagging in his efforts to find a property within his price range that would meet all his requirements; the problem was that Steve had no clear idea of what those were. The only stipulation he had made was that he wanted a view of the sea. That seemed reasonable. If you lived on a narrow sea-girt peninsula, why would you not want that? Take away the sea from Cornwall and there was not much left. The agent had vowed to "factor that in" to his selection of properties, but as Steve flicked through the pile in front of him it soon became clear that his one proviso would be hard to accommodate. The houses that had sea views were mostly on newly built private estates and mostly bungalows. Steve was not sure he was ready for a bungalow yet, and felt that the suburban comforts on offer were more redolent of the Home Counties than the Celtic fringes, and a sea view was not sufficient compensation for that. He also had an uneasy feeling that some of these properties had been spawned by Penpol Investments. The "character properties", as the agent had fawningly described them, were certainly more in harmony with the landscape but did not come without problems. Steve would not have described himself as a cynic but had lived long enough in the world to be wary of estate agent doublespeak. 'Deceptively spacious' meant small and 'some updating needed' was basically telling you the house was falling down. That ruled out most of the available 'houses of character', and the one that looked promising initially afforded only a 'sea glimpse'. Steve knew that would mean you could only catch a distant view of the ocean by standing on a stepladder in the loft. Dispiritedly, he pushed the estate agent's bumf to one side and sipped gloomily at his beer. Nothing, it seemed, was simple.

"Sorry I'm late; been working." Pasco exhaled deeply and slumped down on his chair before drinking noisily and deeply from his glass.

"Thirsty work by the look of it," Steve suggested.

"That's better." Pasco wiped a hand across his lips and sat back contentedly. He twanged the straps on his white overalls. "Catching up. The boy I took on is all right but he's a bit slow."

"Something you've never been."

Pasco laughed. "Well, council's in summer recess now so I can crack on a bit."

"How's it been going?" Steve had been too involved with his own work to have caught up with Pasco recently.

"I'm getting the hang of it." Pasco looked around to make sure no one was in earshot, then spoke softly. "Nothing finalised yet but it looks as if we're getting more council housing in the town."

"That's great. Where?"

"The old spoil heaps at the mine. Going to flatten them, clear the site and put up twenty homes."

"Is that down to you, Pasco?"

Pasco shrugged. "Not just me; got a lot of support from the committee."

"Even Willie Walton?" Steve asked in surprise.

Pasco grinned. "He did suggest that we look for private participation in the scheme."

"And?" Steve prompted.

"I just looked hard at him and raised my eyebrows; in amazement, like." Pasco laughed. "He didn't suggest it a second time."

They both laughed at that.

Pasco drank more sedately from his diminishing pint. "So what you been up to, Steve? Hannah tells Selwyn you spend all day working."

"Got to get everything ready for September. Not long now."

"And when's Eva back?"

"End of next week. I'm going to pick her up from Bristol."

Pasco waited as if expecting Steve to say more, but when no more was forthcoming he switched his attention to the discarded house details. "What you got there?"

Steve followed Pasco's gaze. "I'm thinking of buying a house," he said sheepishly.

"Your cheque come through, then?" There was obviously little Hannah did not confide to Selwyn. "How much for?"

Steve had long since given up attempting to sidestep Pasco's scrutiny. He told him the amount and Pasco whistled in surprise.

"Should be able to get something decent for that."

"Maybe, but it's finding the right thing. I don't want some soulless modern bungalow but I also don't want a picturesque ruin falling down around my ears."

"Choosy bugger, aren't you?" Pasco teased.

"And I want a sea view. So there." Steve sat back defiantly.

Pasco laughed but then fell silent before wrinkling his brow and sucking on his lip in an outward display of some inner calculation. "Tell me again how much you got to spend."

Steve told him.

Pasco digested the information before coming to a conclusion. He smiled at Steve. "I think I might be able to help you."

"What?" Steve sat up straight, but then frowned. "This isn't going to be like the car business, is it?"

Pasco smiled at the memory. "No chance; these are good people. But it might suit them and you."

Steve looked at him blankly.

"This morning I was finishing off a bit of decorating for the Fosters."

"Who?"

"Jim and Sally. Nice old couple, but getting on a bit so they're moving closer to their daughter in Falmouth," Pasco explained, and then drained the last of his beer.

"And?"

"They're smartening the place up a bit, not that it really needs it, before putting it on the market. They've had it valued; could be in your price range."

"Really?"

"Old coastguard cottage, so you get your sea view all right."

"Yes, but old. That means problems," Steve insisted.

"Wrong. They've done a lot to it over the years: a new extension, a loft conversion, rewired; the lot."

Steve was daring to become enthusiastic. "It sounds promising, I have to say."

"Plenty of space; three bedrooms." Pasco smiled. "Should you have company."

Steve tried to ignore the subtext. "And you think they might be up for a private sale?"

"Why not? You've nothing to sell so you're ready to move in. Save them a few quid on the estate agent. Everyone's a winner."

Steve grimaced slightly. "I remember you saying that about the car purchase."

"And was I wrong?" Pasco protested.

"I suppose not."

Pasco feigned indignation. "You're an ungrateful bugger!"

"Never let it be said. I'll buy you a pint." Steve reached for Pasco's glass, which was willingly surrendered.

As he made for the bar, Pasco took out his phone and called to Steve. "I'll just give the Fosters a bell. See if we can go round this afternoon."

THIRTY-SEVEN

The arrivals board showed that the Bucharest flight had landed. It was one of the last of the day and the airport was unusually quiet. It would soon be midnight, and the rows of empty check-in counters and the echoing footfalls of the few weary travellers mooching about the concourse were far removed from any fantasy of the romance of travel. Steve had endured a gruelling drive up from Cornwall, with bottlenecks on the motorway as the Department of Transport had perversely decided that the busiest weeks of the year were the ideal time to undertake extensive roadworks. He had sat resignedly in the exhaust-choked queues of cars inching their way homewards; many with bicycles on their backs and surfboards and canoes on their roofs to be stored in sheds and garages until next summer. At least, he consoled himself, the journey home should be easier. The schools were going back now and Sam's aperitif people would be replacing the boisterous families, and Steve did not anticipate that many of them would be travelling in the small hours of the night.

In spite of the drive up and the hectic workload of the past few days as he had battled to be ready for the challenges ahead, Steve did not feel tired. His mood was a mixture of nervousness and anticipation, both fuelled by adrenaline.

The anticipation was at the prospect of seeing Eva again. She had only been away for two weeks but he had missed her; even immersing himself in work had not driven her from his thoughts. Hannah had noticed his distraction and teased him for being lovelorn. Steve had tried to laugh that off, but out of curiosity had familiarised himself with the definition of that somewhat archaic term he associated with lachrymose Victorian swains. The dictionary had reminded him that affection was unrequited when it was not reciprocated equally. That had been research of a purely academic nature, but as he stood waiting at the arrivals gate the nervousness he felt was rooted in that uncertainty. He found it hard to articulate his own feelings, let alone guess at Eva's. He had hinted as much to Hannah but she had shaken her head in despair and told him to trust his heart. That all sounded very simple, but gnawing at his confidence, he told her, was the fact that following his feelings when he was young had not prevented twenty years of marriage crumbling around him. Hannah had not been impressed by that; it had merely increased her exasperation. "You can't throw away a chance of happiness now because of what might happen in twenty years' time!" That had been her forceful parting shot to him that morning before he set out for the airport.

Steve was thinking of that when the first passengers from the Bucharest flight began to trickle into the arrivals hall. His mouth felt dry and his heart was definitely stepping up its beat. They saw each other simultaneously. Eva waved and ran the last few steps towards him. Steve had no time to consider his response; he simply opened his arms wide and they hugged. Eva looked up at him with laughter in her eyes, and Steve smiled back at her and remembered how beautiful she was. They hugged again with an intensity and self-absorption which shut out everything around them, and only released each other when they became aware of other passengers needing to manoeuvre their wheeled bags around them. Steve nodded his apology but received only smiles and even a wink in return. Composing himself, he took Eva's suitcase in one hand and, linking the other around her arm, led her out of the airport. Neither of them had spoken a word. There was no need.

As Steve had anticipated, the motorway traffic was light. Driving was now stress-free and conversation possible. Eva told him about her time at home. She explained that her mother was already getting into a state of nervous excitement about Steve's Christmas visit, wondering what he would eat and what he would think of their simple home. Steve laughed and told Eva to inform her mother that he had spent the past year living in a hovel. Anya, too, was excited. Eva had shown her the picture taken in The Excalibar. "She said you looked nice," she told Steve.

"She is clearly a very good judge of character," Steve replied.

Eva laughed at that. "I taught her some English conversation. She is going to practise on you."

"She is clearly a clever girl." Steve looked innocently at Eva. "I wonder where she gets that from?"

Eva smiled but said nothing. She looked out of the window for a moment at the dark fields and scattered lights of the sleeping villages. The thrum of the tyres on tarmac filled the silence. When she looked back at Steve she was no longer smiling; her expression was serious, even anxious.

Steve frowned, concerned. "Are you OK? Is there a problem?"

Eva gave a small shrug. "It's Anya."

"What? I thought she had recovered—"

Eva interrupted him. "Not her health; she is well."

Steve relaxed a little. "Good." He briefly took his eyes off the empty road ahead and glanced at her. "So what is the matter?"

"Next year she will start at high school." Eva paused and seemed to be choosing her words carefully. "It is a big change for her." She looked resignedly at Steve. "I need to be with her, Steve."

Steve felt all the exhilaration of the past few hours drain from him in an instant. He clutched at a straw. "Of course, but perhaps your mother can—"

Eva was shaking her head. "Cristian, my brother. His partner is pregnant. In a few months the baby will come, and soon after that my mother will have to help. They both need to work."

"I see." Steve could not keep the disappointment out of his voice.

Eva looked resignedly at him. "What can I do? Perhaps I hoped for too much."

"Perhaps we both did." Steve spoke almost to himself. Then he tried to lighten the mood. "But at least for a year you can stay; get on with the new job. Can't you?"

"Yes." Eva managed a smile. "I spoke with my mother. She wants me to do this work. She can manage for a year."

"Well, that's something." Steve did his best to sound positive, although his thoughts were whirling. "I have been getting everything ready; we'll need to go through it all in the next few days."

"Of course." Eva, too, had managed to move into a more upbeat space. "And I will look for a new place to stay. It is not possible to work where I am; I will need a room of my own." She seemed almost cheerful again. "At least now I will have the money to afford it." She looked at Steve for confirmation but he was staring ahead at the road. She thought perhaps he was concentrating on the thundering articulated lorry which was passing them at a speed far in excess of the limitation posted on its tailgate, but his mind was on many other things.

The traffic was even lighter as they entered Cornwall. They had spoken little after Eva's depressing acceptance that her new-found fulfilment would be short-lived. Each had been absorbed in their own thoughts; the euphoria of their reunion at the airport dissipated. Eva had fallen asleep, her gentle breathing barely audible above the metallic purr of the engine. Steve had to force himself to focus on his driving, but that did not prevent thoughts tumbling through his mind. He tried to organise them into a logical scenario but had to accept that logic was fighting a losing battle with emotion. He stole a glance at Eva; she looked even more beautiful in repose. The thought that she would be gone from his life in a few months was agonising. He had not really dwelt too much on how their relationship would develop; he had lazily assumed that they had plenty of time to see how things went. He was only now emerging warily, blinking at the light, from the dark depression of his collapsed marriage, but he knew that Eva had played her part in leading him out of that darkness. He remembered his despair when she had vanished back to Romania and he'd thought he would never see her again. Such thoughts quickly vanquished calm reason and logic. If he was to lose her again it would not be without a fight. What he was planning, even rehearsing, as the miles slipped by might end in a humiliating defeat but at least he would not have to live with the guilt of not trying.

His mind made up, he looked for the next lay-by, and when one appeared he drove into it and turned off the ignition. The silence of the empty night was disturbed only by the clicking of the cooling engine. The stationary car was no longer the somnolent cocoon which had lulled Eva to sleep, and she stirred, blinked to clear her vision, and turned questioningly to Steve.

"Are you OK? Do you need a rest?"

Steve shook his head and took a deep breath. "No, Eva. I do not need a rest, but what I do need is to talk to you; to tell you what I have been thinking for the last few hours. You will probably think I am crazy, and I apologise now if what I am going to say is embarrassing or ridiculous, but I must say it, so please hear me out. Will you?"

Eva was looking at him in confusion, but she nodded. "Of course I will."

Steve plunged on. "I am buying a house." Eva made to speak at this announcement, but he held up a silencing hand. "It is bigger than I really need, but it has what I am looking for. I am sure you would like it, and it seems silly that you have to look for a room when I have two spare bedrooms and it would be convenient for our work." Conscious that he had begun to gabble, he paused for breath.

Eva seemed to be processing this information, and looked at him in surprise but with a smile.

Encouraged, he continued. "Of course you could come and go as you pleased. It would be your home but," he paused awkwardly, floundering for the right words, "but there would be no pressure on anybody to be, you know, more than just, well, whatever..."

Eva came to his rescue with a joke. "Just line manager and lodger?"

Steve shook his head at his own crassness. "Something like that. But there is more." He composed himself again. "I thought that if it worked out, you might think about Anya joining you. There is room and it would be a good time for her to start high school here. I know it is a big step and a lot to think about. We could discuss it with your mother and

Anya at Christmas if you think it might be possible. Maybe it's a mad idea, but I knew if I didn't say it I would always regret it."

He felt the relief of having spoken what he had been thinking. He looked at Eva, who suddenly released her seat belt to move closer to him.

Nervously, he began to speak again. "Of course it might seem a ridiculous idea and you need time to—"

He got no further because Eva held a silencing finger to his lips and speech became impossible as she kissed him slowly and gently. They held each other close until the headlights of an approaching juggernaut briefly illuminated their embrace and its driver delivered two celebratory blasts on his air horn.

Summer's lease had finally expired. It was early September and the sun was setting earlier, and its rays, although they suffused the beach with golden light, had little warmth. So they donned sweaters and sat closer to the spluttering embers of the fire which had fuelled their barbecue. It had been Pasco's idea to mark the end of summer like this. The end of summer, perhaps, but also a time of beginnings. Hannah would be leaving in the morning to spend time with Linda in her new flat in Cardiff before going off to university. Steve and Eva would be starting work together in a couple of days, and Pasco would be back on council duty in a week. In honour of the occasion, Tamsin had produced freshly caught mackerel for them to grill and, more prosaically, chicken drumsticks which she had cooked at home as, she told them, she was no fan of salmonella. Hannah had prepared bowls of salad; Pasco had provided the beer and Steve the wine. They had made considerable inroads into the alcohol as Pasco proposed more and more toasts. They had drunk in celebration of Selwyn and Hannah's success in getting into university, and Steve and Eva's new jobs. Pasco had then proposed a subsidiary toast to the new couple's happiness in their new home. Steve had looked nervously at Eva at that point, but she had merely squeezed his hand reassuringly. Encouraged, he'd ventured a toast of his own by drinking to Pasco's achievement in getting the council to back the new housing project on which work had already started. To conclude the celebrations, Pasco proposed a toast to the Pirates and their hope of promotion in the new season. He reminded Steve to buy a season ticket, but was told that that had already been done. Tamsin said she was pleased to hear it because Steve could try to stop Pasco "behaving like a hooligan" now that he was a councillor. That provoked general laughter and served as a cue to start packing things away. Eva helped Tamsin carry the leftover food back to the car park whilst Hannah and Selwyn wandered off to the far end of the beach and sat on the rocks, watching the tide come in.

Pasco, on his knees, paused his raking over the embers and pointed at his son sitting with his arm around Hannah's shoulders. "They're going to miss each other, those two."

Steve looked at him. "I know."

"But Bristol and Exeter are pretty close."

"True, but you know how it is. Nothing stays the same."

Pasco looked up from poking at the charcoal. "That's your trouble, Steve. You're a gloomy bugger. Sometimes the sun does shine, you know; good things do happen." He looked hard at Steve. "Like you and Eva."

It was hard to argue with that. The Fosters had moved out and within days the legal details of the house purchase would be completed. Steve already had the key and had taken Eva to see the house. She had been entranced by it. The Fosters could not take their furniture to their small flat in Falmouth and Steve had been happy to buy it for a few hundred pounds. He and Eva had pulled two armchairs in front of the sitting-room window and sat for over an hour, mesmerised by the endless rippling ocean.

When they had gone upstairs Steve had offered Eva the use of the master bedroom when they moved in, but she had teased him that it should be reserved for the 'master' of the house. They had looked silently at each other. The physical attraction between them had yet to find its full expression, though circumstances rather than choice had so far been the cause of their restraint. Neither of them doubted that soon they would share the master bedroom but Steve was happy to wait; there was no need for the nervous planning and urgent manoeuvres of the sexual encounters of his student days which had invariably ended in frustration or embarrassment. He and Linda had found mutual pleasure in the bedroom in the first years of their marriage but he could not deny that as time passed his libido had diminished. Perhaps it was familiarity that had blunted his appetite. Linda had suggested that they spice up their sex life by "trying something new", and had pointedly shown him articles in the Sunday supplements offering guidance on novel practices for the bedroom. Steve had not been impressed. He failed to see how anyone with a sense either of humour or of the ridiculous could possibly indulge in such fantasies. Indeed, some of the allegedly erotic antics discussed seemed possible only for Olympic gymnasts. So, through stale weariness and passivity, he had driven Linda into the arms of Jason. Personally, he still blamed the Northern Line. But with Eva his desire had awoken and could not be long denied.

"You not finished yet?" Tamsin and Eva had returned from the car. Impatiently, Tamsin snatched up a pair of barbecue tongs and began worrying the last of the ashes. "It's getting cold out here."

Pasco got to his feet. "You're right." He pulled his sweater tighter around him. "You two coming back for coffee?"

Steve looked at Eva. "In a bit, if that's all right?" He gestured across the empty beach. "We'll just watch the sun go down." He extended a welcoming hand to Eva.

Pasco laughed. "Walking off into the sunset. Just like in the movies."

Tamsin poked him reprovingly with the tongs. "Ignore him. He's about as romantic as a dead sheep."

As Pasco protested at the comparison, Steve and Eva walked down to the edge of the wet sand where it confronted the encroaching water. The sun was now half submerged, spilling its orange blood into the devouring sea. They stood in silence for a moment, awed by the spectacle, then looked at each other in wonder.

"I think I may be in a dream," Eva said quietly.

"I know what you mean."

"A year ago I could never have believed this would happen to me. That I could be so happy; have so much to look forward to."

"You deserve it, Eva."

"No more cutting cauliflower; no more stupid men shouting at me to hurry up. Now I have a proper job, a lovely house to live in..." She paused and looked up at Steve. "And I have you. A kind, honest man."

Steve, typically, covered his emotion with a joke. "What about handsome? You forgot about that."

Eva punched him playfully on the shoulder. "You can't have everything."

They were quiet again, watching as the sun slipped lower. Steve broke the silence. "Do you know what I keep thinking?"

"What?" Eva asked.

"If all those months ago I had driven past a few seconds earlier or later, none of this would have happened."

Eva understood. "Chance. Is that what you call it?"

Steve shook his head. "I have a better word. Happenstance."

"Happenstance." She said it slowly. "I do not know this word."

"Pasco does," Steve laughed. "It means a chance meeting ending in a good result."

"Perfect. I will remember it." She repeated it slowly as if to commit it to memory. "Happenstance."

Steve smiled at her and, putting his arm round her shoulder, pulled her close and together they stood in silence until the sun finally surrendered to the sea.

 Matador

For exclusive discounts on Matador titles,
sign up to our occasional newsletter at
troubador.co.uk/bookshop